Holding Out for a Hero

By Codi Gary

Holding Out for a Hero

A MEN IN UNIFORM NOVEL

CODI GARY

AVON IMPULSE
An Imprint of HarperCollinsPublishers

Excerpt from *Along Came Love* copyright © 2016 by Tracey Livesay.
Excerpt from *When a Marquess Loves a Woman* copyright © 2016 by Vivienne Lorret.

EPub Edition NOVEMBER 2016 ISBN: 9780062441263

Print Edition ISBN: 9780062441270

Avon, Avon Impulse, and the Avon Impulse logo are trademarks of HarperCollins Publishers.

AM 10 9 8 7 6 5 4 3 2 1

*To My Beautiful Nieces, Lana, Shelby,
Brittney, Kimberly, Gabrielle, Jordyn, and Ayla.*

May you never give up on Happily Ever After.

Chapter One

BLAKE KLINE WAS having a really shitty day, and it wasn't even eight in the morning.

He'd woken up late and only realized that there was something wrong with the hot water when he'd stepped into his shower and had his balls frozen off. He'd gotten ready in half the time, but when he'd gone out to his car, he found the driver's side window smashed and his stereo gone. God, he had to move. The area kept getting worse, and the apartment manager was always slow about fixing things. The only reason he'd stayed so long was because he hated moving.

The only bit of luck he'd had was that the cop who took his statement had been in the neighborhood, so he'd ended up with enough time for his morning run or breakfast at his favorite diner.

He'd chosen breakfast. If anything was going to right the trajectory of his day, it was his usual from Dale's…

And one of Hannah's smiles.

Blake grinned to himself as he parked his car in front of the white and red old-fashioned diner. It was right off the running trail he liked to take, and he'd been going here before work for just about a year. From the first time he'd stepped inside, the whole place had been warm and inviting, including the young, shy waitress who had first served him. For some reason, he'd spent that entire first visit trying to make her laugh.

After that, teasing Hannah, talking to Hannah, and finally, having her tease him back had become the highlight of his day. Hell, his week. It wasn't that he didn't like his job at Alpha Dog Training Program. He got to work with his friends, dogs, and kids all day. The program had been set up as a community outreach program to train nonviolent juvenile offenders in the care of animals, so they would have a focus other than getting into trouble when they left. The dogs, who were saved from being euthanized, were trained as search and rescue, military, police, and therapy dogs. It was admirable work that made him feel as though he was making a difference.

But it didn't chase away the black mark on his soul the way Hannah's laughter did.

He walked through the door, and to his disappointment, his favorite waitress was nowhere to be seen.

"Hey ya, Blake." One of the other waitresses, Chloe, came sauntering over with a smile, her dark hair in a messy topknot. Blake was friendly with everyone at Dale's and knew Chloe was a single mom in her early forties with two teenaged boys who drove her nuts, but the last thing he wanted to hear about today was whatever mischief Thing One and Thing Two had done over the weekend.

"Go ahead and grab your regular booth, and I'll bring you some water," she said.

Trying not to show the irritation he felt, he did what she said, and against his own volition, asked as she set the water down, "Is Hannah out sick today?"

Chloe gave him a sly grin, and he felt his neck and ears burn. He hadn't meant for it to come out like that, didn't want her to get the wrong idea. He wasn't interested in Hannah romantically; he just enjoyed her company.

He hadn't been interested in anyone since Jenny.

"She's just out back on break. You're a little early today, but I know she won't want to miss you."

The teasing note in her voice made him shift uncomfortably. "It's no problem; I was just curious."

"Sure you were. Want me to head out back and let her know you're here?"

"Nah, really, I'll just have my usual with a cup of coffee."

"You got it, boss." Chloe went to put in his order, and Blake sat there, trying not to glance toward the back of the diner where the staff disappeared to take their breaks.

Instead, he pulled out his phone and saw a text from Megan Bryce, one of his coworkers.

Hey, did you bitch out on our run this morning?

Blake rolled his eyes. Bryce liked to crash his morning runs, no matter how many times he'd told her he preferred to run alone. He liked the smart-ass brunette. She was just one of the guys. But his run was his Zen time, and she just wouldn't take the hint.

I had a shit morning and decided to skip it. You should do it though. Best mentioned your ass was getting a little fluffy.

Sergeant Tyler Best had said no such thing, but Blake was really hoping that when he got to work, Best would get his ass kicked by Bryce, just for laughs. Blake needed a good laugh today.

How dare you?! My ass is fucking perfect. I'll kill him, and you're next.

Blake laughed as he responded.

Hey, don't shoot the messenger.

Less than two seconds ticked by before she responded. Damn, she was fast.

The message sucked and should have never been repeated, douche-nozzle.

"Hey, Blake." Hannah's breathy greeting made him jump.

Her expression was slightly sheepish, and her hazel eyes twinkled behind the black framed glasses she always wore. "Sorry, didn't mean to sneak up on you."

"No, you're fine. I was just texting my coworker. With any luck, there will be bloodshed when I get to work."

Hannah laughed, shaking her head, and he watched the light dance off the highlights in her ponytail. Hannah's hair looked like milk chocolate and caramel swirl, and he loved the contrast.

"You are evil."

"Speaking of evil, what are you reading today?" Blake plucked the book peeking up from her apron pocket and ignored her soft protest as he read the title. *"A Loving*

Scoundrel." He glanced over the candy-ass-looking dude on the cover and snorted.

Suddenly, the book was snatched from him, and she smacked him on the shoulder with it. "It's good. Reading improves your vocabulary, your imagination, your—"

"I think they are talking about reading literature, not smut."

Hannah's face turned violet, and Blake was surprised to find her hazel eyes shooting daggers at him.

Holy shit, he'd pissed her off. He hadn't meant to. He'd been teasing Hannah about her romance novels since the first time he'd seen a book poking out of her apron. Usually she just rolled her eyes and scolded him, but she was really mad.

"It is not smut. It is a beautiful love story. Maybe you should try reading one before you poke fun at me."

She started to walk away, and he grabbed her wrist, the softness of her skin rubbing against his palm like a swatch of velvet. Damn, he'd never noticed that before.

"Hey, I'm sorry. I wasn't trying to be a jerk." He tugged a little until she was standing next to the table. "Can you sit for a bit? I promise I won't tease you about your books anymore."

Her lips pursed. "I've got to work."

He gave her a cajoling smile. "Come on, there is no one else here. Sit a spell. I've had a really bad morning, and I could use a little friendly conversation."

HANNAH YORK COULDN'T shake the warm imprint of Blake's palm on her wrist, no matter how irritated she was with him. Maybe it was the way his hazel eyes twinkled boyishly at her or the contrite smile on his tan, handsome face, but she couldn't say no.

She sat down with a heavy sigh. "You really shouldn't give people a hard time."

"I know. I'm sorry. It's a personality flaw."

And here I'd almost convinced myself that you didn't have any.

From the first time that Blake had set foot in Dale's, she'd been drawn to him. Usually, she was pretty shy around men, and things with Blake had been no different. Only he hadn't let it stay that way. He'd teased her, told her jokes and stories, and before long, she'd begun watching the door every morning she worked, waiting for him to walk through it and sit in her section. She'd never had a male friend before, and Blake was great, most of the time.

Sometimes he came in with a dark cloud hanging over him, and on days like that, she just tried to smile and listen. Occasionally, he would open up about stress at work, but she always thought there was more to it than that. There was a deep-seated anger and sadness in Blake beneath the friendly exterior, but she was too afraid to pry, usually.

Today, though, she was too irritated to worry about pissing him off. "So, what's going on? Why are you in such a contrary mood?"

"Contrary, huh?" There was that smile again, liquefying her insides.

"I told you. Broadens the vocabulary."

"Fine, next time I'm at Walmart, I'll be sure and grab a copy of one of your…romance novels and see what's what."

"Just make sure it's not erotic romance, or you'll be in for more than you bargained for."

Oh God, now he was giving her a searching look that made her cheeks warm. "How will I know it is erotic romance without reading it?"

Hannah cleared her throat, fighting back her embarrassment. "Usually, it will have an object on the cover, like a mask or pearls. Sometimes a couple...embracing."

Ugh, I'm going to die.

"Maybe I'll have you text me some suggestions."

A zing of surprised pleasure zipped through her. In the eleven months that he'd been coming in, they'd never exchanged numbers. They talked about a lot of stuff in the mornings, but never outside of Dale's.

"You'd have to give me your number," she whispered.

"Order up!" Kenny called from the kitchen.

Hannah patted the table with a smile. "I'll grab your food and get you some more coffee."

She got up from the table before he could say anything, sweat breaking out all over her body. The last thing she wanted was to make Blake think she was into him, although it was obvious to everyone at Dale's she was over the moon for him.

Of course, she didn't really think he felt the same. If he did, he'd have made a move by now, right? She didn't have a lot of experience dating, but the guys who had asked her out in the past hadn't waited long to invite her to dinner or a movie.

Hannah grabbed the plate of food, and Chloe came up beside her, bumping her with her hip.

"Just so you know, he came in wondering where you were."

There was that zip of excitement again. "He did?"

"Yeah, he seemed put out to have me wait on him, which, by the way, is slightly offensive. I'm freaking delightful."

Hannah laughed and bumped her back. "You are. We're friends, though, and he's having a rough day, which is probably why he wanted to talk to me."

"Ha, friends, yeah. Sorry, but I can't imagine any red-blooded American female being just friends with that hot slab of man meat."

"You're gross." Hannah walked away from her friend and grabbed the coffeepot with her free hand. Chloe wasn't wrong about Blake's attractiveness, but *man meat*? It just wasn't dignified.

Hannah set the plate down in front of him and refilled his cup. "So, you were going to tell me about your day..."

Blake shrugged at first, but when she sat down across from him once more and gave him an impatient *hmm*, he cracked like a one-dollar folding chair.

"It has just been rough from the start. Woke up late, and my water heater must be broken, because I had to take a freezing cold shower. Then I walked out to find my car had been busted into and my radio was gone."

"Oh my God, that is awful. I am so sorry."

He sipped his coffee before answering. "It's just another reason I should really think about moving, but I'm lazy about it. I hate change."

Hannah could understand that. It was probably why she'd stayed so close to where her parents lived. The thought of being too far away was hard. She hadn't even gone away to college, not because she hadn't wanted to, but because her dad was a professor at the junior college and she couldn't turn down the free education she got being a professor's kid.

Still, she would never stay somewhere that wasn't safe.

"So, what are you going to do then? Are you planning on staying here, or do you think you'll get deployed?" *Please say no*.

"No, I doubt it. Not unless another war breaks out; they really want Alpha Dog to succeed, so they need as many hands on deck as they can get in order to expand. Right now they are working on opening a girls' facility."

"That's fantastic." She glanced up and saw an elderly couple come through the door, disappointment churning in her gut. She really wanted to stay and talk to Blake, but the Johnsons were some of her regulars. "Sorry, duty calls. I'll stop by to check on you."

That had been the plan, at least, until the place exploded with activity. After the Johnsons came in, a group of eight women from the technology college walked in, and every minute or two after, a new customer arrived. It was great for business, but when she dropped Blake's check off to him, she hardly had time for more than an *I'll be right back* before someone was waving her down.

When she came back to take his money, he was walking out the door with a wave, and she smiled when she saw he'd left her a ten-dollar tip, more than his meal had even cost. Crazy man.

She went to put his money in the drawer and noticed the writing on top of the receipt.

Don't forget to send me those book recommendations. Blake. 916-777-0912

He'd left her his number.

Hannah wanted to do a little dance behind the register but was too afraid of drawing attention to herself. She settled for smiling like a crazy person for the rest of her shift, and then it was time to head to her second job as a substitute teacher. She changed in the bathroom into a pair of slacks and a soft, gray sweater with a printed wool circle scarf. She pulled on her boots and walked out of the bathroom, her yellow Dale's uniform shoved into her tote bag.

"See you guys later," she called out, and Kenny waved from the little opening. Chloe and Paulette, the server who came in to relieve Hannah, said good-bye but were too busy for any other pleasantries.

Hannah pulled on her coat as she stepped outside and shoved her hands in her pockets. The receipt with Blake's number crinkled in her hand, and her heart picked up speed, excitement pulsing through her body with a steady drumming.

Once she was inside her car, waiting for it to warm up, she pulled the receipt out and punched the number into her phone. Her thumb wavered over the text message icon. Was it too soon to send him suggestions?

She put the phone back into her coat and sighed. It was probably better to wait until after work to text him. The last thing she wanted to do was seem overeager.

Chapter Two

BLAKE DIDN'T WANT to admit to himself how many times he'd checked his phone after he left Dale's and got to Alpha Dog. At least a dozen times, maybe more, before he left the program at nine thirty that night. It wasn't until he was on his way to Mick's Bar to meet up with his friends that his phone beeped.

Blake pressed a little harder on the gas, refusing to reach for his phone until he stopped driving, but it was hard not to pull over right then. Best, after punching him in the gut for telling Bryce he'd called her fat, had asked him who he was waiting on earlier, and Blake had lied, of course. All of his friends were a bunch of nosy bastards, and if he told them about Hannah, they'd start teasing him, even if nothing was going on.

Everyone at Alpha Dog knew he wasn't dating, that he had no plans to, but lately, he had to admit he was thinking about it more. With Best and his other two friends,

Sergeant Dean Sparks and Sergeant Oliver Martinez, in serious relationships, he'd been spending more and more time in his crappy apartment alone. At least dating would get him out more often and leave less time to drink alone. He hated to admit how much he missed his friends; they used to hang out after work at Mick's several times a week, talking shit and drinking beer. Now he was lucky if they met up a couple times a month. Yeah, he saw them at work, but it wasn't the same.

The problem was, every time he thought about signing up for online dating or even asking one of his friends to set him up, he thought of Jenny. Jenny, his beautiful high school sweetheart, then his wife. They'd married when they were barely into their twenties, yet they'd grown together instead of apart. She'd been there for him after his parents had died in a fatal car accident and stuck around while he'd done three tours during their first five years of marriage.

When he'd finally come home and put in for a job that would keep him stateside, he'd lost her.

Lost. It was a shitty word to use when someone died. People had repeated over and over at his parents' funeral how sorry they were for his loss and again at Jenny's. It was such a casual term to convey a moment that had forever changed his life and destroyed his happiness.

Taken. That was a better way to describe his wife being killed in the middle of their Base Exchange. A Texas military base should have been the safest place for her to be while he was at home, waiting for his next assignment. He'd been drinking beer with his friends and watching football while she'd run out to get something to make them all for dinner.

He'd always expected that someday, she'd get the knock on the door and the notification of his death.

Not the other way around.

Blake picked up speed on the freeway, his grip tightening on the wheel until his fingers throbbed, giving him something to focus on instead of his dead wife. For two years he'd been trying to run away from his misery. He'd moved across the country, away from everything that reminded him of her and his past, and still she haunted him.

It was why he was still hesitant about dating. He hadn't even been out with another woman in the two years since he lost her, let alone slept with someone else. Jenny was the only woman he'd ever been with; it was enough to make any man gun-shy about hooking up with someone new.

For some reason, Hannah's angry face flashed through his mind. Since the first time they'd met, he'd seen her shy side, seen her smile and laugh, seen her act happy or shocked by his teasing.

But today, when she'd appeared ready to throttle him, he'd felt a shock of something he hadn't even recognized at first until he'd walked out of Dale's.

Interest.

Hannah's fury had stirred up something inside him. He liked Hannah, had always noticed she was pretty—he wasn't blind, after all.

But he'd never been tempted to cup her face in his hands and kiss her until she was smiling again.

The image was why he'd booked it out of there so fast, not bothering to wait for her to come around and say bye.

He was still shocked he'd left his number for her. He'd been joking about the recommendations, and then she'd been so eager, that spark in her eyes, that rush of excitement at possibly sharing something she was passionate about with him.

He hadn't been able to resist.

Blake pulled into the parking lot, and as soon as he turned off his car, he picked up his phone to see if it was her.

Where are you, dick munch? I got a bone to pick with you.

Damn it, the text was from Bryce.

He didn't even bother texting her back, just climbed out of the car and headed into the bar. The loud blast of classic rock vibrated the floor as he made his way through the crowd and down the stairs to where his friends usually hung. The first thing he saw when he reached the bottom was Best and Sparks playing pool, while Martinez and Slater hung by the table watching.

And then Bryce was in his way, punching him in the gut, her blue eyes flashing in the dim bar lights.

"Bastard. Best said you were full of shit."

It really hadn't hurt, just caught him by surprise. Standing back up with a laugh, he said, "You're really going to believe Best?"

"Hell yeah I am, and you're lucky I am such a benevolent and forgiving person."

"Sure I am." Patting her shoulder a couple of times, he added, "I'm sorry I said that about your ass."

"Ha, you better be, especially since I was nice enough to invite someone to meet you."

Blake's blood ran cold as he searched the bar for Bryce's special guest. He noticed a pretty Asian girl talking to Slater Vincent, one of the other trainers at Alpha Dog, and growled.

"Bryce…"

"What?"

"Why do you keep ambushing me with all of your single friends?"

Bryce frowned at him as if he was the annoying one. This was her second attempt at setting him up, and while the first woman had been perfectly lovely, he hadn't been able to stop thinking of Jenny, thus reaffirming his conviction that he wasn't ready.

And yet, here they were again.

"Come on, just say hi to her. I didn't tell her I was introducing her to anyone. I just invited her to come out with some of my coworkers. There's no pressure."

"Except that Slater and I are the only single dudes, so she's going to get some kind of idea about who she's here for." Blake ran his hands over his face with a sigh. "Why do you have to make me the bad guy?"

She threw up her hands as if she was surrendering to something unreasonable. "Fine, I won't introduce you."

Before Blake could thank her, though, he glanced over and saw Jane walking toward them, a wide smile on her face.

"Megs, I thought you ditched me."

Bryce gave him a look that clearly said *whoops, too late.* "Sorry, just saying hi to Blake. Blake, this is Jane. Jane, Blake Kline."

Jane held out her hand to him eagerly. "Hi, Megan's told me a lot about you."

Blake didn't even want to know what the lot was. "I'm Blake, good to meet you." He took her hand and gave it a firm shake before releasing it.

"Why don't I get you two kids some drinks and leave you to chat?" Before Blake could protest, she'd shimmied up the stairs faster than the weasel she was and left him alone with Jane.

"So, Megan tells me you work with search and rescue dogs. That must be cool. How did you get into that?"

Asking questions about his interests. Yep, definitely a setup.

"My dad trained hounds while I was growing up and taught me everything he knew." Wishing he had a drink in his hand at the moment, he tried to at least be personable. "How do you know Bryce?"

"Oh, we went to high school together, and we kept in touch. She's awesome."

I'd argue that point.

"Yeah, she's something." Catching Best and Sparks watching them with barely smothered grins, he knew one or both of them had a hand in this. "So, what do you do for a living, Jane?"

"I'm actually in the UC Davis veterinary program. I've got another two years, but I love animals, so I'm excited. Hoping to eventually work at a surgical center, but I might go large animal. It all depends."

"Here we go." Bryce popped in with two drinks, one a fruity cocktail and the other a frothy beer, which she handed to him. "How are things going?"

"We were just talking about our careers," Jane said.

Before Bryce could respond, Blake jumped in with a means of escape. "Will you ladies excuse me a minute? I've got to talk to Sparks about a problem with one of our trainees."

Before Bryce's withering look set him on fire, he walked away, coming up alongside Sparks.

"You could have at least warned me Bryce was plotting revenge."

Sparks shrugged his linebacker shoulders before leaning over the pool table to take his shot.

"Dude, you told Bryce I called her fat. You deserve far worse than a hot girl," Best said.

"I said you called her ass puffy, not fat."

Best made a face at him. "Dick." Sparks missed, and Best tipped back his beer until his glass was empty. He wiped his mouth with the back of his hand before lining up his shot. "Your problem is that it's been so long since you've even seen any ass that you've forgotten how to talk to chicks. I'll try to control Bryce, but as your friend, I need to tell you that bottling up the boys and never achieving release is *no bueno*."

Normally, Best's jackass comments wouldn't have spiked Blake's temper, but it wasn't as if he'd been dumped by some woman who'd broken his heart. Jenny was everything he'd ever wanted, and they'd had eleven amazing years together.

Two years might seem like a long time to Best, but to Blake, it was a blip.

As much as these guys were his brothers, there was only so much they could understand about what he'd been through. Combat, fears about not coming home, or regret over those they'd left behind—that they could empathize with, but losing a spouse to violence?

If they really understood, they would get why he was so pissed.

Before he could vent his frustrations, though, Best clapped a hand on his shoulder. "Hey, I'm sorry, man. I know I can be an insensitive prick sometimes, and I'm trying to work on it—"

"Try harder," Blake said through gritted teeth.

Best grinned sheepishly. "Fair enough. I'll make sure Bryce backs up off your shit, and we'll try to…be more empathetic to your needs."

Best sounded as if he was almost choking on the words, and Sparks looked at him from across the table crossly. "What's this *we* shit? I've been telling you to leave him alone, so don't include me in your actions. I'm just an innocent bystander."

Blake couldn't help but laugh. "Where the hell did you learn a word like *empathetic*, anyway?"

"Therapy."

Blake grimaced. "I'm sorry."

"Don't be. It's actually helped a lot. Plus, the therapist gave me these exercises to help me deal with shit, so, you know, making progress."

Although he was happy for Best, Blake couldn't imagine actually enjoying therapy. Even when they were all stuck in group together, Blake hid behind his friends to avoid participating. It didn't always work, but then he said as little as possible. Hashing out his emotions with a stranger had never been something he'd deemed helpful.

Best leaned in, apparently unable to refrain from one last remark. "By the way, say hello to Sally Palm and her five sisters later."

Sparks, who was standing next to them, spewed his beer, erupting in a cough that sounded suspiciously like smothered laughter. Blake shoved his middle finger under Best's nose, but his friend escaped in order to take his shot.

Blake hated to admit it, but Best wasn't far off about that. Blake had been spending a lot of extra time jacking off lately, usually early in the morning as he showered. He also hated to admit that more frequently, his fantasies had included a woman who bore a striking resemblance to Hannah.

Blake took a long pull of his beer. Maybe he did need to just push the guilt back and at least settle for something physical. A little relief so he wasn't so pent up and having dirty thoughts about a woman who was supposed to be a friend.

Glancing Jane's way, he took a large gulp of his beer before checking his phone again. No new messages.

"What the hell," he muttered. Talking to a pretty woman didn't have to mean anything.

Besides, he really didn't want to go home to his quiet apartment again. Maybe Jane was interested in a little mutual sexual relief, too.

This time, Jenny's face swam behind his closed eyeballs, and he cringed. It seemed as though every step he took to try to move on was thwarted by thoughts of her, which inevitably led to mountains of guilt.

Slipping his phone back into his pocket, he polished off his beer and went to talk to Bryce's friend. Tonight, he was going to forget about everything else and just live a little. It had been two years, right?

Just because he was alive and Jenny wasn't, that didn't mean he deserved to be this miserable.

Did it?

HANNAH PULLED HER phone out of her purse for the eighteenth time, desperately wishing for the nerve to text Blake. What was the harm?

"Are we keeping you from something?"

The question came from the surprise date her best friend, Nicki, had arranged without her prior knowledge. What was his name? Mark?

He was giving her a sort of vacant grin, and she noticed the hunk of spinach between his teeth, probably left over from the salad they'd had an hour ago. Should she tell him?

"Figured you must have something better to do, since you can't seem to put your phone down."

Hannah's eyes narrowed. That wasn't true at all. He was the one who'd been pretty curt and rude to her from the start, and okay, yeah, she'd been checking her phone a lot, but he didn't have to point it out.

Screw it, he could save the spinach in his teeth for later.

"No, sorry, I am a substitute teacher, and so I have to keep checking for available jobs," she said.

He seemed to buy the excuse and turned back to Nicki's date, Garret, talking about football. Hannah caught Nicki's exasperated look, but Hannah had warned her she wasn't in the mood for an impromptu dinner date with a guy who had hardly spoken to her except for a few awkward attempts at small talk earlier. Now it seemed he was just as irritated about having to be there as she was.

It wasn't that Mark or Matt or whatever his name was wasn't cute; he was, spinach teeth and all. He just wasn't…

Hannah grabbed her purse and gave the table an apologetic smile. "I'll be right back."

She got up and wasn't surprised when Nicki followed, hot on her heels.

"You better not be sneaking out of here," her friend warned.

"I'm just going to the bathroom. Relax."

"You're being really antisocial toward Max."

Aha, I knew it started with an M.

"I am not. We just don't have a lot in common, and he's a little bit…" *Rude? Obnoxious?* "He just seems a little disappointed playing wingman."

"Oh, shut up! He totally thinks you're cute, but you've hardly said two words to him."

Hannah pushed into the bathroom with a sigh. "I have said more than two words, but I am tired. I am cranky. I have been up since four, and all I wanted to do was go home and curl up in bed with a book."

Hannah locked herself in the stall as Nicki kept talking. "That seems to be all you do lately! Read, work, and stay home. You're not an eighty-year-old grandma, you know! You are a young, nubile chick who needs to get some action."

Hannah pulled out her phone, leaning against the stall door as she scrolled through and stopped on Blake's name. "Just because I don't throw myself at every guy you send my way doesn't mean I'm not looking for action. I'm just picky about it."

She pressed down on the text message icon while Nicki kept ranting on the other side. Before she lost her nerve, she tapped out a message.

Hey, it's Hannah. If you're really interested in giving romance novels a try, here are three of my favorite authors. Let me know what you think.

Hannah listed the names and hit send.

"Geez, are you taking a crap in there? Come on!" Nicki said.

"Coming." Hannah slipped her phone inside her purse and said a silent prayer that she hadn't just made a terrible mistake.

SHIT, I'M DRUNK.

Blake had known that drinking seven beers was probably a mistake, but for some reason, he'd just kept tossing them back. Jane had also had too much to drink, as her voice got much higher the more intoxicated she became.

And it was actually grating on his nerves.

God, he hadn't had this much to drink since the Alpha Dog Christmas party, and that had been a colossal mistake. Not only had he nearly screwed up Best's relationship with his girlfriend, Dani, but he'd almost lost Best as a friend. Since then, he'd laid off having more than one beer, until tonight.

He'd had the second beer, hoping for enough of a buzz to chase away any reservations he'd had about talking to Jane, but it hadn't helped, so he'd downed another. By his fifth, he knew it wasn't about Jane; although he'd talked to her a bit, there had been no spark, no interest whatsoever.

Maybe thinking about Jenny so much today had increased his need to drink.

It could also be that I was hoping Hannah would text.

"Want another drink?" Jane asked, giggling.

Why was her voice so shrill? Hannah's was low and husky, and it washed over him pleasantly, while this woman's sounded more like a peacock's cry.

"No, I'm good. I gotta drive."

"Yeah, I don't think so, buddy." Martinez came up behind him and put his arm around his shoulders. "What do you say I give you a lift home?"

Blake tried to think of a reason why that wouldn't work, but his brain was too fuzzy. "Fine, it's not like there's anything left in my car to steal."

"We'll stop by it, just to make sure. Say good night, Blake."

Their group hollered good night, and Blake wasn't surprised when Jane slipped him her number. When they reached the top of the stairs, Blake tossed it in the trash.

Martinez gave him a thoughtful look. "I take it you're not interested?"

"No."

Martinez didn't say another word until they reached his car. Blake grabbed his duffle out of the trunk and tossed it into the back of Martinez's SUV. He climbed into the passenger seat, the cold sobering him up slightly, and grumbled, "It's colder than a witch's tit, man. Turn up the heat."

"Dude, you turn into a caveman when you drink." Martinez cranked up the heater, and Blake sighed back into the seat.

"I'm sorry, man. I know I'm being a jerk."

"If you know you're doing it, then why don't you stop?" Martinez backed out of the parking space, and the sway of the car made Blake's stomach turn. He must have groaned aloud, because Martinez glanced his way and warned, "If you puke in my car, you're cleaning it up."

"I'm not going to puke." At least, he hoped not.

He thought about Martinez's question as they drove down the street toward the freeway. *If you know you're doing it, then why don't you stop?* He wasn't sure, really. Maybe he was just a jerk who wanted to make everyone as miserable as he was.

His phone vibrated in his pocket, and he struggled to pull it out, his vision blurry as he stared at the screen.

Hey, it's Hannah.

He could hardly read the rest of her message, something about book titles, but by the time Martinez dropped him off, his cheeks were aching.

"Dude, why are you grinning like that? It's fucking creepy."

Blake climbed out of the car and said, "Because I'm going to go inside and order something called *Blitzing Emily*."

"The fu—"

Blake shut the door before Martinez could finish his sentence and climbed the stairs to his apartment. He kept hearing this high-pitched whistling noise as he opened the door and realized that it was him. He wasn't a whistler.

As he flopped onto his back on the bed, he stared up at the screen of his phone, her number right there.

Don't do it.

Before his brain could firmly process what he was doing, he had pressed the green phone icon.

Chapter Three

HANNAH WAS CURLED up on the couch in her Scotty dog flannel pajamas watching the newest episode of *Pretty Little Liars* when her phone rang.

At first, she ignored it, sure it was Nicki wanting to rip into her again for being a bum on the date, but then she realized that wasn't her friend's ringtone.

It was "Have a Nice Day" by Mindy McCready. The ringtone she'd assigned to Blake that morning when she'd put his number into her phone.

Diving for the phone with the desperation of a bear after a fish, she slid her thumb over the screen quickly. "Hello?" God, she sounded as if she was panting.

"Did I wake you?"

His voice was rough and a little slurred. Was he drunk?

"No, I was just watching TV. How are you?"

"Better now that I'm talking to you."

Her heart somersaulted in her chest. "You…You are?"

"Yeah, I had a bad night. My friends tried to set me up."

"Oh…" That was good, right? That he hadn't been interested in the other woman and was calling her now? "I'm sorry. Was she nice?"

"Yeah, she was fine, but she had this real shrill voice the more she drank, and I just couldn't take it. It's nothing like yours."

Whoa, what did that mean? "Mine?"

"Yeah, your voice is low. Smoky. Daddy like."

Hannah couldn't hold back her laughter. He was definitely wasted, but she'd heard people were actually more honest when they were drunk. He could mean everything he was saying.

Even the incredibly goofy stuff.

"I think you're a bit hammered."

"You would be correct, partner," he said, a thick twang in his voice. "I just got your message and was thinking about you. Waited all night for you to text."

"You did?"

"Mmm-hmm. So what did you do tonight?"

Hannah lay back on the couch with a sigh. "Well, my wonderful best friend decided it would be a good idea to get me out of the house and set me up on a terrible blind date. So I suppose our nights were about the same."

The phone was dead silent. "Hello? Blake?"

Suddenly, a sound came through, faint and guttural. Like a snore.

Oh God, it was a snore. He'd fallen asleep on the phone with her.

"Good night." She flicked the red phone icon with the tip of her thumb and ended the call, staring up at the ceiling with a smile. She didn't care that he'd drunk dialed her and fallen asleep. The fact that he'd been thinking about her was enough to keep her up all night.

Unable to concentrate on what A was doing to the Liars now, she got up from the couch and sat down at her laptop, powering up the Mac as she pulled her hair back into a messy bun. She opened her manuscript and read through the last page she'd written the night before, the scene playing through her mind.

She'd started writing a middle-grade novel last year, after going through an old box at her parents' that was filled with pictures of the foster kids who had come before they had adopted her. She'd been placed in Patty and Gilbert York's care when she was taken into foster care just shy of a year old. She didn't remember her life before, but when her birth mother stopped making her visitation, she'd become available for adoption, and the Yorks hadn't hesitated. They had never kept the fact that they weren't her biological parents from her and told her everything they knew when she became curious in her early teens. That was all it was, though. She'd never had any desire to meet the woman who had given birth to her; she'd been loved and cherished and protected. She didn't need anything else.

But looking into the faces of those other kids, some who appeared almost haunted and others who stared mutinously at the camera, as if they were afraid to be happy, had hurt her heart so much. That night she'd come home and started writing about Legonia Marie Phillips, or Legs for short. Legs was a foster child with special powers who protected the world and other kids like her.

It had been just for fun, something to do when she was home alone and couldn't shut her brain off, but before she knew it, she'd finished the first draft. And started a second manuscript.

By the time she'd concluded the third book, she'd had another story formulate in her mind about a young monster hunter named Cameron Fisher, who'd been adopted by normal folks. After his uncle shows up to explain that he's not crazy, that he's really seeing scary, supernatural beings, Cameron soon starts being trained on how to protect the people he loves from things that only he can see.

It wasn't such a surprise that she'd fallen in love with these types of tales; her mother had loved to read to her until she'd learned to read on her own, and the books they always chose had plenty of adventure, fanciful creatures…

And romance, of course.

Before she realized it, she'd written four thousand words, and her eyes were so heavy she could hardly keep them open. Finishing the sentence she was on, she walked into her bedroom and crawled into bed, grimacing as she looked at the angry red numbers on her alarm clock.

It was 3:47 a.m. She had to be up in twenty minutes for work.

But even the realization that she was going to be freaking exhausted couldn't chase the smile from her face as she thought of Blake's silly phrase.

Daddy like.

Hopefully, he'd still feel the same when he was sober.

BLAKE'S ALARM HAD gone off too fucking early, and despite the water he'd chugged and the Excedrin he'd tossed back, he was moving like a lumbering ox. As he jogged along the trail, sweat pouring off him despite the chilly January morning, he tried to focus on his breathing and the Three Doors Down track currently playing through his earbuds.

Anything but the nightmare that had jarred him awake that morning.

He should have known better. Every time he drank too much, she crept into his dreams. This time, he'd been there that day at the Base Exchange instead of safe at home with his friends. He'd stood only a few feet away and watched helplessly as a faceless man had held a gun to his pregnant wife's head.

And then he'd shot her. The sound, the warmth of her blood spraying across his face and hands had felt so real that when he'd woken up, he'd been screaming Jenny's name.

Despite the forty-degree temperature outside, his long-sleeved T-shirt clung to his chest and arms, drenched with sweat. His breath fogged out in front of him as he passed by several women walking toward him, not even glancing their way. He tried to remain focused, tried to push the dream and all the events from the night before far away.

Suddenly, someone slammed into his shoulder from behind. He stumbled forward as Bryce spun around, grinning at him as she jogged backward. He pulled out one of his earbuds and glared at her.

"The fuck, Bryce?"

"Kline, you're moving like an old man today. Best get to stepping. I see a little flab showing up on your midsection."

Blake grimaced at Bryce's taunting. She was like the annoying little sister he'd never wanted, and as much as he usually liked and respected her, he was still pissed about the sneak attack set up with her friend.

"Ha-ha, I get it, payback's a bitch. Well, you're on my shit list now. Maybe I'll let Slater know about how you hijack my runs just to go on and on about how hot he is."

Blake reinserted his earbud, so he didn't hear exactly what she said, but he was pretty sure it rhymed with *hick*.

Despite his obvious foul mood, Bryce kept up with him, and he had to give her props for not giving up when he took off on her, trying to outrun his dark thoughts. He finished his run and walked off the trail, Bryce right beside him.

He glanced her way and pulled his earbuds out, finally addressing her again.

"You're a brat—you know that, right?"

"So I've been told," she said. "Listen, I didn't hijack your run to bust your balls. I wanted to apologize before we got to work, because I do not want Best to know that I even know how to say I'm sorry. But I am. You've told me that you aren't ready to date, and I didn't listen to you. It's been pointed out that I never listen, so I'm sorry, and I will not try to set you up anymore."

"What about my runs?"

Bryce grinned and punched him in the arm, exactly the way Sparks did. "Oh no, I'm still crashing the hell out of those."

Blake laughed; he couldn't help it. She was incorrigible, but it was hard not to like Bryce. They reached his car, and he glanced toward the front of Dale's Diner. He'd read through Hannah's text this morning, chuckling at the titles of some of her suggestions, but he'd ordered the first one to read on his Kindle app before he left the house. He wanted proof that he wasn't just blowing smoke up her ass about wanting to read what she enjoyed.

As he stripped off his sweaty shirt, Bryce whistled. Blake glared at her as he pulled a clean T-shirt over his head.

"Oh, Kline, I just love it when you get all broody on me."

He shut the door to his car and locked it. "Thanks for the apology. I'll be sure to remind you of it when I need blackmail."

As he headed up the steps toward the diner entrance, she called after him, "Aren't you going to invite me to join you?"

"Hell no."

Bryce laughed and waved as she climbed into the red Civic next to his car. He waited until her car disappeared out of the parking lot before he went inside. Anywhere else, he would have invited Bryce in to join him, but Dale's was special.

Plus, he didn't want her teasing him about Hannah or embarrassing him in front of her.

He walked through the glass door and passed by the SEAT YOURSELF sign to his usual booth. He looked around for Hannah and saw her come out of the kitchen, wagging her finger at the cook, Kenny, a wide smile on her face.

There was something different about her appearance, and he couldn't put a finger on what. Her hair, instead of being in its usual ponytail, was loose with the front twisted along her temples and gathered at the back of her head.

Then it struck him. She wasn't wearing her glasses, and she was all made up. He hardly ever noticed Hannah wearing any makeup, but this morning, smoky eyeliner and mascara highlighted her hazel eyes, making the golden flecks pop. Her lips were a glossy rose color, hardly noticeable, except Blake had been studying Hannah for the better part of a year and knew every feature by heart. The round, rosy cheeks, the delicate curve of her lips, the fan of her lashes. Hannah came over in her yellow uniform, the white apron tied around her curvy waist, and his palms started sweating as he gripped the table. Her uniform stretched across her ample chest, and the little skirt flared out over her rounded hips, which seemed to be rolling seductively as she walked.

Blake's jaw was hanging down so far, he could practically feel it resting on his chest. He'd always known Hannah was pretty, but right now, she looked like a pot of honey ready to be licked clean.

An image of his tongue running along Hannah's neck made his cock twitch against the light fabric of his running pants. Shit, that was all he needed; sporting wood while she bent over to fill his coffee. With his luck, she'd probably notice, and then he'd be really fucked.

She set down a mug of black coffee and a tall glass of ice water without being asked, her gaze never leaving his face. "Hey there. You feeling okay today, or do you need me to have Kenny whip you up his hangover cure?"

Blake's mouth snapped closed. How the hell did she know he was hungover?

"What makes you think I'm hungover?" He took a long gulp of his water, draining the glass. Had her uniform always molded so nicely to her curves?

She cocked her head to the side, her brow furrowed. "You called me last night. Don't you remember?"

His heart picked up speed, and he set the glass away, wrapping his fingers around the coffee mug instead. Almost immediately he realized his palms were slick with sweat. He had called Hannah last night? Fuck, what the hell had he said?

Clearing his throat, he mumbled, "I'm sorry about that. I don't even remember doing it."

For a second, she appeared almost crestfallen, and his throat closed up as he racked his brain for any memory of their conversation.

But as fleeting as the look was, it was soon replaced by a reassuring smile and a pat on his shoulder.

"It's okay, you just said hi and immediately passed out. If I'd known where you lived, I probably would have driven over to check on you." Her expression was overly bright, and he knew she was lying. "I'll just go put your order in."

As she walked away, Blake's gaze dropped to her ass, and he watched the sway of that teasing yellow skirt, mesmerized.

Shaking himself out of the lust-filled trance, he tried to remember what in the hell he'd said last night on the phone, but he could hardly recall leaving the bar. Just bits and pieces.

She kept her back to him, and he realized it was a view he'd probably never get tired of. Hannah had a really nice, round butt.

Daddy like.

The words flew through his mind like an echo, and he grimaced.

What the fuck is wrong with me?

Chapter Four

Stupid, stupid, stupid.

Hannah wasn't a bold, brazen flirt and never had been. She'd had an awful stutter growing up and often found it was easier not to talk than it was to listen to other kids taunt her.

As an adult, she would have patted herself on the back for being so cool about a completely awkward situation, if she wasn't so horrified. She'd spent half the morning daydreaming of what he'd say when he saw her, her makeup on point, her glasses nowhere to be seen, and her hair loose like he'd never seen it. For a moment, he'd looked at her so strangely, she'd thought maybe he really did have feelings for her.

But clearly that had just been her naiveté at work. Her face burned, and she was so glad she had her back to him. The last thing she wanted was for Blake to see how embarrassed she was for actually thinking a drunk dial from a man meant something.

Kenny put the plate of food up on the counter and rang the bell. "Wake up, sunshine. Your order is ready."

Hannah laughed as she grabbed the plate. Kenny was in his midfifties and was always calling her names like *sunshine* and *sweetie pie,* but she didn't take offense. She knew he wasn't making a pass at her; that was just how he talked to everyone. He was like the sweet Southern waitress who called everyone *hon,* only he was a man with a gray ponytail who could make a mean Denver omelet.

"Thanks. I think I need more coffee," she said.

"I think you just got a little too much of *that* on your brain." Kenny pointed his spatula past her to where Blake was sitting, and her cheeks heated once more.

"Stop that," she hissed, walking away from his laughter. As she approached Blake, she knew that Kenny was right. Her appreciation for his hazel eyes and broad shoulders had slowly turned into real feelings with every exchange they had. She knew about his work, about his day-to-day activities and the way he took his coffee…

But what do I really know about Blake? His life? His family? Isn't that something friends should discuss?

Hannah had created a whole fantasy about this guy. She'd imagined herself as this wonderful, sweet friend to him, when really, she was just the girl who brought him his coffee.

She set his plate down and refilled his water, refusing to meet his gaze.

"Hannah, I don't know what I said last night, but if any of it was offensive or made you uncomfortable—"

"Let's just forget it, okay? It wasn't a big deal. I just thought it was funny. I mean, the first time we talk on the phone, you're drunk as a skunk and telling me you like the way my voice sounds…"

She noticed his shoulders stiffen, and she cringed. "Sorry, I shouldn't have told you that."

"No, it's okay. Just seems like I have more to apologize for than I thought."

I don't want your apology. I want you to swoop me in your arms and tell me you meant every word.

When he picked up his fork, she shifted her feet awkwardly and mumbled, "It's fine."

Wanting to get as far away from the conversation as possible, she turned and set the water pitcher down. She headed around the counter toward the back door, which she pushed open with a sigh. There were a couple of plastic chairs set up for the staff, who would often come out there to smoke. Hannah came out when she needed some quiet.

Right now, she was hoping for a quick, painless lightning bolt to come from above.

She glanced up at the clear sky and sighed in disappointment. She sat down in one of the chairs and pulled out her phone, sliding her thumb across the screen. Hannah was almost tempted to call Nicki and tell her what an idiot she was, but as much as she loved her best friend, she'd never understood Hannah's romantic notions about love and dating. She'd just tell her to get over it and be off to set her up with someone else.

The problem was that very few men had ever given her that warm fluttering in the pit of her stomach. Not the way being near Blake did.

The sound of footsteps on pavement startled her, and she turned to look down the narrow alleyway behind the diner.

A figure in a dark blue hoodie stood several feet from her, a gun held shakily in his outstretched hand.

"If you keep quiet, I won't hurt you."

Hannah's heart slammed against her breastbone in rapid succession as she stared down the black barrel that inched toward her. She couldn't move, couldn't speak. When she'd thought about being struck by a lightning bolt, she hadn't been serious.

She definitely didn't want to be shot.

As he drew closer, she got a better look at him; deep hollows in his cheeks gave him an almost skeletal appearance, as did his pale blue eyes sunk back in his skull.

"I…I…" God, she couldn't even get a sentence out, she was so terrified.

"Come on, we're going to go inside, and I want you to lock the front door. If you scream or try to signal anyone for help, I will shoot you and everyone inside. All right?"

She nodded and climbed up the steps into the diner. She didn't look back over her shoulder or acknowledge Kenny as she passed by the kitchen. Hannah just stared straight ahead, quickening her steps toward the door.

Just as she reached the glass, Blake stood up and tossed down several bills onto the table. Sweat trickled down her forehead and neck, and she held the door, hoping he'd hurry. The last thing she wanted was to have him caught in here. Somehow she doubted he'd sit back and follow the gunman's orders quietly.

"Have a nice day, Blake," she said, glancing back to see if the man had moved up front yet.

Blake shot her a look as he approached, placing his wallet into the pocket of his running pants.

"You okay, Hannah? You're really pale."

"I told you to lock that door!"

Hannah's stomach dropped as she recognized the hooded man's high nasally voice, and she shut the door, locking it with a click.

Blake's gaze met hers, but despite the slight widening of his eyes, he remained passive, calm. Why wouldn't he be? He'd probably faced off against men with guns for years, while besides her dad's, she'd never even seen anyone holding a gun, let alone pointing it at her.

"I'm sorry." She turned away from Blake to face the man's wrath, but he was addressing the rest of the diner, his gun pressed against the side of Kenny's head. He was visibly shaking, and Hannah was afraid he might pull the trigger, he trembled so badly. Was he just pumped up with adrenaline or on something?

"Everyone set your cell phones and wallets on the counter in front of me. If anyone gets any ideas about being a hero, I will blow this man's brains out."

Hannah cried out, but a firm hand on her arm stalled her from moving forward. She looked up to find Blake had moved in next to her, watching the gunman with narrow-eyed determination.

"Come on; get a move on. I don't have all day," the gunman snapped.

The five customers, including Blake, did as he asked. The only one missing was Chloe, and hope flashed through Hannah as she imagined Chloe calling the cops from inside their tiny bathroom.

"Your cell phone and whatever tips you got hidden in that apron."

Hannah realized the gunman was talking to her, and she set the black phone next to the others.

"I said give me your tips."

"They're in the jars next to the register," she said. "There should be three of them, with our names taped to the outside."

While he grabbed a plastic to-go bag from under the counter and started shoveling the phones, wallets, and purses into it, Hannah glanced toward Blake. His jaw was clenched, his gaze glued on the hooded man.

In any of the books or romantic movies she loved, this would be the moment that the heroine would turn to the hero and say something clever like, "If we make it out of this, we're going on a date. You're buying."

But this was real life, and there was a good chance once this man got what he wanted, he was going to just open fire and take them all out.

Once the cash register and the tip jars had been collected, the man shoved Kenny to the ground roughly. "You stay down there. And you"—he pointed his gun at her again—"get over here. You're going to see I get out of here safely."

Hannah took a step toward him, her feet heavy, as if she was sporting cement blocks for shoes.

She gasped when Blake stepped in front of her.

"You don't need her. You got what you wanted, so why don't you take it and go?" Blake said.

As the black gun swung toward Blake, Hannah's world tilted. She couldn't let Blake get shot because of her.

"Stop, please, I'm coming." She pushed past Blake and moved until she was right in the line of fire, walking slowly toward him. "You don't have to shoot anyone."

"Hannah…" Blake's growl rumbled behind her, but she kept her attention on the gunman.

"I'm going with you. You don't need to be scared. No one is going to hurt you." She spoke as if she was talking to a wounded animal or one of her kindergarteners, slow and easy.

The man didn't seem to be listening, still focused on Blake, waving the gun up and down unsteadily.

"I said no heroes. Believe me, she ain't worth dying over."

As soon as she was within arm's distance, the man pointed the gun right into her back, and she led him down the hall.

Please, if you get me out of this, I will do anything. Just…

Blake's smile…his eyes…and the last angry glare he'd sent the gunman's way flashed through her mind.

Please, let me see Blake again.

A STONE SETTLED into the pit of Blake's stomach as he helplessly watched Hannah disappear, the gun trained on the middle of her back. If the man's finger pressed that trigger, the shot was too close not to be fatal.

Blake still couldn't believe she'd stepped in front of him. He'd given her the perfect opportunity to escape and let him handle things, and she'd put herself right back in harm's way.

The minute Hannah and the gunman were out of sight, Blake moved. Turning the lock on the door, he raced out the front and around the side of the building, his footsteps slowing even as his heartbeat picked up speed. He listened for the sound of approaching feet and knew that the gunman had to bring Hannah back down this way; the other side of the alley was a dead end into a brick wall.

Blake tried to remain calm, but he'd seen the pale white of Hannah's cheeks, the usual rosy hue leached away by terror, and he imagined Jenny in her place. Had Jenny tried to intervene when the gunman had entered the Base Exchange, or had she been quiet? Following his instructions and just hoping she made it out alive?

He heard footsteps approaching and knew that even if it meant he didn't make it, Hannah was going to walk away unscathed.

Hannah stepped out first, and before she even noticed him, he pulled her toward him. He pushed her past him, out of the gunman's sight.

"What the fu—"

Blake didn't wait for the gunman to figure out what had happened. As quick as the Flash, he grabbed the gun and with a swift twist of the man's wrist found himself in possession of the firearm, pointing it directly at the other man's chest.

"Toss the bag this way and get on the ground with your hands behind your back." Blake kept sight of Hannah out of the corner his eye, the sick feeling in his stomach easing the farther away she got from danger.

The man's hands flew up, sweat trickling down his temples. "I wasn't going to hurt her, I swear—"

"On the ground or I *will* hurt you," Blake snapped.

The sound of sirens drew closer as the man did what Blake said. Blake kept his attention solely on him, even as he spoke to Hannah.

"Are you all right?" he asked gruffly.

"Y…Yes. I'm fine."

He nodded curtly, the last of the worry for her draining out of him. "Take the bag inside, and let everyone know it's okay. I'll stay with him."

Hannah picked up the bag from where he'd thrown it, and Blake sensed her hesitation, then felt her hand briefly touch his arm.

"Thank you."

This time, he couldn't stop himself from looking at her, taking in her wide eyes, her brown hair around her shoulder in loose, thick waves. Her lips…

Snapping his gaze away from her, he practically growled, "Go inside."

He couldn't let his emotions distract him, although they had played a large part in his response to the robbery. He hadn't been able to leave Hannah at the hands of the gunman, not after she'd put herself in the midst of the danger.

To protect me. She did it so that the gunman would take his sights off me.

Two cruisers pulled up, and when the officers got out, their weapons drawn, Blake held his hands up.

"Drop your weapon!" a tall officer with a shiny bald head shouted.

"Yes, sir!" Blake slowly tossed the gun away from him and the man on the ground and called out, "My name is Sergeant Blake Kline with the United States Army. This man attempted to rob Dale's Diner and take a hostage before I disarmed him."

"That is quite a story, Kline. Don't shoot him, guys; he's probably telling the truth." Officer Zack Dalton came out from behind the open squad car door with a wide grin on his face, holstering his weapon while his shiny-headed partner kept his gun on Blake. Dalton had been hired at Alpha Dog Training Program several months ago to assist with training the police dogs, and everyone at Alpha Dog respected the young officer with the wicked sense of humor.

Blake kept his hands up in case the other officers didn't take Dalton at his word. "There are witnesses inside, including the girl this man held at gunpoint. Her name is Hannah, and the rest of the customers will vouch for me."

Dalton walked past him and knelt next to the hooded man, securing handcuffs on his wrists behind his back.

"You have the right to remain silent. Anything you say can and will be used against you…"

"Can you please put your hands behind your back, sir?" Blake hadn't even heard the officer come up but did as he requested. "I am going to secure you with handcuffs as a precaution until we get a witness to corroborate your story."

Blake complied, letting the officer secure the steel cuffs on his wrists.

"Hey, what are you doing?"

Blake and the officer turned at the sound of Hannah's outraged cry. She was racing down the steps with an angry scowl on her face.

"Ma'am, you need to go back inside—"

Hannah ignored the officer and stopped a few feet away, her hands on her hips. "And *you* need to let him go right now!"

A surprise laugh escaped Blake even as the officer behind him stiffened and Blake thought he heard something unsnap. Was he actually going to pull his gun on Hannah?

"Ma'am, you are interfering with a police investigation, and if you don't step back inside, I will be slapping a set of cuffs on you, too."

Dalton stepped up then. "I'm sure that won't be necessary, Officer Blount." He smiled at Hannah, and Blake tensed when he thought the other man's eyes did a quick once-over. He must have liked what he saw, because he took off his hat and stepped closer to Hannah. "Ma'am, I appreciate your concern for Sergeant Kline, but rest assured, he's a friend of mine, and we'll get this sorted out quick."

Hannah's hands fell from her hips, and her voice turned pleading. "I'm sorry for being disrespectful, but this man is a hero. He saved my life, and it just doesn't…doesn't seem right…"

Hannah's lips trembled, and fat tears threatened to spill over her lower lids. Blake found himself taking a step toward her, his first instinct to comfort her, only to be jerked back by Officer Blount, who cleared his throat. Even without seeing his face, Blake could tell he was uncomfortable.

"Ma'am, please, just go back inside, all right? Someone will be in to take your statement, and until then, the sergeant is just going to cool his heels in the back of one of our squad cars. Once we do that, you can rain all the gratitude you want on him."

The snide way the officer said it made Blake want to swing his head back and break his nose, but then Dalton might really arrest him.

Dalton shot his partner a dark glower, which Blake appreciated, and turned his attention back to Hannah. "Why don't I escort you back in? I'll go ahead and take your statement now, Miss…"

"York. Hannah York." Hannah backed away reluctantly, casting one more look his way before going back inside. He saw Dalton's hand rest on the small of her back, a gentlemanly move, but Blake didn't like it.

Blake's jaw turned to granite, and he gritted his teeth painfully as Officer Blount opened the back door of the police cruiser and helped him in. "You just sit tight, hero."

He closed the door, and Blake cursed. He hadn't done anything that any man with his training wouldn't have. It didn't make him a hero.

He glanced toward Dale's and saw Hannah standing by the window, watching him earnestly. Between all the terror and fighting to save her life, he hadn't had a chance to dwell on his reaction to her earlier and the knowledge that he had drunk dialed her and probably said a host of things he shouldn't have. It didn't take a genius to realize he was attracted to Hannah, but she was more than just a pretty woman. She brightened his day, was the one thing he looked forward to.

But he couldn't make a move on her. Not with how completely fucked up he was. He'd had a few beers, and after one conversation with her he couldn't even remember, his subconscious had triggered a violent, gut-churning nightmare. If that wasn't the universe telling him he needed more time to work out his shit, he didn't know what was.

Now, he just needed to find a way to ease away from Hannah without hurting her.

Chapter Five

HANNAH SAT WITH Officer Dalton, recounting everything that had happened after the gunman had approached her outside. She was right next to the window and kept glancing outside, concerned about Blake.

She was still in awe of him. She'd never seen anyone move that fast, and the sheer strength with which he'd twisted and laid out the other man was beautiful. He was like a lion taking down a gazelle. He was a hero, and they were treating him like a criminal; even the officer who knew him was allowing it.

"Officer Dalton, when are you going to take the cuffs off Blake?" she asked.

The young officer's dark eyes twinkled. He was really good-looking, resembling Will Smith a bit, especially with the little mustache. She hadn't been oblivious to his friendly overtures, but she wasn't interested in anyone but Blake.

"You don't have to worry about Sergeant Kline. I'll tell Officer Blount to release him just as soon as I get an awkward pic of him to show the rest of the guys at Alpha Dog."

Hannah shook her head. "He saved my life. He should be getting medals and awards, not sitting in the back of a police car with his hands behind his back. I can't imagine that's comfortable—"

He interrupted her with his hands in the air, as if he was surrendering to her. "All right, Miss York, I'll go give the word that Kline is in the clear. You just sit tight."

He got up from the table and went outside, walking down to the cop car where Blake was sitting. He really did pull out his phone and take a picture, but then he took the cuffs off him. Hannah had no idea what the two men were saying, but when Blake glanced up toward the window, she smiled and gave a little wave.

He looked away without acknowledging her.

Hannah's stomach sunk like a rock. Did he blame her? Think that all this was somehow her fault?

Blake spoke to the officers a moment or two longer and then got into his car and drove away.

"Hannah?"

Kenny's voice made her jump, and she realized her eyes were blurry with tears. Wiping at them shakily, she sniffled, "Hey, Kenny, sorry, I was—"

"No need to apologize, sweetie, I was just going to see if you needed a ride home. Dale's on his way, and I thought you might be shaken up."

Hannah hadn't been surprised by the round of hugs or that their boss was rushing in to check on them. The employees at Dale's were more of a family unit than just coworkers.

"Thanks, but I think I'll be okay. I have an interview this afternoon that I can't miss, so I think I'll just go home and unwind for a while."

"All right, darlin', but you call if you need anything, you hear?"

"Yes, sir."

Hannah walked out of the diner, not nearly as calm as she'd pretended. The truth was, her heart was pumping so hard it actually felt like it may burst. Just as she reached her car, a news van pulled up behind her and a woman jumped out.

"Miss, miss. We received a tip that a gunman was disarmed and restrained by an active military man before the police arrived. Is this true?"

Hannah's mouth opened and closed for a moment as a young man in a loose beanie and a scraggly beard shoved a camera in her face.

Well, if Blake didn't want to stick around to hear how grateful she was in person, then at least she could tell him now.

"Yes…Yes, his name is Sergeant Blake Kline, and he saved my life."

BLAKE CUT OUT of there as soon as the cuffs were off, hauling ass back to his place to change into his uniform.

He couldn't wait for Hannah to come out of the diner; he was already late for work, and besides, he didn't think he could look her in the eye, not with the thoughts that had been racing through his mind about her.

If he was being honest with himself, he'd been tempted to break the gunman's arm after seeing the guy manhandle and threaten Hannah. It was a knee-jerk, violent reaction and one he hadn't been prepared for.

It had scared the hell out of him.

He'd thought all he'd felt for Hannah was friendship, a mild affection even. Now, he knew it was more than that.

He was attracted to her. Even cared about her as more than just a friend.

And the guilt twisting up his insides was more than he could stand.

It had only been two years since Jenny's death. How could he want to be with anyone else? Jenny was his soul mate, his high school sweetheart, his best friend.

Two years of mourning was pitiful, and he hated himself for it. Looking for someone to just pass the time with, a little physical comfort, that was one thing. But getting emotionally involved with Hannah when he was still so fucked up would make him feel worse, not better. And it wouldn't be fair to her.

He pulled into the parking lot of Alpha Dog and saw Best getting out of his SUV. He tapped his horn once as he parked and caught up with his friend.

"How you doing?" Best asked, sounding almost exactly like Joey from the show *Friends*.

"Fine, except Dale's Diner, that place I always eat at after my run, got robbed this morning. Made me late."

Best's eyes widened as he looked Blake over. "Geez, that is crazy! Is everyone okay?"

"Yeah, everyone is fine." Blake didn't really want to tell Best all the details.

"Well, that's good." Best grabbed the door and held it for Blake to go through first. "By the way, did you hear about the fundraiser Eve has planned for us?"

Blake grimaced, just imagining what the Alpha Dog publicist might have cooked up this time. "No, I make it a habit to avoid all of Eve's bright ideas."

As their publicity expert, Evelyn Reynolds was in charge of making sure people learned about the good Alpha Dog did, so they could expand to other cities across the country. She also happened to be the daughter of their commanding officer, General Reynolds, and the girlfriend of their friend Martinez. Which made it a little hard to tell her to stuff it when she asked you to dress up like a clown to visit the children's wing at Sutter Memorial.

"Well, you're just going to *loooove* this one." Best drew out the word, indicating that Blake was going to hate whatever it was Eve had in mind.

His mood still amped up from the diner, Blake snapped, "Either tell me what it is or get the fuck out of here."

Best grinned, and Blake wondered if he was deliberately torturing him.

"She wants us to have a Valentine's Day singles' event. A ball. Fifty bucks a ticket, and guess who's the entertainment?"

Blake grimaced. "Us?"

"Bingo. We are to dance with the ladies, fetch them drinks, and all around make them happy."

"Pass."

"No can do, dude. It's mandatory. Even the guys with girls are being ordered to step up," Best said.

"I don't care. I'm not going to spend the night flirting and catering to a bunch of women."

Best pulled open the door to leave. "Please let me be there when you tell Eve that."

The door shut on Best's laughter, and Blake sat down at his desk, shaking his head. The whole morning had been a trial, and now this ball thing…

God, couldn't he just get a little peace? All he wanted was to go to work, run, read, sleep, and eat. He didn't want to go to balls or take down robbers. He just wanted to be left alone.

An image of Hannah's smile rushed through his mind. Until this morning, he hadn't minded being around her. Hell, he'd actually looked forward to it. Hannah was sweet, and she put him at ease.

But she'd looked at him a little differently today, and it had unnerved him, made him feel things he thought had died with his wife.

Or was it because she looked at you the way Jenny used to? As if you could conquer the world?

Blake had let Jenny down when she'd needed him the most. He should have been the one to go to the store, not her. If only…

Blake pushed that thought away. Today, he'd been there for Hannah, but he couldn't give her what she ultimately wanted. His heart hadn't been his since he was sixteen, and what was left of it was a hollow shell.

Hannah deserved more.

Chapter Six

THE NEXT MORNING, Blake skipped breakfast at Dale's. Avoiding Hannah seemed like the best course of action under the circumstances.

But despite knowing it was a bad idea, he drove by the diner after his run, staring into the window to catch a glimpse of her. He'd had a rough night's sleep, and it just wasn't the same going into work without seeing Hannah's smile.

God, he was such a selfish prick. Just because he had issues didn't mean Hannah should be punished. He should just be honest with her, tell her that he hadn't meant to give her the wrong impression. That he wasn't ready for anything more than friendship. He could say that, right?

Sure, because women love the "let's just be friends" speech.

Besides, it wasn't just Hannah's feelings that scared him, but his reaction to her and the guilt eating him up because of it.

He parked in front of Alpha Dog, and as he got out, he heard Best yelling his name from the front door.

"Why the fuck are you ignoring our calls, hero?"

Hero? Blake shut his door. "I left my phone here last night. Why, what's up?"

"What's up is that the girl you saved yesterday was on the news, singing your praises. The program's phone has been ringing off the hook from reporters trying to get interviews with you! Eve is drooling about getting you on camera to help drum up some press about Alpha Dog. You, my friend, are a local celebrity."

Blake wanted to run back to his car and disappear. He didn't want to do camera interviews. He just wanted to come to work and do his job.

"No, I'm not doing any interviews. I just did what anyone would have done—"

Best slapped him on the back and broke in. "No go, *mi amigo*. Not everyone would have gone outside, disarmed a man with a gun, and saved the girl. You are a knight in shining armor, and Eve is going to milk the shit out of it."

Blake greeted the guys working security and walked away from Best, who yelled after him, "You can't escape your destiny, man!"

Blake saw Eve standing outside Sparks's office talking to Martinez and Sparks and cursed silently. What were the chances he could duck into his office without any of them noticing him?

"Blake!"

Eve's cheerful call made him wince. Too late.

He watched her approach, giving her what he hoped was a formidable scowl. He must have been losing his touch, because she just continued to give him that wide, red-lipped smile.

"I am so glad I caught you. You've been getting interview requests all morning on what happened yesterday, so I took the liberty of scheduling Channel Three to come out and interview you. Maybe watch you in action with the kids and the dogs. It will be great exposure for the program and you…"

Blake's skin pricked as she went on and on about everything she had planned for him, and finally, his temper snapped. "I don't want any exposure. I did what needed to be done, and that is it. I'm not a trained monkey to sing and dance for you or anyone else."

"Kline!" Sparks barked. "My office."

Eve stared at him as if he'd suddenly grown horns, and he couldn't blame her. Most of his friends' girlfriends thought he was this quiet, mild-mannered guy with a sad past.

That wasn't the whole picture, though. He hated to be pushed and had a bit of a temper—even he could admit that. So did every guy here, and right then, Sparks and Martinez were watching him as if they wanted to unleash theirs on him.

He walked past Eve and Martinez, following Sparks into the office, and closed the door behind him.

Sparks's thunderous expression had eased slightly, and he waved his hand. "Sit down."

Blake did it, mostly because he had a feeling he wasn't going to like what Sparks had to say and he'd be less likely to throw a punch if he was sitting.

"I get that you don't like being in the spotlight, but I've been getting questions from the higher-ups on whether or not you even belong here."

Blake stiffened. "What does that mean? I'm here. I work with the kids and teach them how to train the dogs. Exactly what more do I need to be doing?"

"For starters, you've been at the program a year, and yeah, you help out, but if you haven't noticed, our squads are getting bigger, and we actually need you to take on your own. And you need a dog, man. You need to at least pretend as if you give a damn about this place and want it to succeed. You've been going through the motions for a year, but it's time to commit to something."

The muscle under Blake's eye ticked furiously. "What are you talking about? I'm committed. My apartment just won't let me have dogs, is all."

"You bitch and moan about that shit hole all the time, but you won't leave because I think you're afraid to actually settle in here. As if your whole life is just temporary now, but eventually, man, you will meet someone new and things will be good—"

"I don't need a life coach, Sparks."

Sparks's expression darkened. "Fine. As the director of Alpha Dog, I'm telling you that part of your job here is to train a dog to use for demonstrations. That your *job* means you do everything in your power to spread the word and make sure it succeeds. So, you're going to suck it up and do the interview. You're going to be charming and say whatever Eve wants you to. And, you're going to start looking for a place that accepts dogs and get with the program, or the next time the general wants to transfer your ass, I won't go to bat for you."

"I never asked you to," Blake snapped.

"You didn't have to. We're all friends, and we've been through a lot. But while the rest of us have been slowly putting our lives back together, you—"

Blake slammed his hand down on Sparks's desk, cutting him off. He knew that he was disrespecting his friend and his boss, but at the moment, he wasn't thinking rationally. He was thinking about the blood pounding in his ears and that Sparks and the rest of his friends couldn't compare their baggage to his.

"Don't try to act as if we're all the same. Just because we were in group therapy together doesn't mean you know how I feel or have any say on how I conduct my personal life. You want me to pretend I'm some perfect guy that saves lives and has nothing but patience, fine, I can play, but don't start dictating how I choose to continue living after my wife was *murdered*."

Sparks leaned across the desk, his dark gaze full of pity, and Blake hated him for it. "I'm not telling you that.

I'm worried about you, as are the other guys. In fact, the general suggested you go back to mandatory therapy sessions three times a week—"

Blake shoved his chair back then. "I don't need a fucking shrink. I'm not a head case."

"No one is calling you that, Kline…Kline!"

Blake stormed out without looking back, needing to breathe more than anything.

Escaping to the kennels where they kept the dogs, he walked past several barking animals, pausing in front of a huge bloodhound mix named Charge, who bayed at him as he leaned against the fenced door. The black and tan dog had to weigh nearly a hundred and fifty pounds and was taller than a purebred. His fur was wiry, even on his long, droopy ears.

Sadly, the dog was yet another reminder of a past he'd rather leave buried.

When he'd first been offered the position at Alpha Dog, it had been based on his experience with search and rescue dogs, like the ones his dad had trained while Blake was growing up. He hadn't worked with a dog in ten years, not since he was a senior in high school, but his dad was a trainer people had respected and loved. He'd been famous, winning national competitions, and Blake had been proud to learn from him.

His mother had been an elementary school teacher, but no less cherished by their small Texas town. They'd been driving home early from a weekend trip and been hit straight on by another car. They hadn't even made it to the hospital alive. Blake had struggled for years to remember the last thing he'd said to either one of his parents, but he just couldn't.

All he knew was, like with Jenny, he'd never imagined that the last time they spoke would be the final time.

Blake walked straight into an empty cage next to Charge and sat at the back, sucking in calming breaths as evenly as he could manage. The thought of going in to speak to someone one-on-one was worse than group therapy. At least in group, he could hide behind the guys who wouldn't shut up.

One-on-one, the focus would be all on him.

Deep down, he knew Sparks was just trying to help. He was a good friend, but Blake was already confused and struggling with feelings he never thought would surface again. Maybe he'd be better off asking for a transfer instead of getting more involved in the program.

But Blake loved working at Alpha Dog. He enjoyed the kids and the dogs. He was just being a selfish dick again. Thinking about his feelings before anyone else's.

Charge the bloodhound stuck his nose through the chain-link kennel, sniffing at him. Blake slipped his fingers through the small hole and stroked the dog's soft black and tan muzzle, laughing as he pushed harder against the fence, attempting to get better pets.

"I see you're already acquainted with your new trainee."

Blake glanced toward the front of the kennel where Best stood watching him pet Charge.

He climbed to his feet with a grunt, ignoring Charge as he jumped up onto the side of the kennel. "I can't have a dog in my current place."

"I understand that, but I also know that Sparks told you to start looking for one." As Blake walked out of the kennel, glaring at him, Best grabbed the leash off the door. "Look, I've got my hands full, and you're the only one not fostering. Besides, this guy is perfect for you."

Best got the door open, and an ear-splitting howl erupted from Charge, who pushed past Best and flew at Blake. When the dog placed his massive paws on Blake's shoulders, it knocked him flat on his back. The hard cement floor knocked the wind out of him, and he lay there frozen for a second, wheezing.

As he tried to breathe again, he found himself staring into Charge's loose-skinned face, the animal's brown eyes hidden beneath the folds.

The dog panted in his face, his breath noxious. And then he was howling again.

He could hear Best cracking up. "Well, aren't you two getting along like two peas in a pod."

Blake reached up and grabbed the dog's long ears, pushing them back. "Get this thing off me."

Best dragged Charge off him, and Blake sat up slowly. "What the hell is he?"

"My best guess is Irish wolfhound and bloodhound mix. He's been here three weeks, but most of the trainers were intimidated by his size."

"Yeah, I understand. He's massive. I can't take him home with me! My landlord will shit himself."

"This guy has no training as far as I can tell but is a natural for search and rescue. I shoved your sweatshirt under his nose earlier, and he went straight for you."

"Even if I find a place, it will take time to move in. I'm just not ready for him."

Best's face lost its smile. "We'll keep him here for now, but he's yours to train. When you're here, I want you working with him. If you want to prove you're committed to the program, now is your chance."

Best held the leash out to him, and Blake took it reluctantly.

"Fine, I'll train him."

"Good. Because I have an ulterior motive."

Blake suppressed a smile. "Of course you do."

"I want to use you two this summer in the Hound It Search and Rescue Tournament in Montana. If you win, it could mean national coverage for Alpha Dog, and we could open two more locations."

Blake looked down at the hound's lolling tongue. "You want me to have this guy ready for a national competition in five months?"

"Yeah. Figured it would be easy peasy for you."

Before Blake could scoff, Bryce popped her head in and sighed loudly. "There you two are! If you're done diddling each other, maybe you could actually do some work so the rest of us don't have to babysit your kids, too?"

She shut the door without waiting for a response, and Blake caught Best's scowl.

"Sometimes I think Megan's cool, just one of us...and then it feels as though I've got another annoying sister to watch out for."

Blake chuckled, as he had the exact same feelings about their coworker.

"Okay, well, I'll go get my squad under control, and you bring Charge out when you're ready. I've assembled a nice collection of brats for you to mold and shape in your image." Best paused and frowned. "Okay, maybe not your image. Someone cheerier. Like me."

"Fuck you."

"See. Always so grumpy." Best took off toward the door before Blake could take a swing, leaving him alone with Charge.

He looked down at the big dog again. He should start looking for a new place. Somewhere in Orangevale or Roseville; not too far from Highway 80, but in a nicer area, where his car was less likely to get broken into again.

This was the last of his self-involved wallowing. Once he left the kennel, he'd start acting like he gave a damn and take the first step in moving on. He'd go to therapy and fake it until the doctor assured Sparks and the general that he was in perfect mental health. That he was committing to Alpha Dog wholly.

Finding a new place was the best way to show that. It was also the least terrifying of the steps he could be taking.

Chapter Seven

HANNAH CLIMBED THE steps to her parents' home, ringing the bell. Since she no longer lived there, she always knocked or rang the bell, and it drove her mom nuts. Holding the Chinese food she'd picked up for dinner, Hannah chuckled as she heard Uncle Miggons, her parents' spoiled Pomeranian, barking hysterically from the other side.

"Shut it, Migs!" her dad snapped from inside the house, and then the door swung open. He looked down at her from his impressive height with feigned annoyance, his bushy white brows drawn together. He still kept his hair in a military buzz, something that hadn't changed since he was honorably discharged from the army when she was fifteen.

"Is there a reason you can't use a doorknob?" he asked.

Hannah stepped inside and stood on tiptoe, kissing his rough, whiskered cheek. "Nice to see you, too, Daddy.

I figured it was locked. It's not safe to leave your doors open when any crazy person could just stroll in."

Her dad scoffed. "And I've got a thirty-eight that will be happy to greet them."

Hannah didn't bother responding. Her dad reminded her of a character from a John Wayne movie; a tough-talking man with a rough exterior and a heart of gold. At least, that's the way her mom described him. Hannah had never actually watched a single John Wayne movie, despite numerous attempts by her parents to force one of the classics on her.

Hannah carried the bag of food into the kitchen, while her dad headed back to the living room. She noticed the slump of his shoulders and the hitch in his step, concern tightening her chest. Her parents had been in their late thirties, early forties when they'd adopted her, and they were getting on in years. After her dad's bout with prostate cancer last year, Hannah was afraid they wouldn't tell her if they were really sick until they had to. They tended to still treat her like she was twelve instead of a twenty-four-year-old adult.

"Hey, Mom," she called.

Her mom was in front of the dishwasher, putting away dishes as she hummed along to Sam Hunt's "House Party."

"Hi, baby!" Her mom actually shimmied over before hugging Hannah, which she thought was a little weird.

"You're in a good mood. I thought you hated the way new country sounded?"

"I just wanted something with a beat. It's hard to get motivated to put away the dishes anymore. Most of the time, I don't even want to wash them. Just want to chuck them and buy new ones."

Hannah pulled back from her mom's embrace, more than a little surprised. "You do?"

"Mmm-hmm." Her mom went back to putting plates in the cupboard, Uncle Miggons sitting at her feet, watching her intently. "You know, I was thinking maybe for our anniversary this year, I'd drag your father on one of those senior cruises. What do you think?"

Hannah studied her mother. Her parents had never stepped foot on a boat to her knowledge or had any interest in group activities. And she'd never complained or put off housework before.

"Well?" her mother prodded when she hesitated.

I think you're an alien who's taken over my mother's body.

"Pretty sure Dad will hate the idea. You know how he feels about forced socialization."

Her mom sighed loudly, pushing her glasses up with her wrist. "You're probably right. Maybe we'll do a trip to Tahoe, just the two of us. He does like the area. And a good buffet."

There was definitely something weird going on. "Mom, is there a reason for the flurry of activity and vacation planning?"

"Well, I was just thinking that eventually it's going to be harder for us to get around and do things, and then when you get married and have kids of your own, I'm going to want my grandbabies as much as possible. Right now we're kidless and fancy-free; figured we'd get a little wild in our old age."

The word *wild* was terrifying in association with her parents, but Hannah didn't say so. Who was she to tell her mom that her dad barely tolerated all the senior functions she dragged him to now? There was no way he was going to be down with a string of vacations. It would take him too far away from his Fox News.

"Oh, I saw that young man who saved you on the news tonight, by the way. You never mentioned how good-looking he was."

Hannah's skin warmed as a blush crept up her neck and cheeks. "Because it's not like that." At least, she was pretty sure it wasn't like that, especially after he'd taken off yesterday and hadn't bothered coming in today. Hannah was convinced she'd probably scared the crap out of him. She hadn't realized how much she'd gushed on the news until she'd seen the broadcast last night. Geez, could she have been a bigger idiot?

"Well, he was on the news talking about the program he works for and how it helps stray dogs and troubled youth, and I have to say, it takes a special kind of man to do that kind of job."

As if I didn't already know that.

"Yeah, I know he's great."

"Well, let's get our plates and watch it. You know we always tape the five o'clock news, and when I realized who he was, I figured you'd want to see it."

Hannah nearly groaned aloud in frustration. She'd spent last night tossing and turning, convincing herself to forget about Blake, but it seemed like the universe was mocking her with him.

They filled plates for themselves and her dad, and when they walked into the living room, her mom said, "Turn on the five o'clock news."

"I'm watching this!" Her dad hated having his nightly TV regimen ruined.

"And Hannah hasn't seen it yet, so stop being a grump and turn it on."

Hannah hid her smile in her sweet and sour chicken. Since she could remember, her parents had always bickered with each other, but it was never serious. At least, she'd never seen them seriously fight.

"Fine." He scrolled through the DVR and pressed play. "I'm getting a little tired of your harping, woman."

"And I'm done with you thinking you're king of the remote. Now shush up."

Her dad continued to grumble, but Hannah tuned him out as the newscaster came onto the screen. Her hair was artfully styled and her pretty face and trim figure perfect in every way as she stood next to Blake, introducing him. He appeared relaxed, but she'd been around him often enough to know when his eyes wrinkled at the corner he was either smiling or tense.

And he definitely wasn't smiling.

"Sergeant Kline, can you tell me what was going through your mind when you made the decision to go after the armed assailant with nothing but your combat skills?"

Blake cleared his throat and shifted from his left to right foot.

"To be honest, Tamera, I just knew I didn't want him taking Hannah off the premises."

"Hannah is the woman he held hostage. So, this was personal to you?"

Hannah saw Blake's cheeks redden, and she was mesmerized by the sight.

Until he spoke again. "No, I would have done the same for anyone in danger, but it's not like what I did was that special. If someone thought they could help, they would. I'm just an ordinary guy who was in the right place at the right time."

"Oh, I don't believe that's true, Sergeant." The reporter put her hand on Blake's arm and practically purred at him. "In fact, I think the majority of our audience would agree that what you did was extraordinary."

Hannah winced as Blake smiled at the reporter, albeit stiffly. "It was what I was trained for, ma'am. Nothing special about it."

The story cut to the Alpha Dog Training Program, showing video of teenagers and dogs, along with instructors demonstrating techniques for the kids. The voiceover explained how Alpha Dog was coming up on a year of being open and how it had assisted nearly one hundred kids in finding employment and specialty programs after completing their sentence.

The last clip was of Blake again, telling the reporter, "The real heroes are the men and women who launched this program and are determined to keep it going so that other kids can benefit from it in other states. They are amazing."

Hannah's eyes teared up a little at how humble he was.

"He seems like such a nice young man," her mom said.

"Now can I get back to my program?" her dad growled.

Hannah ignored the bickering, her mind on Blake and how she'd told herself to just forget about him.

But with a guy like Blake, that was easier said than done.

THAT NIGHT, BLAKE sat on his couch, scrolling through Realtor.com and absently munching on his Jack in the Box tacos. There were several listings that he'd printed out, but they would deplete everything he had from his parents' estate. It was crazy how expensive houses were now.

Taking a break, he clicked on the other window he had opened and pressed play on the video of Hannah's news interview. The reporter stood next to her, introducing her while Hannah smiled nervously, her cheeks pink.

"What was going through your mind when that man held a gun to you?"

Hannah's hazel eyes flicked to the camera and back to the reporter. "I just thought that this was it. That he was going to kill me as soon as he got away and I was never going to see the people I loved again."

Blake's eyes pricked at her words. He'd watched the video a dozen times today, at work and at home, but it still made his gut clench with sadness. Jenny had probably thought about the people she loved in her final moments. About him.

Maybe Hannah thought of me, too.

Blake stood up from the table, the tacos he'd eaten sitting like rocks in his stomach. Grabbing a bottle of whiskey from the cupboard, he poured a glass over ice and downed it. He should not be thinking about Jenny and Hannah in the same span of thought, but he couldn't seem to stop himself.

There was a knock on his door, and after pouring another glass, he walked over to answer.

On his porch stood Best, Sparks, Martinez, Dalton, and Slater Vincent.

"Was there a party I don't know about?" Blake asked.

Best slapped a deck of cards against his chest as he passed. "We decided you needed a poker night."

"*You decided?* What if I had plans?" Sparks walked by with two twelve packs of beer.

Dalton patted his cheek like he was an amusing child. "You never have plans, buddy. That's why poker is at your place."

Slater nodded at him, the only one who actually looked abashed at barging in on him. "Sorry, man. I got food, though."

When Slater disappeared behind him with sacks of groceries, Martinez was the last one left to come inside.

"So, what did you bring?" Blake asked.

"This."

Martinez sent a fist into his stomach.

Blake bent over with a wheeze, trying to catch his breath.

"The fuck was that for?" Blake rasped.

"For disrespecting my woman."

Martinez stepped over the threshold, patting his back as if to say, *Sorry, buddy, but you deserved it.*

Finally, able to stand straight again, he shut the door. "Sorry about the thing with Eve this morning."

Martinez nodded at him. "I know Evie can be a pushy pain in the ass, but she's *my* pushy pain in the ass. Nobody talks to her the way you did without a serious ass kicking, so be grateful I love you, 'cause you got off light, my friend."

"You're right. I'll apologize to Eve, too."

An awkward silence stretched across the room.

Well, except for the crunching sounds Best was making while he scarfed down one of Blake's tacos.

"We good then?" Best asked around a mouthful.

"Dude, you are an animal." Sparks picked up Blake's laptop to move it out of the way, and Blake knew the moment he noticed the video on his screen. He paused, his eyebrows hiking up his forehead.

"What's the look for? Kline watching porn or something?" Dalton walked over to stand next to Sparks's shoulder, and he made a clicking sound. "Ah, Miss Hannah York. She definitely thinks the sun rises and shines out of your ass."

"Shut up. She was just grateful." Blake took the laptop from Sparks and shut it with a snap.

"So, what, you're watching her news clip for an ego boost?" Best had finished the taco and was currently licking his fingers, so he missed Blake's murderous look.

"Dude, I didn't come over here to cluck like a bunch of hens," Vincent said gruffly. He set a bowl of salsa and chips on the table and sat in the chair, his dark eyes shooting about the room. "So either shut up and play or I'm going to help Kline kick your candy asses out."

The whole room was shocked as hell, if their silence was any indication. Including Blake. He hadn't worked with Vincent very long, only a couple of months, and most of what he knew about the guy came from Megan gushing over him. It was the most the burly black man had ever said at once.

"Easy, brother, we were just fucking with him." Dalton sat next to Vincent and cracked his neck. "I'm ready to take all your asses to the cleaners anyway."

Loud protests and shit talk erupted around the table as they sat down, and Kline glanced at Vincent, giving him a nod of thanks. Vincent returned the gesture and then took the beer Best handed him.

As the night wore on, Blake started to relax and just enjoy the time with his friends, guilt over Jenny and worry over Hannah pushed to the back of his mind as they played.

But when they all filed out near midnight, Blake looked around his empty apartment. The silence was deafening. Grabbing one more glass of whiskey and his laptop, he went to his bedroom. He already had a pretty good buzz from the two glasses earlier and several beers, but he wanted to fall asleep fast.

He got undressed and crawled under the sheets, trying to relax as he took a drink. He opened his laptop and tapped on the video.

"What about Sergeant Kline? What can you tell us about him?"

Blake studied Hannah's face; the way her eyes lit up and her full lips parted into a sweet smile.

"Blake is amazing. He moved so fast. I never knew anyone could move like that, except for maybe Jet Li."

He chuckled and caught himself.

"Do you know him personally? Is he a friend?"

"Yes, he's my friend." He saw something flash across her face, but it was gone too fast to identify. "But Blake is the type of guy who would risk his life for a stranger. He is just a good man. A hero."

Blake shut off the video as the reporter started talking again and closed his laptop. Once he turned off his bed-side lamp, he lay in the dark, his eyes closed. Hannah's rich, husky voice played through his head, and he found himself reaching for his cock, stroking it.

Oh, Blake.

Hannah's mouth, her eyes, and the mass of hair he wanted to stroke teased him as he got close.

Then, it was a different face. Jenny's. Her wide blue eyes filled with terror and her mouth open, calling to him.

Blake threw off the covers and sat on the side of the bed, his head in his hands. He was breathing so hard he was trembling, tears sliding from between his closed eyelids.

God, what the fuck? He could watch porn or think about bendy Eliza Dushku in the shower, but one mild fantasy about Hannah, and Jenny crops up.

Blake finished off his whiskey and crawled back into bed, determined not to think of Hannah or Jenny anymore.

But just as he slipped off to sleep, he replayed the last part of the interview in his mind.

"He is just a good guy. A hero."

God, he wanted that to be true.

Chapter Eight

Two days later, Hannah was doing her grocery shopping while trying to carry on a phone conversation with her mom. As she reached out to grab a bag for her lettuce, a woman next to her gave her a foul look, as if being on the phone was somehow disturbing her.

"No, Mom, I don't think *Good Day Sacramento* is going to want to interview me."

"And why not? You went through a traumatic experience, and I bet they would want to hear all about it."

Hannah groaned aloud. Ever since she'd seen Blake being interviewed, her mom had gotten a burr up her butt about Hannah telling her story in detail.

"Because I'm not that interesting."

"That's a load of bull, Hannah Banana. You just don't see yourself the way I do."

Hannah rolled her eyes, silently agreeing with her. Her mom was constantly telling Hannah everything she could do with her life; crazy, far-fetched dreams that Hannah had no desire to pursue. Like auditioning for *American Idol* or *The Bachelor*. Hannah just wanted to get a full-time teaching position and maybe someday submit her books for publication. Not parade around in front of TV cameras and have what little self-confidence she had shredded for entertainment purposes.

Maybe she should be a bit disturbed that her mother actually enjoyed shows like that.

"If they wanted to talk to anyone again, Mom, it would be Blake." Cranky lady was pushing her cart away, still shooting shade Hannah's way, and she was tempted to make a face right back, but she refrained. "He was the real hero."

"Yes, he is! Have you seen him since?"

"No, he hasn't been in." Hannah tried to keep the disappointment from her tone, knowing her mom would latch onto it like a boa constrictor.

Guess he didn't want to deal with my hero worship anymore.

"Well, when you see him, tell him I want to have him over for dinner some night to thank him for saving my baby."

"Mom..." Hannah started through gritted teeth.

"Oh, sweetie, I have to go! We're heading over to Linus and Mary Pat's to play bridge."

Hannah almost released a depressed sigh. It was really sad when her parents had better social lives than she did.

As if sensing her train of thought, her mother asked, "By the way, what are your plans for the evening?"

Hannah grabbed a couple limes and stuffed them in a bag before answering. "Not sure yet."

"Well, whatever you do, be careful. Your father and I were watching ID network the other night, and there was this horrible story about a girl who got separated from her friends, and this man kidnapped her, raped her, and cut off her—"

"Okay, thanks, but that's enough of that. Seriously, you guys need to stop watching those shows or at least stop *telling* me about it."

"I'm only saying, you're a young woman living alone, and I worry."

Hannah sighed. "You have nothing to worry about, really. What happened this week was an anomaly. I was just out back when he walked up. That's it. I can't live in a bubble."

"I know, sweetie, but I'm your mom. It's my job to care."

And Hannah was really glad for that.

"I know, and I love you for it."

"I love you, too, Hannah Banana. I'll talk to you tomorrow."

"Night, Mom. Tell Dad I said hi."

"I will. Bye."

Hannah made sure the call ended and slipped the phone into her purse. Retrieving the shopping list she'd made and a pen from inside, she started checking off what she'd already grabbed. She'd planned on making a chicken salad recipe she'd seen on Facebook earlier in the week, but a salad just didn't sound as good as a plate of mile-high beefy nachos.

Of course, if she ever wanted to squeeze back into her size fourteen jeans again, she needed to change something. She'd thought about joining a gym, but between waitressing at Dale's Diner and substitute teaching, it was hard to justify spending fifty bucks a month for something she might make it to twice a week. Walking with a friend was out, too, since most of them were just as busy as Hannah, if not more so.

She just needed the discipline to do one of her workout DVDs in the morning or evening. She had a whole shelf of them, but gathering the energy to shake her booty at four in the morning or seven at night was hard.

"Excuse me," a deep voice behind her rumbled just before a long, muscular arm reached past her toward the limes.

Hannah turned sharply and found herself face-to-face with Blake, who appeared as surprised as she was.

"Oh!" She stumbled back against the limes, and a dozen or so escaped from the display, falling to the ground with little bounces.

"Shit. Sorry." She dropped her list and pen into her cart and immediately knelt down to gather up the limes.

"Hannah, Hannah, calm down. They're just limes." He squatted next to her and helped, their hands brushing as they reached for the same limes.

"I'm so sorry!" Her cheeks burned as she jerked her hand back. She noticed several shoppers turning their way, staring at them, and heat spread down her neck.

Well, they were staring at her mostly. She was the one acting like a grade A spaz.

Focusing on Blake again, her gaze drifted over him appreciatively. He wore a gray sweatshirt over dark blue jeans and white sneakers. He had a ball cap on his head with a logo she recognized, though she couldn't remember what sports team it was for.

God, how did he make casual so freaking sexy?

Blake's handsome face was stretched into the gentle smile that had been turning her bones to mush for a year. "I'm the one who should be sorry, Hannah. I didn't mean to scare you, I just needed some limes."

They stood up and put the limes back. Hannah picked up her list again, but her pen was missing in action. "Of course, and here I am, just standing in the way blocking them. I was too busy checking stuff off my list and got lost in thought."

Hannah caught Blake looking over her list. "I can see why. You've got kind of an eclectic assortment of groceries on there. What are you making?"

"Just a recipe I saw online." Before she lost her nerve, she asked, "I never did get to say a proper thank-you for saving me the other day. I'd love to take you to dinner, or I could even make you something." There was no way she was going to mention her mother wanted to cook for him, too. She'd suffered enough embarrassment to last a lifetime.

"It's really not necessary, Hannah. Anyone would have done the same. Besides, the news story they did on me because of you really helped Alpha Dog, so I should be thanking you."

"Not just anyone would have put themselves at risk for me," she said softly.

His hazel eyes stared into hers, and for a moment, she thought he almost looked...afraid? Of her?

"Then if you won't accept dinner, I'd at least like to buy you a cup of coffee. There's a Starbucks at the front of the store." She glanced down at the two cases of Corona in his cart. "Unless you have somewhere you need to be?"

After what felt like the hesitation that would never end, Blake nodded.

"I've got some time."

WHY HAD HE said yes? He was all set to hightail it out of there, to wave off her gratitude as no big deal, but the way she'd looked at him, those big eyes luring him in like a fish on a line, he'd been powerless to stop himself from caving.

He took over pushing the cart for her, and her shy smile was lethal when paired with her soft, husky, "Thanks."

Damn, he really liked her voice. "Not a problem. My beer is causing most of the weight, anyway."

"What's all of it for? You having a party or something?" she asked.

"It's the Super Bowl this weekend. I'm heading over to a friend's to watch on Sunday, and it's bring your own beer."

"I should have guessed. My dad loves football." Hannah's eyes got wider. "You're drinking all of that in one day? Your poor liver."

Blake burst out laughing. "No, there's a pretty dense crowd of people I work with coming, so I figured I'd buy extra. I'm not an alcoholic, I swear."

She probably didn't believe him after he'd drunk dialed her, but over explaining would just make him sound guilty, which he wasn't. He liked having a beer or two, but he only drank heavily when things got to be too much.

"That's good." They stepped into line in front of the Starbucks shack, and she looked at him expectantly. "What do you want?"

"I can get my own coffee—"

"It's a thank-you coffee. You wouldn't deny me the chance to buy you a single cup of gratitude, would you?"

Blake felt his mouth twitch in amusement. "Of course not. I'll just take a large coffee. Black."

"Boring." Her teasing tone made him relax. Things didn't have to be weird between them. He was making it that way.

They made it to the counter, and she ordered his drink, plus a tall caramel macchiato. He still didn't like letting her pay for it, but when he started to reach for his wallet, she shot him a dark, warning look so out of place on her normally friendly face that he chuckled and put his hands up in the air.

"Sorry, I'm just not used to a woman paying for me."

"It's a small repayment for what you did."

Blake shifted his feet, uncomfortable again.

Once she finished, they grabbed a table in the small sitting area and settled in across from each other. Blake studied her covertly, liking casual Hannah. Out of her usual yellow uniform and in a pair of blue jeans, a soft-looking blue sweater, and a patterned scarf, it was no wonder he hadn't recognized her. Her hair was half up, with the long caramel waves rolling over her shoulders and down her back.

"You look different outside of work," he said.

Her hand flew up, playing with her scarf. "Is that a compliment?"

"Yes…I mean, you don't look bad at work. It's just different."

She looked up at him from beneath those thick lashes, and his heart raced.

"Thanks," she said.

The barista called Hannah's name, and as she left to get their drinks, Blake stood up with her, wiping his sweaty palms on his legs. What the hell? Why was he so nervous? It's not like this was a date or anything.

Hannah came back and handed him his cup, shooting him a puzzled grin. "Why are you standing?"

"Because it's rude to sit when a woman leaves the table."

"Where'd you learn that?"

She sat down, and he did the same. "From my dad, and then the military just instilled what was already there."

"That's nice. Gentlemanly."

"Thanks."

She took a sip of her drink, running her tongue discreetly across her upper lip. He wasn't prepared for the shot of lust that raced through him in response to that simple gesture. Damn.

Shifting in his chair, he tried to focus on anything but her mouth.

"So, do you come here often?"

"Yes, it's right down the road from my house. How about you? Have we been shopping at the same grocery store for a year and just never crossed paths?"

He shook his head. "I normally shop over at Winco, but it was pretty packed today, so I decided to change it up."

"Lucky me."

Blake took in her coy smile, and his heart kicked up another notch. "How is that?"

"Well, because I finally get to give you a semi-proper thank-you, since I haven't seen much of you the last few days."

He glanced away awkwardly. "Yeah, I've been busy, looking for somewhere to move to."

"Really? That's amazing, Blake. Any prospective places?"

"Still working on it." He didn't really want to get into his lack of success on the real estate front, so he changed the subject. "What's been going on with you outside of the diner? I know you're just subbing for now and that you want to teach kindergarten, but why? Why not high school?"

She glanced down at the table, and he noticed the nervous way she fidgeted with her cup. "I find any grade above fifth a little…intimidating."

Blake nodded, understanding. When he'd started coming into Dale's, the first thing he'd noticed about Hannah was her rather timid nature. "Hell, I work with teenagers all week, so I don't blame you. Some of them can be challenging."

"That's right. How does your program work, again?"

"We take judge-recommended juvenile offenders who have committed nonviolent crimes and teach them to train dogs in obedience. Most of the graduates have gone on to continue their education in animal health or work with animals at shelters and veterinary hospitals."

"That is awesome. It's good that you give them a chance to make better decisions with their lives. A lot of kids get lost in the system and never catch a break."

The way she said it sounded personal, and he was genuinely curious about her.

"Did that happen to you?" he asked.

"Me? No. I mean, I *was* in foster care, but I was too young to remember. I was placed with my parents when I was just a baby, and they adopted me when I was three. But I did an internship at McClatchy High School, and some of the kids... You could just tell they'd given up."

The vulnerable sadness on her face had him reaching toward her before he could stop himself.

As his palm covered the back of hers, heat radiated along his skin. He was completely aware of her; her sweet, fruity perfume, the flecks of gold in her eyes, and the way her lower lip was twice the size of the top.

He jerked his hand back and knocked his hot coffee back onto his lap and front.

"Shit!" The loud curse carried as he stood up, cringing as the painfully hot coffee soaked through his jeans to his thighs, lower abdomen, and dick.

His stomach rolled against the pain, and he fought back the urge to hurl.

"Oh my God, Blake, are you okay? Come on." She picked up her purse and took his arm. "Let's get you cleaned up."

Oh, hell no, if his hand caught fire just touching her skin, he could only imagine what her cleanup would do to him.

"I'm okay," he said hoarsely.

"Are you sure? That coffee was really hot, and it's all over your...well..."

Several snickers close by let Blake know that they had drawn an audience, and he sucked in a deep breath as he straightened.

"I'm good. I should be going, though."

"Oh, okay. Well, it was good catching up with you. I guess I'll see you at the diner."

"Yeah, sure. See ya."

He picked up the empty coffee cup and threw it in the trash before retrieving his beer and limes from her basket. He couldn't even look at her; not when he'd acted like a complete idiot.

There was one thing for sure: He was never going back to Dale's Diner. Hannah was too dangerous for his peace of mind.

And my genitals.

Chapter Nine

THE NEXT MORNING, Hannah got called into work at the diner, and without anything better to do, she took the shift. She needed the money, anyway.

Plus, she'd been hoping Blake might come in.

God, she was so pathetic. He'd spilled his coffee on himself just to get away from her. If that wasn't enough to tell her he wasn't interested, she didn't know what was.

"Kenny, I'm taking the trash out."

"No, you let me do that! Crazy girl," Kenny muttered as he flipped several pancakes on the griddle.

"I'm fine. If I'm not back in three minutes, you can lead the rescue mission." She shook her head, tired of everyone's worried expressions and mollycoddling.

She opened up the back door and jumped when she saw a man standing near the Dumpster, a roll of duct tape in his hand.

Hannah screamed without thinking, and the guy dropped the duct tape and ran back down the alleyway, his black Windbreaker flying behind him like a cape.

"Hannah!" Kenny yelled right at her back. He grabbed her arm and jerked her behind him, waving his butcher knife around as he looked from left to right. "What happened?"

Hannah tried to calm her heavy breathing before answering, but her response was still pretty breathless. "Sorry, there was a guy by the Dumpster, and he just startled me, that's all."

"This is why you should have let me do the trash, you are still recovering—"

Hannah huffed as she pushed past him and climbed down the steps, but in all honestly, Kenny might have been a little right. She was jumpier behind the diner than she used to be.

As she approached the dropped duct tape, she noticed the box he had been taping. She tossed her trash bag up on top and reached down to pick up the box.

Idiot! What if it's a bomb or something?

Hannah forgot the ludicrous idea the minute the box whimpered and shook.

She nearly dropped it, it scared her so bad. Instead, she set it back on the ground and yelled for Kenny.

"Bring me a box cutter!"

"What for?"

"There's something alive in here!"

"Then why the hell would you want to open it? It could be a skunk or something!"

She started pulling on it, ignoring his worry, but it was wrapped too tight. A few moments later, she heard Kenny's footsteps and his steady puffing before he passed the closed box cutter over her shoulder.

Hannah took it, opened it, and carefully sawed through the silver tape. When she got the ends open, she could see something yellow moving on the inside.

Finally, she pulled the lid open, and the sight inside brought a lump into her throat, outrage pouring out of her in waves.

It was a puppy with short golden fur. The poor thing's front and back legs were taped together, along with his little muzzle.

The puppy whimpered and tried to struggle, but she laid a hand on his side and shushed him.

"Don't move, sweetie. I'm going to get this off you."

"Holy shit," Kenny said behind her.

"Do you have your phone on you?"

He gave it to her, and when she asked him to grab some oil from the kitchen, he didn't ask why, just did it.

Hannah took a few pictures to document what had been done and then dialed 911. She explained why she was calling and gave a description of the assailant to the dispatcher, who said she would contact animal control to come out.

When she got off the phone, Kenny was back with the oil, and slowly, Hannah coated the tape along the puppy's muzzle, trying not to get it in his nose or mouth.

As she slowly removed the tape, the puppy tried moving again, and she spoke softly, cooing to him so he would remain still.

"Kenny, can you get his legs? Be easy."

Together, they worked the tape off until Hannah had the pup's mouth free. He'd lost some hair, and there were some abrasions, but otherwise, he seemed okay.

In fact, with his paws and mouth free, he was trying his best to lick Hannah everywhere he could reach.

"I better get back in there before Marcus starts having a meltdown," Kenny said. Marcus was their other cook, only he hated to actually work. "Why don't you bring him in, and we'll put him in the storage closet until animal control arrives."

Hannah snuggled the puppy into her arms as she stood up, guessing he was probably around fifteen pounds or so. He was already bigger than Uncle Miggons and he couldn't be older than a few months.

"You're a big boy, huh? Will you be good while I finish my shift?"

Kenny laughed as they climbed the steps to the back door. "That little guy isn't going to the shelter, is he?"

As the puppy rolled onto his back in her arms, exposing his smooth tummy, her whole body turned to melted butter. He turned his head, gazed up at her, and she knew Kenny was right. There was no way she'd let anyone else take him when those big brown eyes were staring at her as if she was the best human in the whole world.

I'm going to call you Milo.

The kind animal control officer showed up just before her shift was over, and Hannah texted him the pictures she'd taken with Kenny's phone. He'd assured her they would keep her updated if they made any arrests in Milo's case.

After work, she'd carried Milo out the back and around to where her car was parked. Once she got the door open, she slid in, closed it behind her, and set Milo on the passenger seat.

"What do you say we go see the vet? Huh?"

Milo tried to climb into her lap, but she sat him back on the seat gently. She started the car and headed up the road to Highway 80. She'd called the vet as soon as they opened, asking if Dr. Standen could squeeze them in. Her parents had taken all of their animals to him, and Hannah trusted him.

Twenty minutes later, she turned into Watt Avenue Veterinary Clinic and carried Milo and her purse inside. She passed by a white van with camo and black lettering on the side and paused in surprise.

Alpha Dog Training Program Mobile Transport.

Her heart thudded in her chest, and she nearly skipped her way to the door. As she stepped inside, she noticed a man standing at the front desk in a pair of black boots, camo pants, and an army-green T-shirt.

Only he had blond hair, not Blake's dark strands.

Disappointment zapped through her as she sat down and began stroking Milo's ears and neck. He'd tensed up when they'd entered the veterinary hospital, maybe because of the distant barking in the back, but Hannah continued to comfort him.

The double doors heading into the back swung open, and Hannah caught her breath as a giant hound pushed through, dragging Blake behind him.

"Damn it, Charge, slow your roll!"

The blond man at the counter laughed as Blake struggled with the dog, and Hannah found herself giggling, too, covering her mouth with her hand. Blake hadn't noticed her yet, and she wished she'd bothered to check her appearance before heading into the veterinary hospital.

Suddenly, the dog spotted Hannah and Milo, and to Hannah's surprised terror, stood up on his hind legs and launched himself toward them. Blake looked up as he struggled with the dog, but when his gaze caught hers, his grip seemed to go a little lax and his jaw dropped.

"Hannah?"

Nothing for it now. She stood up with Milo, avoiding Charge's eager nose. "Hi, Blake. How are you?"

"I'm good. Just brought this guy in to get neutered." Blake pulled Charge back toward him and nodded at Milo. "Who do you have here?"

He didn't seem upset seeing her, just surprised. "Milo. I found him duct taped in a box this morning behind the diner, and I'm having Dr. Standen make sure he's okay minus a little hair."

Now Blake's expression was thunderous. "You were back there alone?"

She blinked at his furious tone, shaking her head slowly. "No, I mean, I was taking out the trash, but when I saw the guy, I screamed, and Kenny came running—"

"You don't need to be going back there by yourself. Why didn't Kenny take the trash out?"

Hannah opened her mouth to answer, but Georgia, Dr. Standen's longtime tech, walked into the lobby behind Blake and called out her name.

"Hannah, is that you? Girl, I haven't seen you since we put Misty to sleep four years ago. Come give me a hug."

Hannah obliged, her head still spinning at Blake's reaction to her being behind the diner alone. As if he cared about her.

"Hey, Georgia, it's good to see you."

"You, too. Hey, how're your folks?" Georgia asked.

"They're good." She turned to Blake, about to apologize, but he spoke first.

"I'll see you later, Hannah."

Hannah was absolutely flabbergasted. The man almost blew a gasket because she'd taken the trash out alone and then turned around and took off before she could even properly digest it all. Was he for real?

She should be mad at him for being so all over the place with her, but as she followed Georgia back, listening with half an ear, she couldn't seem to stop smiling.

Blake cared about her well-being. How could she be mad about that?

He shouldn't have lost his cool there.

Blake watched Hannah disappear into the back with Georgia, the double doors closing behind the two women. He couldn't fathom it. He had just been thinking about her, and then suddenly, boom, there she was, holding onto that yellow Lab puppy and looking just as good as he remembered.

Damn it, every time he saw her, it just made it that much harder to forget her.

"Hey, who was that? She looked familiar." Best eyed Blake suspiciously, and he tried to appear casual, knowing Best was like a shark; if he smelled blood in the water, he would get frenzied.

"She's a waitress at Dale's Diner."

"No, I've seen her somewhere…wait." Best's eyes widened, and he slapped Blake's shoulder. "That's the chick you saved. The one who was gushing about you on the news."

"Shut up."

"I will not, this is classic. That girl is in love with you, and you hate it."

"She is not in love with me."

And I only wished I hated the way she looked at me.

"No, but it's a strong like."

"Shut the fu—"

"Oh, shit." Best was watching him closely. "Are you into her?"

"No. I've told you, I'm not interested in dating anyone."

"That girl isn't just anyone though, is she?"

Before he could respond, the receptionist finished helping the older man next to them and waved them forward. As Tyler paid, Blake kept checking the double doors, even as guilt gnawed at his gut. This attraction to Hannah seemed like a betrayal to Jenny, and he hated it. Hated feeling as if he was cheating on his dead wife by looking at another woman.

"All right, all paid up. You ready to head back?" Best seemed to catch the direction of his gaze and, in a surprisingly cool way, shrugged and said, "Or we can hang out for a bit. See if her dog's okay."

Blake was going to shake his head and say no, that they should get Charge back to Alpha Dog, but instead, he nodded. "Appreciate it."

"Well, why don't Charge and I go grab some coffees, and I'll be back to pick you up in about ten, fifteen minutes?"

Blake was leery of Best's suddenly chill attitude, but he really wanted to talk to Hannah. At least apologize for getting pissed at her about going out back alone. It was none of his business what she did or how she lived her life; he had no say in what she did or didn't do.

But why did she have to be so reckless with her wellbeing? There was no reason why Kenny couldn't take the trash out, or at least she could grab one of the other girls to go with her. He'd thought that after having a gun pointed at her, she'd show a little more caution.

And he really didn't want to get into all that with her in front of Best.

"Sounds good. Black coffee."

"Yeah, I know, dude. I've been getting your coffee for over a year."

Blake grinned as Best and Charge took off out the door, and he went to sit down in the corner, his foot tapping impatiently on the tile floor.

This was insane and probably bordering on stalking. Would she even want to see him after he'd flown off the handle with her?

Ten minutes later, when Hannah came through the double doors, the puppy snuggling his nose in the crook of her neck, his question was answered. When she caught sight of him, her eyes brightened and she smiled before turning to speak to the receptionist. With her back to him, his gaze slowly traveled over her length, his eyes lingering on the little flared yellow skirt and the way it swished above her long, curvy legs.

Realizing she could turn around any second and catch him staring in the direction of her ass, he jerked his gaze up and caught the puppy watching him over her shoulder, a surprisingly suspicious look in its dark eyes.

Blake laughed aloud at the absurdity, and Hannah turned, frowning.

"What's so funny?"

Blake got up, moving in next to her now, and reached out toward the puppy, who actually growled and released a high-pitched bark. "Nothing, I was just thinking it was funny that we keep bumping into each other."

"I was thinking the same thing, although... It's not so strange, if you think about it. We work in the same area, so it would make sense that we would bump into each other every now and again."

Blake supposed that was true, but he couldn't help thinking that maybe Hannah kept getting thrown in his path for a reason.

"I stuck around so I could apologize for talking to you the way I did. Most of my friends have been telling me I'm hard to be around lately, and I had no business acting as though I had the right to dictate how you live your life."

Hannah smiled sheepishly. "I guess I can let it slide, considering you saved me once. I can understand why you wouldn't want to have to do it again."

"No, it's not that…" Blake struggled for a moment, trying to formulate his answer carefully, so that there wouldn't be any confusion. "I wouldn't want anything bad to happen to you because I like you. You're a sweet girl, and you deserve to be safe and happy and live a long life."

For some reason, she almost seemed disappointed by his words, and when he started to ask what he'd said, the receptionist handed her the bill. While Hannah paid, she turned enough so he got a good look at the puppy again. His small golden muzzle looked raw with red bumps and bald patches, but other than that, he appeared to be in good health.

Blake reached out toward him again, planning to run his hand over his shiny head, and the puppy actually bared his little white teeth at him as he snarled.

His jaw clenched. He couldn't really blame the little guy for not trusting him, especially if it was a man who had hurt him. What the hell was wrong with people? There were other solutions if they decided they no longer wanted their pets, but abusing them or leaving them to die a painful death was just evil.

"It's a good thing you found him. He looks like a Lab or a Lab cross."

Her hand stroked over the puppy's back soothingly as she turned back to him, cooing at her new pet. "I don't care what breed he is. He's just Milo to me."

Blake's eyebrow hiked up. "Milo? Like the orange cat from that kid's movie with the pug?"

"Yeah, so what? I think it fits." She took her card back from the receptionist and slipped it into her purse.

"That was my favorite movie as a kid. I just think it's funny."

She looked up at him, and he caught the slight smile playing across her lips. "It was mine, too. It's—"

Whatever she was about to say was cut off when Best poked his head in and nodded at Blake. "Hey, Kline, we got to go."

Blake really didn't want to leave, but he was at a loss for anything else to say. "If you ever need a lesson in obedience training, there are some great classes at PetSmart."

"Thanks, Blake. I'll probably do that."

"Great. Well, I guess I'll see you."

"Why don't I just walk out with you? I've got something to ask you anyway."

Blake's heartbeat raced as a thousand possible scenarios played out in his mind. Was she going to ask him out? Maybe to coffee again? She did seem nervous, so that would make sense.

"Yeah, sure. Sounds great."

Blake held the door for her, an unintentional curse escaping as a blast of cold air hit him.

"Man, I was just starting to think that it was warming up a bit, and then this morning happened."

"Yeah, sometimes we get a little cold front moving through, but it doesn't really last long."

Look at them, discussing the weather as if they were just a couple of acquaintances who had absolutely no interest in each other.

Which was complete bullshit, at least on Blake's end.

He saw her shiver out of the corner of his eye and shook his head. "Why aren't you wearing a jacket?"

"I just forgot it in the car. I figured I was only walking ten feet, and it seemed like a lot of hassle for just a few-second walk. I didn't expect to bump into you or find myself standing out here, incredibly nervous."

"Why are you nervous?" Blake waited, his stomach actually fluttering, for fuck's sake.

"Well, I know you're really busy, but I was wondering if you ever teach self-defense classes?"

Blake was blown away. That was the last thing he'd been expecting.

Because I was hoping for something else.

"You want to take a self-defense class? From me?"

Her cheeks turned that pink color he'd grown to really like, and she nodded. "It's just, the way you handled that gunman the other day…Since then, I've been jumpy, and my parents are worried, and I just thought if you could teach me a few things to put their mind at ease…" She caught his gaze with her big hazel eyes, and her black lashes swooped over them several times, innocently enchanting him. "Plus, you seemed so concerned for me before, I thought you might be willing to help."

She paused, studying him, and he had no idea what expression was on his face, but it made her backtrack. "You know what, never mind, it was a crazy idea anyway."

Hannah started to turn away, but he reached out and touched her shoulder, stalling her.

And setting the protective little shit off with a series of high yips.

"Milo, stop."

The puppy settled, tiny rumbles emitting from his chest as he turned his head, keeping Blake in his sights.

"I wasn't going to say no. If you want me to teach you a few things, I'd be happy to."

Hannah's warm smile was back, and so were the butterflies. Damn it, he hadn't had those since high school, since...

Since the first time I saw Jenny.

Blake pushed back the rush of guilt, telling himself this was about something important. It wasn't a date, and it wasn't about sex or feelings. This was a necessity, to keep Hannah safe and out of trouble.

"My best days are usually Sunday and Monday, although sometimes I pick up substitute teaching jobs on Mondays." Hannah seemed oblivious to his sudden mood shift, thank God, and he forced a smile.

"Good to know. I'll figure out where I could train you and give you a call on Monday."

"That's perfect. Thanks, Blake."

"Yeah, sure."

"Oh, how is house hunting going?" she asked.

"Um, no luck yet."

"Well, I hope you find something. We'll talk soon."

"Bye, Hannah."

She was already walking toward her car, and this time, he was sure if the puppy had fingers instead of paws, he'd have been flipping Blake off. When Hannah opened up her passenger door and put the puppy on the front seat, he could almost swear he saw a flash of blue lace panties.

For fuck's sake, stop being a damn pervert!

Turning away, he climbed up into the van and tried to avoid Best's gaze, afraid he'd be able to tell how bad Blake was fighting a grin.

"So, what was that about? It looked pretty friendly."

He glanced at Best and saw the telltale twinkle in his blue eyes.

"It was nothing. I'm going to show her some self-defense moves. She's still a little freaked about what happened the other day."

"I'll bet those aren't the only moves you're gonna show her." Best wiggled his eyebrows at him before starting the van up.

And he's back to his barely mature self.

"You're an idiot."

"Should we tell Bryce you're back on the wagon?" Best asked as he backed out of the parking spot.

"Hell no, don't tell her anything. That girl is a monster, and the sooner the female center opens and she's no longer all up in my business, the better."

"Come on, Bryce's not so bad. She just likes attention and for everyone to like her. I can relate."

Blake's jaw dropped before he recovered. "All you do is mess with people!"

Best sent him a wink. "But I do it in a friendly, likable way."

"Says you."

Blake settled back into the seat as Best chuckled, and he realized that he was actually more excited for Monday than the Super Bowl.

"Not to be a Debbie Downer, but Sparks says the general is insisting you go to counseling."

All of Blake's good humor evaporated. "You had to bring this up when you've got me trapped in a car, huh?"

"I just wanted to say that it probably isn't the worst idea. It really helped Sparks and me. Since Carlos pulled that gun on us in November, I've been going to Dr. Stabler, and I don't know, man, sometimes just having someone to bounce feelings off can really help."

"When did you become the poster boy for the heart-to-heart talk?" Blake knew he was being an asshole, but the last thing he wanted to talk about was his appointment on Tuesday.

"Don't be a douche. I know I like to pretend I never take things seriously, but it seems like since we haven't been hanging as much anymore, you've been kind of..."

"Relieved?"

"Depressed."

Best's somber delivery of that single word raked over Blake like hot coals on skin. "I'm not depressed."

"You're drinking more and losing your temper too often."

"Well, if I'm such a bummer to be around, then why do you bother?" Blake knew he sounded like a petulant child, but fuck, the last thing he needed was a lecture on what else was wrong with him.

Best seemed to be counting under his breath for several seconds before he finally spoke again. "If you don't want to acknowledge the fact that you are unhappy and need help, there's nothing I can do, but if you aren't ready to fix yourself, then I agree; you aren't ready to date anyone."

Neither of them said anything else for the rest of the drive back to Alpha Dog, but Best's words had demolished all of the light, happy feelings that seeing Hannah had elicited.

Dick.

Chapter Ten

IT WAS AFTER noon on Monday, but Hannah struggled to keep her bleary eyes open as she stared at her computer screen, scrolling through her Facebook feed idly. When her mother had told her raising a puppy was like having a newborn, Hannah had scoffed, but now, after a fitful four hours of sleep, she could easily imagine the little golden terror in diapers and a bonnet.

She leaned down and peeked under the table where Milo had fallen across her feet in an exhausted sleep. Apparently, whining half the night, chewing on Hannah's feet at one and three in the morning, and piddling on the kitchen floor after she'd just taken him outside had been a lot of work for him, because even when she removed one foot, he continued to snuffle.

Hannah turned back to her computer screen and saw her friend Gretta Kent had changed her profile picture to what looked like a sonogram. When she clicked on it, sure enough, there was a whole album with the title "And Baby Makes Three." There were several pictures of Gretta and her husband, Dave, holding a pair of white baby shoes and a sign that read ARRIVING IN JUNE.

Wow. Gretta was a year younger than Hannah. They'd met in English class their first semester at junior college, but while Hannah had transferred to continue her education, Gretta had stopped at an associate's degree and married Dave, her high school sweetheart. Dave was only twenty-five and already a store manager with Safeway, while Gretta sold Jamberry Nails and Younique Makeup.

Hannah mused at how happy Gretta was and how she already had everything Hannah was now dreaming about: a house, a husband, babies. But she'd wanted to finish her degree and get her career in order before she concentrated on her personal life. Several of her friends had gotten serious when they were too young and regretted it.

Hannah had even made a point of waiting until she was really in love, maybe even engaged, before she had sex. But most of the guys she'd dated had barely lasted a month, and of those, none of them had really gotten her motor running anyway.

She could still remember sitting on Gretta's couch with Megan and Courtney, listening to them talk about their boyfriends and all the things they'd done. She'd laughed along with them, but now, as she continued looking at her old friends' walls, she realized she was the last to do everything. The last to get married, have kids, get a career-focused job…

She was only going to be twenty-five at the end of April. When had everyone suddenly gotten their life together?

Her cell phone buzzed on the table, and she glanced at the screen. A number she didn't recognize flashed, and Hannah's breath caught. Maybe Blake was calling her from his work phone?

Sliding her thumb across to answer, she put the phone to her ear. "Hello?"

"Hello, is this Hannah?"

Hannah's shoulders slumped as she heard the feminine voice on the other end. "Yes."

"Hi, Hannah, this is Georgia at Watt Avenue Veterinary Clinic. How are you doing, girl?"

"Hi. I'm tired but doing okay. How are you, Georgia?"

"Oh, fine. Dr. Standen just wanted me to call and let you know that Milo's blood work checked out just fine, but we'll need to see him back in a month for his boosters and another dose of dewormer."

Hannah glanced down at the sleeping pup fondly. "Sure, I'll call you back when I know my schedule better."

"All right, dear. But hey, it was good to see you."

"You too, Georgia. Take care."

"Good-bye, Hannah."

Hannah set her phone down and stood up. She might as well make something to eat and then take a shower instead of waiting around for some guy to call. Why did she keep putting herself through this?

After that, maybe she'd check for available teaching jobs again. She didn't really think she was going to get the job she'd interviewed for, so she might as well continue applying. As much as she loved Dale's, she needed to move on.

Grabbing a banana and a package of strawberry Pop-Tarts, she sat back down. It was stupid to think that the fruit somehow made up for the sugary breakfast pastry, but she loved them too much to give them up.

She peeled the banana and took a large bite as she closed Facebook. She opened up Microsoft Word, planning on starting the next chapter of her book, when her phone started singing "Have a Nice Day."

She chewed quickly, trying to swallow the wad of banana as she glanced at the screen.

Blake's Cell.

Excitement zipped through her. He hadn't forgotten.

Trying to chew the banana in her mouth, she finally gave up and answered.

"Hewow?" she said around the glob.

"Hello, Hannah? It's Blake."

He sounded completely unsure, and no wonder. She sounded like Chewbacca. Why the hell had she answered the phone with a mouthful of food? She should have just let it go to voicemail and called him back.

"Hang on." At least, that's what she tried to say, although it came out more like "ham hon."

"Are you okay?" He sounded as if he was laughing.

"Mouf fool."

"I'll give you a minute to swallow." Then, she heard a noise that sounded suspiciously like a stifled laugh. Another sound and Hannah grimaced. Yep, that was a definite chuckle.

She got it down and took a drink of her coffee. "Sorry, I had just taken a bite of a banana when you called."

"It's okay, sorry to catch you at a bad time."

"It's fine, really. What's up?" Did she seem too eager? It was hard not to be when she'd been waiting two days for him to call.

"Well, I wanted to let you know that if you're available tonight at seven, I can teach a couple moves."

Hannah's heart slammed in her chest. "Tonight?"

"Yeah, sorry for the late notice, but I just got permission to use our training room at the program. So, what do you say? You up for it?"

Was she up for rolling around with Blake, letting him put his hands all over her?

Milo had finally woken and started sharpening his puppy teeth on her big toe. "Ow!" she cried, jerking her foot back. "You little punk."

"Did you just call me a punk?" he asked.

Hannah's whole face caught fire in mortification, and she was so glad he couldn't see her. "No, sorry. Milo bit me, and his teeth are really sharp. Tonight would be great. I just need the address."

He rattled it off, and she typed it into Google Maps on her laptop as he spoke. It wasn't very far from her place, maybe ten minutes.

"Great," she said. "And this might be a bit of a girly question, but what should I wear?"

He laughed again. "Just comfortable clothes, sweats or yoga pants and sneakers."

"Thanks. I really appreciate you doing this. It's just, after that man held a gun on me, I want to feel like I can take care of myself again, you know?" She stood up and grabbed Milo when she spotted him sniffing suspiciously, carrying him to the front door so she could take him out to go potty. "Not that I didn't appreciate your timely rescue, but since I haven't see you in the diner after the whole saving-my-life thing, I thought you might not be coming in anymore."

As she hooked Milo's leash on his collar, she realized Blake was dead silent on the other end and replayed what she'd just said in her head. Had he taken what she'd said the wrong way? Did he think she was keeping tabs on him?

"I just meant because of what happened. I don't know if I'd frequent a restaurant that was robbed again, no matter how good the food was."

Finally, he spoke up. "I'm still coming into the diner. I've been busy the last few days, is all."

Hannah didn't fully believe him, but there was no use in talking about it anymore. He'd called her and was offering to teach her self-defense. That had to mean something, right?

Yeah, that he is a good guy who doesn't want me to not be able to defend myself.

"Well, then, I'll just see you at seven," she said.

"See you then. Bye."

She slipped her phone in her pocket and set Milo down before opening the door, the urge to whistle a merry tune while she skipped around the yard overwhelming.

"What do you think, Milo? Isn't it going to be a beautiful day?"

The puppy peed on the lawn in response, but Hannah was excited. Her and Blake, alone in a room. Sweating, gripping each other as their bodies strained against each other...

The sheer imagery made Hannah wish seven o'clock wasn't so far away.

BLAKE STOOD IN the lobby of Alpha Dog just before seven, waiting with security for Hannah to show up. Unfortunately, Sparks and Best were standing behind him. Best had told Sparks he thought Blake might like Hannah, so Sparks decided he needed to get a look at her.

"Hey, your girl's got four minutes, or she's late. Girls who run late are high maintenance. Just ask Martinez."

Blake looked over his shoulder and found that Martinez had joined the spectators, thus earning the jibe from Best about his girlfriend.

"You're just pissed Eve is making you flash that pretty smile of yours at the ball," Martinez said mildly.

"No, she's high maintenance. Always got to look on point, even when we're going hiking. Thank God Dani's not like that."

"The way Best talks about her, you'd think the sun rose and set out of Dani's ass, don't you think?" Sparks asked.

Blake closed his eyes, trying to keep a rein on his temper. Since Best and Sparks had informed him that all of his friends had been discussing his short temper, he'd tried to get it under control. Even when Sparks had stuck a for-sale listing he'd apparently gotten from General Reynolds on his desk. The house had looked nice, but Blake was getting a little tired of so many nosy Susans managing his life. It wasn't as if he hadn't been trying to find a place; he just wanted the right one.

And now, with them all waiting here, ready to embarrass him, it was all he could do to stay calm.

"So, what does this Hannah look like?" Martinez asked.

Blake's eye started twitching as Best jumped in. "She's about medium height, brown hair. She's pretty, with a thick, curvy body, and you should see her—"

"For the love of God!" Blake spun around. "Don't you assholes have anything better to do than stand around being a bunch of nosy sons of—"

"Blake?"

Damn, he hadn't even heard the door open. His three friends were looking past him, and as he turned, he caught Larry Walton's smirk. Larry was army and worked night security at Alpha Dog, and under normal circumstances, Blake liked the guy.

Not so much right now.

Hannah was staring at him with wide eyes behind her glasses, her hair back in a long ponytail.

"Is everything okay?" she asked.

Blake cleared his throat. "Yeah, it's good. Come on through."

Hannah walked past Larry and gave him a tentative smile. Larry tapped the brim of his cap and said, "Ma'am."

Blake put his hand on the small of her back and started to lead her toward the training room, but there was no easy escape. Not when Best moved into their path with a wide grin.

"Aren't you going to introduce us to your friend, Kline?"

Blake glared daggers at Best but managed to grind out an introduction. "Hannah, this is Sergeant Tyler Best, Sergeant Dean Sparks, and Sergeant Oliver Martinez."

"Nice to meet you," she said, taking each of their hands in turn.

"It's nice to meet *you*." Sparks flicked a glance at Blake with a questioning brow, which he ignored.

"You've all been introduced, and we have stuff to do, so…" Without finishing the sentence, he pushed Hannah forward and around his friends.

"Have fun!" Martinez called.

"Jackass," Blake muttered under his breath.

"What was that about?" Hannah whispered.

"They're just messing with me. Don't worry about it."

"Okay, because we're practically running from them."

Blake realized she was right; he'd been propelling her forward so fast she'd had to jog to keep up.

"Sorry." He reached for the door of the training room and led her inside. He flipped on the lights, illuminating the dark weight room. There was a thick blue mat at the edge of the room where they trained the boys in self-defense, which was why he'd wanted to bring her here.

She unzipped her Sac State sweatshirt and draped it over one of the weight benches. Underneath was a purple loose-fitting tank top that, when she turned, showed off a scooped neckline and an inch of cleavage.

God help him.

"So, where do we start?" she asked.

Oh, the responses he had to that question would definitely send her running from him.

Looking everywhere but her impressive chest, he went to the mat, expecting her to follow.

"How about we stretch first, so we don't pull anything."

Blake showed her basic stretches for her arms, legs, hamstrings, and neck. As they did them, he talked, trying to sound as professional as possible.

"The first thing we're going to talk about is prevention. Don't put yourself in a vulnerable position. Try not to walk alone to your car at night, if you can help it, be aware of your surroundings, and if you are unable to avoid a confrontation, make sure that you remain passive until you are ready to strike. What you did with that gunman, giving him exactly what he wanted, was the right move."

She shot him a small grateful smile. "I have to admit, it didn't feel that way at the time."

"When you've got a gun trained on you at point-blank range, there's not much you can do, and it's important to wait for the right moment, especially if it's more than just you. The goal of self-defense is to cause your attacker the maximum amount of damage with the least amount of force so that you can remove yourself from the situation. And remember to use what you have. Walking to your car, place your biggest key between your knuckles.

With enough force behind it, it can be used as a weapon, especially on soft areas like the eyes, neck, and stomach."

She looked up at him from where she was bent at the waist, her caramel ponytail trailing across the floor. "That's actually a really good tip."

Sweat broke out over his forehead as Hannah's shirt rode up, exposing her plump rear end pointing sky-high. Blake was so tempted to walk around her, maybe use a ruse about checking her form just to press against her, but this wasn't a date or a hookup or anything. Hannah had asked for his help, and he was being a horny asshole who couldn't think beyond the hard-on in his pants.

Just keep talking about self-defense. Don't look at her, don't think about her…concentrate.

"If they are wearing thick, baggy clothing or jeans, it won't penetrate it, so you want to look for exposed areas. Once you get free, run and find help."

She stood up, and he showed her how to stretch her arm across her form, ignoring the way it pressed her breasts up. Brownie points for him.

"What about pepper spray?" she asked.

"You're more likely to have that turned around on you. A loud personal alarm or pocket-size air horn is good. It draws attention to the attack, and the air horn can damage his hearing enough that you can get away. The ears and eyes are some of the most vulnerable spots on the body. There's also this thing called a monkey fist you can put on your key chain, and when it hits, I'm told it packs quite a punch."

"I thought the most vulnerable spot on a guy was…"

She trailed off, and he could tell where she'd been going with the sentence by the blush on her cheeks.

"Yeah, that hurts, too, but like I said, baggy jeans can make it sometimes hard to get to, although if he's attacking you from behind, reaching back and squeezing the hell out of his nuts is a good way to make him weak." Blake didn't want to think about the pain associated with that particular move, but he'd promised to show her the best ways to defend herself, and unfortunately, the groin's fragility was just part of the lesson. "If you're stretched out, let's try a couple of moves. Come up behind me and wrap your arm around my neck."

Hannah came around his back as he dropped to his knees.

"Oh, I was wondering how I was going to do that, since you tower over me."

"Hey, I'm always thinking ahead. Go ahead and wrap your arm around my chest."

Only Blake hadn't prepared himself for the press of Hannah's breasts against his back or her warm breath against his ear.

"And now?"

Blake's cock stirred at the low tone, and he almost reached up and flipped her over his shoulder. Then, when he had her dazed and gazing up at him from the mat, he'd lean down and get a taste of that plump, pink bottom lip of hers.

Instead, he tried to think about anything else. Airplanes. Cotton balls. Jenny.

That sobering thought nearly did the trick.

"Now, if someone ever gets you in a hold like this, you have three seconds to get him off. So, from this position, the best thing you can do is shift to whichever side is opposite your writing hand and reach back—"

He shifted on his knees to the left and reached back with his right hand, his fingers curled like claws.

"And you grab whatever you can get and squeeze it hard. Do you understand?"

Her breath tickled the shell of his ear, warming it in the most erotic way. "Yes."

Keep it together, man. "An elbow to the face is also good once he releases you, but if he is on the ground and you're afraid he'll chase you, I want you to stomp his ankle. If you need to, use both feet and put all your weight into it. If his ankle is jacked up, he's not going anywhere anytime soon, and you have time to run away and get help. And, once you report it, if he seeks medical attention, he's going to get a big surprise when he's arrested. Got it?"

"Yeah, except the whole stomping thing. What if I freeze up?"

Blake's hand came up to rest on her forearm, and he turned his head so he could look at her. "Then you're going to be hurt. Unless he just wants your valuables, there is no reason for him to try to drag you off. You have to think that whatever he has planned for you is going to be worse than any injuries you might get in a scuffle."

Hannah still looked uneasy, and he squeezed her arm. "I believe that when the time comes, you'll be a fighter."

She smiled brightly down at him, and Blake noticed how close their faces were. Their lips close enough that if he just stretched up a few inches, they'd be kissing.

Her eyes fluttered closed, and he watched her lips part in slow motion. This was happening. She wanted him to kiss her, and hell, he wanted that, too, more than anything.

I haven't kissed anyone since Jenny.

He knew how Jenny liked to be kissed, how she enjoyed being held tight and her lower lip nibbled a little bit until she giggled. What if when he kissed Hannah, she was disappointed?

At the last minute, he panicked, putting distance between them with her arm still around his neck.

"Wanna switch?" he said abruptly, smashing the moment into oblivion.

Hannah blinked at him, surprise and he was sure disappointment flashing in her eyes.

"Sure." Her response was slow, hesitant, and she sounded so confused. He was confused, too, and he was the one who'd pulled the plug.

He stood up when she released his neck and came up behind her, praying she couldn't feel the semi he was still sporting.

"Let's see it," he said.

"I don't want to hurt you, though," she said.

I'm more afraid I'll hurt you.

"You won't."

I won't let you get close enough.

Chapter Eleven

HANNAH COULD FEEL something hard pressing against her back as Blake set up to attack her from behind. Her body hummed with the desire to rub back against him like a cat in heat, and her cheeks burned in embarrassment. God, she never knew how the hot body of a tall, sweaty wall of muscle could make her lower abdomen clench and quiver with need.

"I'm going to come at you, and as soon as my arms go around you, I want you to reach back and grab me." His deep, rumbly whisper vibrated against her ear as his words sunk in, and her heart kicked up a notch.

"Um, you mean, you want me to grab your…penis?"

He sounded strained when he answered. "I've got a cup on, so it should be fine. You don't have to castrate me, just reach back like you would if I was actually attacking you."

"Okay." Hannah waited, her hands out as she rocked on the balls of her feet, anticipating Blake's arms going around her once more.

Suddenly, Blake grabbed her from behind, nearly lifting her off her feet, and she gave a startled yell. It was rougher than she'd expected, and a lump of panic rose up in her throat as adrenaline kicked in. She wiggled and heaved in his arms until he seemed off balance for a split second, then she took the opportunity to twist her arm back and grab him through his pants.

Only her grab was more like a punch, and she winced as her fist hit hard plastic.

Blake let her go, and when she turned, she found Blake on the ground, lying on his side with his knees tucked up to his stomach. Her hand covered her mouth, and she immediately went to her knees beside him, apologizing. "I am so sorry! I didn't mean to—"

Without warning, Blake moved, far too quick for her to react, and she found herself on her back, staring up at him.

"You were supposed to stomp on my ankle and run."

Hannah blinked several times as his words sank in. She hadn't actually hurt him?

Relieved, she started laughing, shaking her head up at him. "I thought I'd hurt you."

"If you'd done that nut punch on me without a cup, my pain might have been real, but luckily, it took the brunt of that hit. Nice move, by the way." Blake reached out a hand to help her up, a wide grin on his face. "But I'm a fantastic actor, huh?"

"Yes, you are," she said, her other hand grabbing onto his bicep to steady herself. As Hannah gazed up into Blake's hazel eyes, she was completely aware that they were alone in this room. That what they were doing could be considered incredibly intimate…

And he was pulling away from her, his hands circling her throat loosely, all business again. Hannah had to admit that she preferred the mischievous, laughing side of Blake more than Mr. Reserved, but since this was what she'd asked for, she wasn't going to complain. At least he was here, helping her and spending time with her. She wanted to know more about Blake, to get to know him outside the diner, and so far, this was working out splendidly for that.

"Now, when you're faced with an attacker who goes for your throat, you need to attack his eyes or even use your knee for his groin while ripping his ears down."

A horrific image popped into her head at those words, and her stomach turned a bit. "Ripping his ears down? What is that?"

"You grab the top of his ears and pull downward as hard as you can. They're sensitive and easily injured."

"That's pretty gross."

"Hey, you gotta get over being squeamish, especially if it's your life on the line," he said.

He was right, but Hannah couldn't imagine ripping off someone's ears.

Hannah checked out Blake's ears briefly, noticing for the first time that they stuck out slightly, an adorable imperfection to his otherwise handsome visage.

"Unfortunately, not everyone is going to have ears so easy to grab onto," he said, practically reading her thoughts.

Hannah giggled and reached up, running her finger over the shell of his ear. "I think they're cute."

Blake's hazel eyes twinkled. "No one has ever called my ears cute. My wife used to…"

His mouth snapped shut, and his face became unreadable.

Hannah's heart squeezed painfully. Blake had been married?

He'd never mentioned a wife before.

"Your wife used to what?"

Blake cleared his throat, avoiding her gaze as he went to the fridge in the corner. He pulled out two bottles of water, not answering right away. Finally, as he handed her the cold plastic, he spoke.

"She used to tell me they looked like catcher's mitts, and I'd tell her it was why I did so much better in school; I caught every word."

Hannah smiled. "That's clever." She hesitated briefly, then asked, "Where is she now?"

By the starkness of his expression, Hannah already knew. "Oh. I'm so sorry."

"Thanks."

"When did it happen?" She couldn't stop the question, even if she'd wanted to. It was the first time Blake had ever given away something so personal about himself, and she wanted to know everything. Was she the reason for Blake's black moods? She had never lost anyone close to her, but she could fully imagine a time when her parents would be gone. That was heart-wrenching enough, but to lose your spouse so young?

"Two years ago."

Hannah opened her mouth to ask more questions but noticed the tense set of his shoulders; causing him more pain was unthinkable.

Then, to her surprise, she boldly stepped into him and wrapped her arms around his waist, laying her head against his chest.

She didn't say anything else, just hugged him, offering comfort and empathy without a sound.

Slowly, she felt him move, his hands sliding across her back until his arms were looped around her waist, holding her against his body.

Hannah closed her eyes, concentrating on the feel of the hard wall of his chest under her cheek, to the thump of his heartbeat steadily drumming. He smelled of spicy cologne and the musk of sweat beneath, something that should have been unpleasant but instead was actually very sexy.

Suddenly, she wanted to snuggle deeper. To chase away his pain and bring back that smile that turned her knees to mush.

Stroking her hands over his back, she turned slightly and, before she lost her nerve, kissed his chest.

They both froze, and it took Hannah a minute or two to work up the courage to look him in the eye. When she did, he was staring at her intensely, his hazel eyes blazing.

And then he kissed her.

BLAKE WISHED HE could call it a mistake, but the minute his lips touched Hannah's, it felt too good to pull back. Her mouth softened automatically, and the kiss was a mix of salty and sweet as their tongues brushed together.

It had been so long since he'd been touched, let alone held, that when she'd put her arms around him so lovingly, he hadn't been sure what to do.

And then she'd kissed his chest, a comforting gesture that had been his undoing.

The moment she'd looked up at him, he knew he was going to kiss her. He might regret it later, but there was no way to resist her after that.

Blake's hands came up to cradle her face, and he slanted his head to deepen the kiss. Shocks of desire raced from his mouth down his body, settling into his groin. The whole time he'd been training her in self-defense, he'd been aware of her. Of his reaction to her, and it was finally too much. He needed to feel that sliver of happiness that only came in her presence since...

Jenny's face surfaced, shattering the moment like a hammer against a mirror.

What am I doing?

He pulled away, nearly stumbling back to put some distance between them.

"Blake?" The way she said his name, husky and dazed, was so fucking hot he tried to push back his qualms, to tell himself that Jenny was gone and he could kiss Hannah without feeling any guilt.

But as he stared at Hannah, Jenny's blue eyes swam through his mind.

Two years was really all Jenny meant to me? God, I'm an asshole.

"Blake? Are you okay?"

Blake blinked at Hannah, clearing his vision, and realized that he wasn't at all okay. That he had no right to drag Hannah into his fucked-up crazy life and kiss her until they were both gasping for breath. His chest was still heaving, partly from panic, but mostly from Hannah and his reaction to her.

Which made her dangerous to his heart and his peace of mind. Hannah was beautiful, kind, and funny. She deserved someone who wasn't still dreaming of his dead wife. She needed someone without baggage.

"I am so sorry I did that."

Blake wasn't prepared for the way her face fell, for the excitement to drain from her eyes and be replaced by hurt and confusion.

"Okay."

Hannah didn't say anything more, just went over to where her sweatshirt was and pulled it over her arms.

"Hannah, wait, it has nothing to do with you—"

"Please don't give me the 'it's not you, it's me' speech." The snap in her tone surprised him, and he took a step back as she spun around to face him. Shy, sweet Hannah had been replaced by a firecracker whose expression said she was ready to give him a piece of her mind. "You can regret doing something, but don't insult my intelligence by kissing me and then saying it was a mistake, that it has nothing to do with me, because it is bull. Kissing someone implies that you wanted to kiss them, but for whatever reason, you changed your mind, so you stopped. That is all it is. You don't have to lie or make up some excuse about why it's not my fault that you don't find me attractive—"

"I do find you attractive. That's the problem."

"Why is being attracted to me a problem?" she asked.

How did he put all of his feelings into words without sounding like a complete head case? Even with Jenny, he'd struggled with communication and putting his emotions into perspective for her. Now Hannah was standing there, asking him to lay his shit bare and tell her all the reasons why he shouldn't want her?

Why did women have to have everything spelled out for them?

"Because I'm not ready for anything beyond friendship right now."

Hannah slowly nodded, walking toward the door. She paused with her hand on the knob and turned.

"Just a word of advice, but if you aren't ready for anything more than friendship, then you shouldn't go around kissing women like that."

She pushed out of the door and out of sight before he could tell her he didn't kiss other women like that. That she was the first since Jenny. But then she might read more into that than he intended.

Just let her go. It's better this way.

"What the hell did you do?"

Blake caught Best standing in the doorway, looking incredulous.

"I kissed her."

Best's eyebrows shot up, and he came in fully, shutting the door behind him. "And your breath was rancid?"

"No, I…I stopped it."

Best dragged in a deep sigh that reeked of exasperation. "Why? That girl obviously likes you, and you've got some weird thing for her."

"Why is it weird?" Blake asked.

"Because if any other woman gets near you, you act as though they have the plague, but you offered to give this girl self-defense lessons. You fucking smell good, dude, which means you snuck into the kid's showers and cleaned up before she got here, which tells me you care what she thinks."

"I do."

"Then why are you standing in here? Go out there and tell her you're an idiot."

Blake shook his head. Best didn't understand. If he chased her down with anything but an apology and an invitation for a date, she was going to be pissed. He'd bungled their first kiss so badly; he wouldn't blame her if she never spoke to him again.

I AM SUCH a stupid, desperate idiot.

Hannah pulled her keys from her pocket and unlocked her car door, slumping into her front seat with a cry of frustration. She usually never lost her temper like that, but she also didn't let people walk all over her.

She was so angry with Blake, but mostly with herself. Why would she think it was okay to let Blake kiss her after he had just told her about his dead wife?

Because you wanted him too much to move away.

It was true, but how in the hell was she going to face him if he came into Dale's? He'd tried to let her down easy, to explain that although he'd had a moment of weakness, he wasn't ready, and she'd blown up at him. She was a jerk.

A knock on her window made her jump, and she turned to find Blake standing outside her car in the dark, waving at her.

"Sorry for scaring you. Can we talk?"

Hannah was so tempted to take the coward's way out and escape, but she was an adult, and avoiding your problems was just something you didn't do.

She opened the door and climbed out, crossing her arms over her chest.

"Sure, what do you want to talk about?"

"Hannah, I'm sorry. I didn't mean to embarrass you."

She couldn't look him in the eye as she scoffed. "Embarrassed? Me? No, I'm fine. Really."

"Okay, well good. Because if you…if maybe you thought…ah, hell. I am screwing this all up. As attractive as I think you are, it's not just that my wife died. She was murdered, killed while another soldier was having a psychotic break in our Base Exchange. It was just the wrong place at the wrong time, but I have a lot of unresolved stuff I'm still working on, and I really don't feel like it's fair to drag you into it. I like you, but I don't want to hurt you."

Hannah didn't want to tell him that she was already hurt; it seemed like a petulant move for such a heartfelt admission.

Hannah reached out to lay her hand on his arm. "I am so sorry."

"Yeah, but it doesn't change anything. She's still gone and I'm still here, and I just…I'm sorry if I gave you the wrong idea. I just got caught up in the moment."

Me, too.

Trying to muster a smile for him, she said, "I'm sorry for flying off the handle. It's just, I've liked you for a while. I still think you shouldn't kiss someone unless you mean it, but I understand that you aren't looking for anything."

His smile spread across his face, a flash of white in the dark. "I like spending time with you. I'd still like to finish our lesson sometime, and maybe we can still be friends?"

Ugh, the f word.

The last thing she wanted was to be just friends with Blake.

But she also didn't want to give up being around him. Of seeing his hazel eyes light up or hearing his amazing voice saying her name.

Dear Lord, she was pathetic.

"Sure, we're good. We can hang out and do things and be just friends." The words were like salmon bones in her throat, hard to get out, and she almost choked on them.

"That sounds really good, actually," he said.

"Then it's settled. You have my number, if you ever want to talk or hang out." At least she sounded cool and casual, if she didn't exactly feel it.

"I will, and thanks for understanding."

She nodded, climbing into her car and closing the door. He moved away from the car, and Hannah gave him a little wave as she backed out of the space.

Of all the ways she'd imagined the night ending, *that* had not been any of the scenarios.

Chapter Twelve

HANNAH'S CELL RANG the next afternoon just as she was getting on the freeway on her way to her substitute teaching job in West Sacramento, and she tapped the answer button on her car's stereo screen.

"Hey, Nicki."

"What's up? You sound down."

Hannah grimaced. It was the third time someone had commented on her sour mood. Kenny had asked her if she'd left her smile at home, and Chloe had asked her if she was okay right before she left. Luckily, Blake hadn't stopped in to see how glum she was.

With Nicki, though, she could be completely honest about what was eating her. Twenty years of friendship had given her that.

"Oh, I'm fine. Just got a big fat *no thanks* from a guy I liked last night. No big thing."

"What a dick! What did he say? I will beat his ass!"

Hannah laughed a little. "No, really, it wasn't like that. He was really nice about it, even gave me the 'it's him and not me.'"

"Oh, hell no, that is some bullsh—"

"Nicki, really, he's got his reasons, and they are good ones. His wife was murdered two years ago, and he's just not ready to date."

"Oh, well, then I'll refrain from trash talking. This is actually good for my next announcement."

Hannah groaned, passing a slow-moving car. "Please tell me you haven't set up another blind date."

"Better! I got us tickets to this awesome single ladies' ball on Valentine's Day!"

"A ball? Like poofy gowns and tiaras kind of ball?"

"Hell yeah!"

"And how is that better?"

"Don't be a party poop head! It's gonna be like freaking prom, baby!"

Considering she'd skipped prom in lieu of a plate of nachos and a *Gossip Girl* marathon, she had no response to that.

"But what about our anti-Valentine's Day? Horror movies? Junk food? You want to give all that up?" It was actually one of her favorite traditions, one that had started when Nicki and she were twelve and weren't invited to Kelsey Wilson's first boy-girl party. Since then, even if Nicki or Hannah had a boyfriend, they would ditch them to have their traditional Valentine's Day together.

"Oh, come on, Han, it will be great. We can break tradition this once. We'll go shopping, and get our hair and nails done. Maybe our makeup. When is the last time you went and got pampered?"

It had been her last birthday. She'd gone to get a pedicure, and it had been great except she'd almost kicked the woman in the face. The curse of ticklish feet.

"It's been a while, but I don't know if I want to spend my Valentine's Day dressed like Cinderella with no prince."

"That is the best part! Princes will be provided. It's some charity event, and they will have a ton of guys from the base there to dance with us and tell us we're pretty."

"Military guys?" Thinking of Blake, a scene flashed through her mind of her in a cream-colored gown, her hair atop her head in a riot of curls, and Blake staring at her as if she was the most beautiful woman in the world.

"Hannah? Did I lose you?"

"No, I'm here."

"So, what do you say? And before you say no, the tickets cost me fifty bucks each and I really want to go, but I need my best friend so I don't look like a loser."

Hannah sighed heavily. "You owe me."

"Yes! I'll make our beauty appointments, and this weekend, we're shopping! Love you, got to go! Bye!"

Hannah didn't even get a chance to say good-bye before Nicki was gone and she was getting off the freeway. For the last few minutes of her drive, she conjured up an epic fantasy to rival Cinderella's happily ever after. She'd show up at the ball, and Blake would just happen to be one of the military guys. He'd see her from across the room talking to some other guy, and he'd make his way over to ask her to dance.

As he spun her around the room, he'd hold her tight and tell her he couldn't stop thinking about their kiss. That he didn't want to just be friends.

Then he'd kiss her once more in the middle of the dance floor.

Hannah parked in the staff lot and walked into the elementary school. Once she was directed from the office to the classroom, she read through the teacher's lesson plan, which was pretty loose considering it was kindergarten. They'd go over the letter O, practice their addition, and have story time with a book that started with O.

Hannah pulled out her laptop, checking the time. The class didn't start for another half hour, so she had some time to work on her manuscript while she waited. Smoothing down her dress as she sat in the chair, she read through the chapter before and started typing.

When the first student arrived, escorted by her mother, Hannah closed down the laptop and smiled at her. The little girl's hair was braided with pretty blue and pink beads that clicked when she turned her head away to hide against her mother's stomach.

"Hello there. I'm Miss Hannah, and I'll be substituting for Mrs. Reichling. What's your name?"

Hannah squatted in her floral dress so she was eye level with the child, who peeked at her with one eye.

"I'm Nita. This is my niece, Tasha," Nita said, her hand brushing lovingly over the top of Tasha's head. "She's a little shy when first meeting people."

"I can completely understand that. I used to be really shy, still am sometimes, but you know what helps me relax when I'm around new people?"

Now two brown eyes were staring out at her, curiosity etched in her pretty features.

Without waiting for Tasha to ask what, Hannah continued, "I make silly faces, and it usually breaks the ice. What do you think?"

Hannah stuck her fingers in the sides of her mouth and pulled, rolling her eyes and sticking her tongue out.

A tiny giggle shook Nita's skirt, and Hannah pulled her fingers out of her mouth, smiling.

"You know what I can't find? The Play-Doh. If only there was someone who could show me where it was."

"What do you think? Do you want to be Miss Hannah's special helper?" Nita asked.

Tasha hesitated, still hanging onto her aunt's skirt. Then, she nodded.

"Great! Let me put some sanitizer on my hands since they were in my mouth, and you can help me set up the Play-Doh before everyone gets here."

Tasha was already making her way over to the cupboard, and Hannah pulled her little container of hand sanitizer out of the pocket of her skirt.

"Thank you for trying to make her comfortable." Nita was an athletic woman in a pair of black slacks, a tan shirt, and black cardigan. She was beautiful, like her niece, but Hannah could see the lines of stress around her eyes and mouth.

"Of course, it's important for children to feel safe at school."

"Yes, it is." Tasha's aunt appeared to have tears in her eyes, but in the next second, they were gone. "Anyway, thank you for taking the class. I need to get back to the office, but I'll be back to get her after school."

Hannah watched the two say good-bye and then held a plastic container of cookie cutters and shape makers.

"Hey, Tasha, what are these things? Do you think we can use them with the Play-Doh?"

Tasha studied what was in her arms, nodding. As Hannah opened it and held it out to Tasha, asking her what the different shapes were, Nita disappeared.

Other students arrived as Hannah and Tasha finished setting up, and when Hannah stood up, Tasha latched onto her hand.

Hannah looked down at the little girl and squeezed her hand. "Do you want to show me where your seat is?"

The relief on Tasha's face made Hannah smile and long for a permanent teaching position. Where the students were hers and she was able to help them long term, not just for a day.

Once Tasha was seated, Hannah pulled a pack of stickers from her skirt pocket and handed Tasha one with Elsa from *Frozen*.

"Thank you for all of your help."

In a tiny voice, Tasha replied, "You're welcome."

BLAKE SAT IN the lobby of Dr. Stabler's office, waiting for his mandatory therapy to start. If there had been a way out of it, he would have tried again, but Sparks had been adamant.

After this appointment, he had a meeting with General Reynolds, and Blake had a feeling that might be more torturous than the therapy. At least in therapy, he could refuse to speak.

"Sergeant Kline?" A woman in her forties appeared from down the hallway, her black hair laced with silver and her face only slightly lined.

Blake stood up. "Dr. Stabler?"

"That's right. Come on back, and we'll get started. Can I get you anything to drink?"

"No thank you, ma'am."

Blake followed her into a small room with three comfy-looking chairs, and as she took the one on the other side of the room, Blake went ahead and sat across from her.

"So, Sergeant Kline, tell me a little about yourself."

Blake rubbed his hands over his face, finally settling them on his knees. "I'm sure you read the file, Doctor."

"Yes, I've read your military file, but I mean who you are personally. For instance, why do you want to continue to work at Alpha Dog? Is it because of the work with search and rescue dogs you were involved in with your father?"

Blake shook his head. He didn't want to get into his parents' death with this woman. "That's why I got the job, not why I stay."

"Then by all means, tell me why you stay."

Shifting in the chair, Blake tried to appear casual, but his shoulders hurt where the muscles bunched tensely.

He hated therapists, always picking apart everything you said, even if there was no other hidden meaning behind your words. It was a bunch of hokum, and he wasn't going to play into this woman's game.

"Because this program deserves to succeed. It had helped a ton of kids, dogs, even—"

"But why do *you* stay? You've been with the program for over a year and have just now started training your own dog and having your own squad. That's a long time to be involved without actually being involved. There are thousands of other jobs you could be doing in the military, so tell me, why is this one important to you?"

It was almost exactly what Sparks had said. Had he put his concerns in Blake's file, or had the general given Dr. Stabler a full report on the issues they were having with Blake?

"With all due respect, I have been looking for a place so I can bring Charge home with me, and I want to be at Alpha Dog because I enjoy it. It's fulfilling. And to be quite honest, I really don't need to be here, talking to you."

"If that were true, then why would your commanding officer and the Alpha Dog director suggest that you would benefit from three sessions a week?"

Blake clenched his jaw, pissed at Sparks's nosy traitorous bullshit.

"I'm sure you know I lost my wife two years ago, and I guess you could say that I struggled the first year, but I went to group therapy. I discussed and dissected my feelings, and I got better. I don't know why they're concerned about me, but I assure you, I am working to alleviate their worries."

Dr. Stabler smiled at him, the expression behind it bland; she was obviously humoring him.

"It's interesting you would say that, because it also says in your file that you've been exhibiting signs of depression."

"I am not depressed," Blake ground out.

"Let me ask you this, Sergeant. What steps have you taken to mourn your wife?"

Blake couldn't believe the brass balls on the woman. "I buried her. I organized her funeral, and I stood by her grave as they leveled dirt over the coffin."

"And have you been back since?" she asked.

"No."

"Have you thought about going back to Texas and visiting her grave site?"

"My wife isn't in that grave. She isn't anywhere. She's just gone."

"Your theology is your own, but many people in mourning find it healing to visit their loved one's grave and even talk to them. Tell them about what is going on in their life as if they were there."

Blake scoffed. "You mean they go to a cemetery, stand over a grave, and talk to themselves? Sounds crazy to me."

She scribbled something down on her little yellow notepad and asked, "What about dating, Sergeant Kline? Have you been out with anyone since your wife passed?"

"Let's be clear. My wife didn't *pass*. She was brutally terrorized and murdered. She didn't die quietly in her sleep. She died scared and alone."

Dr. Stabler sat back in her chair, as if waiting for him to say more, but he was done.

"And the distinction is important to you. Do you blame yourself for the way she died?"

"What kind of stupid question is that?"

She glanced down at his file. "It says here that she was at the store. Where were you?"

His chest squeezed tightly as she pressed him. "Does it matter?"

"I think so. Were you on duty?"

"Doesn't my file tell you that?" he sneered.

"Are you going to avoid my questions or make this easier on yourself? We both have to be here, Sergeant Kline, so we might as well work." Her calm, no-nonsense tone was grating on his nerves. "Now, were you on duty?"

"You already know the answer to that."

"Were…you—"

He cut her off, shouting out in frustration, "No, for fuck's sake, I wasn't on duty. I was watching football with my buddies and asked her to go to the store for more beer and food. I could've gotten off my ass and gone, and she'd still be alive. So no, I wasn't on fucking duty, and yes, I blame myself."

She scribbled something down and met his gaze head on. "But then you might be dead, and she'd be a widow now."

It would have been better that way.

Blake didn't add anything else, knowing he'd already said too much, if the way the doctor went about scribbling was any indication.

"You were going to tell me if you had been out with anyone since your wife was murdered."

"Actually, I wasn't."

Dr. Stabler's eyebrow rose. "Are you embarrassed by the answer?"

"No, I'm not embarrassed. I just don't think it's any of your business."

Dr. Stabler sighed heavily. "Sergeant Kline, let me be blunt. The way that this works is I ask questions, and you answer them. If you don't cooperate, I'll have no choice but to inform General Reynolds and Sergeant Sparks. If that occurs, you may be removed from the Alpha Dog Program. So, if there is any reason why you may want to stay, I suggest you stop fighting me and let me help you."

Blake was so close to telling her to go to hell and leave, but he took a second to think, his fingers running through his hair and rubbing his scalp painfully. He'd told himself he would try, that he'd commit to Alpha Dog and work to benefit the program. He could take a transfer and walk away, but then he'd have to leave his friends. And as big of a pain in the ass as they were, they were the glue that had kept him from falling apart.

Plus, if you left the city, you wouldn't see Hannah again.

"Sergeant Kline?"

Blake took a deep, calming breath and answered, "No, I haven't been out with anyone. My friends have tried to set me up, but I haven't been interested."

"What's holding you back?" she asked.

"It's only been two years. I'm just not ready, I guess."

"Have you been attracted to anyone?"

She must have noticed his hesitation, because she smiled reassuringly. "It's completely natural to be attracted to other people and feel guilty about it. In fact, it is very common."

"If it's so common, then how do you make it stop?"

"The guilt?"

"The attraction," he corrected.

"Ahh. Why do you want to make it stop? Is she wrong for you?"

"Because it's only been two years. My wife and I were together for eleven and knew each other our whole lives."

"What was her name?" she asked.

"What?"

"What was your wife's name? I ask because you haven't said it once in fifteen minutes. You continue to simply call her 'my wife.' Are you afraid to say her name aloud? Is it painful?"

Blake shook his head, disgusted. "Anyone ever tell you that you have the sensitivity of a gorilla?"

Instead of being offended, the doctor laughed. "Once or twice. Are you avoiding the question?"

"Fine, her name was Jenny. Are you satisfied?"

"Yes, for the moment. Tell me about the other woman. Does she look like Jenny?"

Sweat broke out on Blake's forehead; he was uneasy for reasons he couldn't even put together. "Why do we need to talk about her? It's a moot point."

"Why is that?"

"Because I told her I wasn't interested."

"I see. So you lied because you felt guilty that you don't feel enough time has passed for you to be able to move on. What is a decent length of time?"

Blake shifted, ready to jump up and leave. "I don't know."

"Well, historically in Western culture, the proper length of time to mourn a spouse was one year, regardless of the time you were together."

"It's not enough time for me."

"Shouldn't the fact that you're finally feeling attraction for someone else tell you that enough time actually has passed and you are fighting it because you blame yourself for Jenny's death?"

"Do you always jump right into the hard shit with your clients?" he asked.

Dr. Stabler smiled as she wrote something else down on that yellow notepad. "To be honest, I find that working through the hard stuff is easy. It's taking what you learn from that work and applying it to the rest of your life that is the tough part."

Blake didn't understand that for one second, but he was going to do his best to stick it out. Three hours a week of intense therapy wasn't going to break him.

He was determined that nothing would ever break him again.

Chapter Thirteen

HANNAH ENDED UP staying the rest of the week at the school, falling in love with the students in Mrs. Reichling's afternoon kindergarten class, especially Tasha. The parents had been singing her praises; at least, that is what the vice principal, Mr. Jones, had told her on Thursday.

On Friday, though, he'd called her into his office early before class started, and she was really nervous about it.

"Miss York, Mrs. Reichling called this morning, and due to some medical issues I cannot disclose, has chosen to retire early. She'd already cut her workload to the single afternoon class, so it is only a part-time position at this time, but as she has chosen not to return for the remaining school year, I was hoping that you would agree to take on her class until the end of the year."

Hannah was beyond thrilled. She didn't care if it was only part-time; it was a real teaching position. It was consistent and exactly what she needed to get her foot in the door.

"Of course, I would be happy to. I have really enjoyed working with the kids this week. I appreciate the opportunity."

"Good, then we'll get a contract drafted, and when the school year ends, we'll reevaluate and see if maybe we might have a permanent place for you here."

Hannah stood up, wanting to hug the man, but she refrained. "Thank you so much, sir."

"You are welcome."

Hannah shook his hand and went to her classroom, then grabbed her cell from her purse. When she pulled up her contacts, her thumb slowed as her gaze fell on Blake's name. She should just delete it and stop torturing herself. Although Blake told her that they were going to be friends, she didn't actually believe it. Especially since he still hadn't come back to Dale's, and it had been four days since she'd last seen him.

Still, she couldn't bring herself to do it, so she just kept scrolling past until she found her mom's number, trying not to dwell on Blake.

She'd been just about to press the call button when her phone blew up, Nicki's smiling face popping up on the screen.

Hannah answered by swiping the green phone icon.

"Hello, Nic."

"I just wanted to remind you that you have a date with me tomorrow for some girly shopping awesomeness!"

Hannah rolled her eyes. "I know, even if I didn't have you in my calendar, I wouldn't forget."

"Just making sure, because I know how you get. If you can weasel your ass out of this, you will, and I will not allow it!"

"You know you missed your calling as a dictator, right?"

"Who says I can't still rule a country someday with an iron fist?"

"Speaking of jobs, I just got offered a part-time position at Fairview Elementary teaching the afternoon kindergarten I've been doing all week."

Nicki whooped so loudly, Hannah had to hold the phone away from her ear. "That is fantastic, babe!"

"Thanks, I think so."

"Well, congratulations! This just means we'll have more to celebrate when we meet up for shopping tomorrow!"

Hannah grimaced at the reminder of the ball. "Are you sure…"

"Oops, got to go, sweets. There is a cute guy next to me at the light. I'm gonna see if he wants my number. Love you!"

The call ended, and Hannah slipped her phone into her pocket. She'd just gotten a job and was going to spend some quality time with her best friend this weekend. She wasn't going to dwell on Blake or any other guy.

In this moment, life was good.

BLAKE AND A large group of military personnel sat in the auditorium at Alpha Dog while Evelyn Reynolds stood on stage, going over her plans for the ball the next week-end. Apparently, it wasn't just a plan, but an actual reality with sold-out tickets, a booked venue, and a caterer.

"There will be approximately two hundred women at this event, and we want them happy. Ecstatic even. So, I will need at least two hundred volunteers to entertain them. Dance with them, sit with them, and make them feel special. We do not want anyone left out or alienated. Am I clear?"

Eve's commanding voice was answered by a hum of grumbles. He wasn't the only one unhappy about being forced to participate in this farce.

"This event has brought in ten thousand dollars so far, including raffle-ticket sales. The potential is closer to thirty, so please, take this seriously. We are really close to opening a second Alpha Dog location up the road for female offenders, and if we're successful with this fund-raiser, we could be ready as soon as April. The goal here is to help more kids and more dogs, so stop your bitching, Tyler Best—"

Tyler, who was sitting next to him, sat up straight and glared at her. "I wasn't saying shit."

"You were thinking it."

Tyler mumbled something about "crazy," and Marti-nez, who was sitting on the other side of Best, punched him in the arm.

"Please be at the location at six in the morning on Fri-day to help set up and arrive between seven and seven thirty that night to await our guests. Doors will open at eight, and the event will end at one in the morning. Be professional, but attentive. I will be there to handle any problems. You're free to go."

Blake stood up, wishing he could tell Eve and her ball to suck it, but he liked Eve. She was trying to help the program. He could put his comfort aside for that.

"So, how's Hannah?" Best asked behind him.

"There is nothing going on there, I've told you this." And the words were total bullshit.

He was back to avoiding Dale's like a pussy, and after two sessions with Dr. Stabler, he was ready to move to the woods and be a hermit. She kept pressing him about Hannah, Jenny, why he felt guilty about moving on, and he was already exhausted. He would love to avoid his appointment this afternoon, but after his meeting with the general the other day, he knew that wasn't an option if he wanted to remain at Alpha Dog.

"Dude, why the hell haven't you talked to her?" Best asked, bringing him out of his head. "She seems nice, and she's pretty. And all those curves will keep you nice and warm at night—hey!"

Blake had spun around and had Tyler by the front of his shirt.

"Shut. Up."

"Easy there, Kline, don't hurt the guy." Martinez's jovial tone cut through the red cloud of rage, and Blake let Best go.

"Sorry, man."

Best rubbed at his neck with a smirk. "Don't mention it. I totally understand now. You don't like her, and I should just stop talking about her."

Blake gritted his teeth, but instead of rising to Best's bait, he stormed out of the auditorium and toward study hall, where his squad was waiting for him.

Sparks had taken a few kids from each of the other squads and put them with Blake. So far, things had been going well. He had a pretty easy group of kids at the moment. There were eight of them, most of them in for drug offenses, and they had been more than willing to learn what he had to teach them as long as they didn't have to go to juvie. Considering the shit they'd dealt with in the past, this was a cakewalk.

Blake stepped into the room they used for study hall, and they looked up from whatever they were working on.

"Hey, guys, wanna grab your dogs and meet me out back?"

"Yes, Sergeant." Their chorus was followed by the sound of shuffling pages and books.

"Hey, Kline, walk with me for a second?" Sparks said behind him.

"Actually, hold that thought, guys. As you were." Blake followed Sparks out into the hall, and the two of them walked toward the outside training area, neither saying anything.

"How are things going with Dr. Stabler?" Sparks asked.

"Isn't there some kind of doctor-patient confidentiality?" Blake still hadn't forgiven Sparks for recommending he do these therapy sessions.

"I'm just asking because of what just happened in the conference room with Best. I've never seen you put your hands on anyone like that."

"He was being a douche. Besides, it's not as though you haven't tried to take out Best a time or two and vice versa."

"That's true, Best and I get into it, but you are always Mr. Calm and Cool. But it seems like you're on edge the last couple of months."

Blake grimaced, thinking about how he used to think Sparks's and Best's bouts of violence were unnecessary and stupid.

"I guess being around you guys is rubbing off on me."

"Bullshit."

"You know how Best gets up in everyone's business. Seriously, I just grabbed the guy's shirt. No big deal."

"I know you're pissed at me for recommending you see Dr. Stabler, but I really think you've got shit too heavy to carry on your own."

Blake hesitated, knowing that Sparks wasn't completely wrong. He did feel like he needed to talk to someone, and out of the members of their group, Sparks would be the guy to understand where he was with Hannah. Lord knew he'd fought his feelings for his girlfriend, Violet, hard enough.

"If I talk to you about something, I don't want you telling the other guys."

Sparks nodded, understanding in his dark eyes. "Shoot."

"That girl, Hannah...I think I might have feelings for her."

Sparks grinned and slapped him on the back. "That's great, man. What's the problem then?"

Blake sighed as they opened the back doors and walked toward the grass. "Every time I start to think about taking a step in that direction, I think about my wife."

Sparks seemed to be contemplating this and finally said, "Shit, Kline, it's been two years, and you're not even thirty. I know you loved her and you guys had a long history, but I can't imagine she wanted you to mourn her forever."

"It's me. I feel like I'm betraying her. I mean, if it was just about sex, that would be one thing, but with Hannah...I get up and I can't wait to finish my run and get to Dale's. Not even for the breakfast, but just to see her, hear her voice, and just listen to her talk, you know? She's sweet and funny; she likes to make me laugh, and it makes me want to do it, if only to please her. Does that sound weird?"

"No, not at all. In fact, I'm not hearing a problem."

"The problem is that I am afraid of taking a shot with her, realizing I'm really not ready, and hurting her. I've already done that once, and I just feel like it is better to keep things friendly and not cross that line until I'm sure."

Sparks leaned against the wall across from him, crossing his arms over his chest as he watched him thoughtfully. "I get where you're coming from, but how are you ever going to know if you are ready or not if you don't put yourself out there? I did the same thing you're doing; I tried to deny myself happiness because I felt like I needed to atone before I could move on with my life, but I was wrong. I just needed to forgive myself. You need to do the same, man. It wasn't your fault Jenny was killed. Blame the man who shot her."

"I do, every day. But what if that was it? What if what Jenny and I had was the best I'm ever going to have, and say I try with Hannah and can't give her what she needs because I don't have it in me anymore?"

"You are doing a lot of what-ifs for a girl you haven't even been on one date with. You might hook up with her and find out she sneezes like a lumberjack and wipes her nose on her sleeve."

Blake laughed at the image in his head. "You're an idiot."

"Just trying to give you some perspective. It does no good to speculate on what might happen, and besides, you haven't dated for thirteen years. You don't want to jump right into another relationship. Test the waters with Hannah. At least you know her, right? And she knows what you've been through. She seems like she'd be good for you."

Blake had to admit that Sparks had a point, which brought him back to Dr. Stabler's comment about his attraction to Hannah being a part of his body and mind letting him know he *was* ready to move on and try dating again.

If he started to move that way, maybe he could cut back on his sessions with Dr. Stabler. If she thought he was at least trying to move on...

"Yeah, I'll think about it, but don't tell Bryce, or I'm going to be bumping into her entire Facebook friends list at every function."

"Deal."

Chapter Fourteen

ON SATURDAY, HANNAH dropped Milo at her parents' for the day and thanked them for watching the puppy while she and Nicki went shopping. Her mom had been especially excited about the Valentine's Day ball and ordered Hannah to show her everything she'd bought when she returned to pick up Milo.

"Actually, Nicki is coming to pick me up, and I'm going to leave my car here, if that's okay?"

"Oh, sure, sweetie, do you think you'll be back to join us for dinner?"

The sound of a horn honking outside was Hannah's cue to skedaddle. "Probably not. Who knows how long it will take with Nicki in charge."

"Well, have fun!"

Hannah raced out the door before Milo could escape with her and ran toward Nicki's car.

"There she is!" Nicki, her dark hair in a clean A-line bob with burgundy streaks throughout, waved out the window. Hannah climbed into the passenger seat and gave her a hug, pulling away to study her friend's face; Nicki's eyes were lined with kohl and dark shadow, and her lips were the same shade as her hair. She always did her makeup as if they were going clubbing, and today it was a little much for trying on formal dresses.

"Ready to get our pretty on?" Nicki asked, stepping on the gas as she backed out of Hannah's parents' driveway.

Hannah grabbed the *oh, shit* handle and held on for dear life. "As I'll ever be."

"That's the spirit."

The bridal shop was about ten minutes from her parents' house, near the Sunrise Mall. Traffic wasn't bad in the middle of the day, so they didn't have nearly as long to talk before Nicki was pulling into the parking spot in front of the store.

"All right, we have an appointment, and I don't want to hear any whining about the prices, you got me?"

Normally, assertive people intimidated Hannah, but she'd known Nicki too long to let her railroad her. "I won't whine. I'll just take off out the door and wait for you at Starbucks. I'm not blowing my savings on one dress I'll never wear again."

"You're such a poop," Nicki said, climbing out of the car. Hannah didn't take offense, though. For as romantic as she was, she was the more levelheaded of the pair and wouldn't let Nicki go broke over an outrageously priced ball gown, either.

They stepped into the open room filled mostly with white wedding dresses, and Hannah was a little surprised when the elegantly dressed saleswoman walked over to them and gave Nicki a hug.

"Nicki, I'm so glad you came in." She gave Hannah a discreet once-over. "And who is this?"

"This is my friend, Hannah. Hannah, this is Madeline, a friend of my mom's."

"Nice to meet you." Hannah held her hand out, and Madeline placed her soft palm in hers.

"Lovely to meet you. Hmm, what size are you, dear?" Madeline asked.

"She is a size sixteen," Nicki answered for her.

Hannah expected the woman to remain cool and aloof, but instead, her dark eyes twinkled. "I think I have something just perfect for her. Why don't you ladies follow Karen to the dressing rooms, and I will bring you some choices."

Karen, a petite blonde with a vacant smile, motioned for them to follow her.

The first two dresses didn't work for Hannah, but when Nicki squealed, Hannah poked her head out to find her friend looking like a sexual dynamo in a wine-colored strapless dress with a mermaid skirt. The corset back was lined with sparkling beads that matched the top of the bodice and edge of her skirt.

"That's the dress," Hannah called.

"Hell yeah it is."

Nicki received a disapproving look from Madeline and a clucking tongue from Karen. A few moments later, Madeline slipped a dress through the curtain of Hannah's dressing room.

"Try this on. I think it will look amazing on you."

Hannah held up the dress in her hand. It was a gorgeous lilac color with an off-the-shoulder sweetheart neckline. The skirt gathered up with little seed pearls, and the back was a corset, loosened to allow her to step in.

When she had the dress in place, she called out to Madeline, who stepped in to cinch her up. The woman was practically bouncing on her feet as she looked Hannah over.

"I think you'll be pleased when you see the full effect."

Once the dress was tightened just shy of oxygen deprivation, Hannah and Madeline emerged.

Nicki's eyes widened, and her mouth dropped. "Oh, Han, you look freaking gorgeous!"

Hannah's heart kicked into high gear as she stepped up onto the block and let the dress fall around her. Raising her head up to look in the mirror, she stared at her reflection in awe.

In this dress, she didn't lament the pounds she needed to lose or that her legs weren't long enough to pull it off. The dress fit her as if it had been made just for her, and with the right heels…

It would be completely perfect.

"Geez, I can't go with you to this thing. Guys will be fighting just to stand near you."

Hannah knew that Nicki was exaggerating, and she loved her for it.

"As long as you buy that red one, we'll both be beating them off with a stick."

HANNAH WAS SO tired by the time they finished shopping. Once they had purchased their dresses, they'd headed to the Sunrise Mall and gone to Torrid for their undergarments. Hannah found a very pretty white bustier and thigh-high stockings to go with it, while Nicki had gone for black everything. They'd hit three shoe stores before they found the right heels and swung by Claire's for their accessories.

"This is so awesome. I cannot wait."

"You know this was a lot more expensive than staying in and watching movies, don't you?"

"It's only once a year, if we even decide to go again, so stop sweating it. You're killing my buzz." As they stuffed their purchases in the back of Nicki's car, she asked, "What should we do now?"

"I don't know about you, but I'm starving," Hannah said.

"Hell yeah! Wanna hit BJ's?"

It was a little out of the way, being off Arden Way, but it was Hannah's favorite. "Sure, sounds good."

Thirty minutes later, they walked into BJ's Brewhouse. Hannah's feet ached, protesting the walk from the parking lot to the restaurant. She couldn't believe they'd shopped for over six hours; that had to be a record.

"How do you not want to curl up and sleep right now?" Hannah asked.

"Wearing my shoe gels, baby. Gotta dress comfy if you want to shop with the big guns."

Hannah laughed. There were several groups waiting for tables, and as Nicki went to put their name in, Hannah decided it was a good time to go to the restroom.

And then she spotted Blake, sitting on the bench in front of her, smiling at a pretty brunette holding a present. Their heads were bent close together, the way people did in a loud atmosphere or just when they wanted to be near each other.

The bottom dropped out of her stomach as she realized he'd given her the brush-off. All that talk about not being ready to date, that he was still mourning his wife, had been just to spare her feelings.

She wished at that moment that the floor would open up and swallow her whole.

Ducking her head, she rushed past them, praying she made it to the bathroom without him noticing her. Tears were already stinging her eyes and blurring her vision.

There was no reason to cry about this. She and Blake were just friends. No harm, no foul.

If that's really what you think, then why does it feel like someone just ripped your heart from your chest?

BLAKE SMILED AS he pretended to listen to Bryce go on and on about her friend Jill, who would be perfect for him, but he really couldn't care less. He had only come to

Eve's birthday dinner to give her the gift card he'd bought and drink some beer with his friends.

Blake caught movement at the door and did a double take as he spotted Hannah, her caramel waves falling across the shoulders of her black sweater. He almost called out to her, but Bryce said his name at the same moment, drawing his focus away.

"What?"

"I said, who are you staring at?"

Blake glanced over and saw that Hannah was walking past him toward a narrow hallway, presumably to go to the restroom. She must not have seen him.

"I thought I saw a friend of mine," he said.

"If you want to go talk to them, I can wait for everyone else to get here. They said it was going to be ten minutes until we're seated, anyway."

Blake hesitated. He didn't want it to seem as though he was stalking Hannah.

"Nah, I'll just wait until she comes back," he said.

"She, huh?" Bryce gave him a wide grin, her blue eyes filled with mischief as she elbowed him in the ribs. "Is this the same she you gave self-defense lessons to?"

"It's not like that, we're just friends."

"Oh, here comes Slater." Blake didn't miss the way Bryce smoothed down her hair.

"You like Slater, huh?"

"I will kill you if you say anything," she warned.

"I'm shaking in my boots," he said dryly.

"I know you are, you big pussy." Bryce laughed when he glared at her insult.

Slater pushed into the lobby, his smile flashing as he caught sight of them. "Hey, y'all."

"Slater." Blake held his hand out for the other man to take.

"What's up, man?" Slater nodded at Bryce. "Meg, you catch the game last night?"

Bryce said something in response, but Blake was no longer paying attention. Craning his neck around, he tried to see if Hannah had come out of the bathroom yet.

The waitress called their party's name, and Bryce patted his shoulder. "That's us. Do you want to stay here and wait for your friend?"

Blake hesitated. While getting to talk to Hannah would be great, he kept remembering what Sparks had said about jumping into something before he'd dipped his toes back into the dating pool.

"Nah, I'll just talk to her another time."

HANNAH WAS DRYING her face off when Nicki pushed into the bathroom.

"Han, are you okay? What happened?"

"Nothing, I'm just being an idiot." And she definitely felt like one, crying over something as silly as a guy she wasn't even dating. It wasn't as if she'd never been rejected before.

Except with Blake, you fooled yourself into thinking there was something between you.

"Come on, tell me what is going on." Nicki gave Hannah a big hug, rubbing her back. "Seriously, whose ass do I need to kick?"

Hannah laughed. "I just saw that guy I like, Blake, and he's here with another girl."

"Oh, babe, I'm sorry. Wanna grab our food and go?"

"Do you mind?" Hannah asked. "I'm kind of a mess."

"Nah, let's do it. And maybe we can stop by a Redbox and grab a couple of movies to watch. After you tell me all about this mystery man."

"Sure, sounds good."

"I'm going to change our reservation to a to-go order. Come on out when you feel up to it."

"Thanks, Nic."

"Hey, best friends are the people you can be a total crazy mess around and who love you anyway. Don't sweat it."

Hannah laughed, rubbing at her eyes as Nicki left the bathroom. She turned to look at herself in the mirror, dabbing at her puffy eyes when the door opened again and the pretty brunette Blake had been cozy with walked in. She caught Hannah's gaze in the mirror briefly.

"Hey," she said casually.

"Hi." Hannah's voice came out as more of a croak, and she suddenly wanted to get the hell out of there.

She left the bathroom and headed toward the bar, where she found Nicki nursing a margarita. When her friend noticed her, she held the straw out to her. "Want some? It's going to take about twenty minutes for food, so I figured why not have a drink while we wait."

"No, thanks." She didn't want to look around in case Blake was close and noticed her.

"Do you want to go out to the car and wait? I can hang here—"

"Hey, Hannah."

Blake's voice came from behind her and sent a quiver of awareness down her back. She turned around and gave him a tentative smile. "Hi, Blake. This is Nicki. Nicki, this is Blake."

Blake shook Nicki's hand and turned that knee-jellifying smile back her way. "What brings you ladies out today?"

"We were shopping all day and decided to swing by and grab food on our way back home," Nicki said.

She could feel Blake's gaze on her, but she avoided his eyes, afraid he'd be able to tell that she'd been crying.

"Cool, what were you shopping for?" he asked.

Hannah gave Nicki a panicked look, silently pleading for Nicki to make up something else, anything other than the truth, but her friend ignored her.

"We're going to a single ladies' ball, so we were buying our dresses and accessories."

God, Hannah wanted to sink into the floor and die. It was bad enough that Blake could probably tell she'd been crying, but just saying their plans for Valentine's Day out loud made her want to crawl under the counter and hide. Two grown women getting dressed up like princesses to attend a singles event?

He probably thought they were both pathetic.

"A single ladies' ball? The one at the Hilton?" he asked.

Hannah's head jerked up at his question. "Yeah. Why?"

A slow smile spread across his face. "Because Alpha Dog is putting it on."

Her heart pounded so hard it made her wince. "So I guess that means you'll—"

"Be there? Yes. Yes, I will."

Hannah's stomach turned. Blake was going to be there to see her all dressed up and looking like a complete idiot. Probably with the beautiful brunette on his arm.

Faking a smile, she said, "Well, great. It sounds like a lot of fun."

Before he could respond, the brunette came up behind him, smiling at Nicki and Hannah apologetically. "Hey, Kline, we're ready to order. Do you know what you want?"

"Yeah, sure, I'll be right there." When she made no move leave, Blake sighed. "Hannah and Nicki, this is Megan Bryce, my coworker."

Megan took each of their hands, pausing as she shook Hannah's. "Oh! You're the girl Blake gave a self-defense lesson to, huh?"

"Yeah, I am." Hannah shot Blake a puzzled look over Megan's excitement.

"Well, I've heard *so* much about you—"

"Okay, we've got to get back to the table and order. I'll see you guys next week," Blake said. Without giving them a chance to respond, he ushered Megan away.

"What the hell was that about?" Nicki asked.

Hannah just watched them whisper furiously back and forth, wondering what was being said. Had Blake been talking about her?

Hannah was beyond confused, her emotions warring. He had introduced Megan as someone he works with and been talking about Hannah to her. That alone made warmth spread through her chest. But what if it hadn't been good? What if he'd been talking about the crazy waitress who was obsessed with him?

Bile rose up the back of her throat at the thought of him and the pretty brunette laughing about her behind her back.

Come on, Blake isn't like that.

But was she really so sure?

"Hello, earth to Hannah. What was that little interlude about?"

"I have no idea."

Chapter Fifteen

ON TUESDAY MORNING, two weeks since Blake had saved Hannah, Blake's feet pounded the pavement of the walking trail, classic AC/DC blaring in his ears as sweat dripped into his eyes. He was insanely frustrated, and a lot of it had to do with a certain waitress with golden-flecked eyes.

Despite talking himself out of starting something up with her, he knew he liked her. And they'd both agreed to be friends, but when he'd walked up to Hannah at BJ's, she hadn't seemed happy to see him. She'd been distant and cold, and when he'd mentioned that he was going to be at the Valentine's Day ball, too, she'd almost appeared horrified.

What the hell did that mean? That she'd been lying about wanting to be friends? Had she been trying to avoid him? Sure, he hadn't texted or called her or gone to Dale's either, but that was because he was afraid of his reaction to her, not because he wanted to cut her out completely. Especially since Bryce had embarrassed the shit out of him at BJ's last weekend. He'd been tempted to drown her in her beer when they got back to the table but had simply ignored her as he tried to catch another glimpse of Hannah.

Being near her and smelling that insanely good fruity perfume she wore was like a shock wave to his cock. He knew deep down that the more time he spent with Hannah, the more he was going to want her and the weaker he would be. He wanted to be sure before he made a move.

Which was why he'd decided to go to Dale's today. Sparks was right about him knowing Hannah and how understanding she was. If he could just move past his own crap about dating, he thought that they could at least have fun together. Take things slow.

But maybe he'd completely screwed things up between them by telling her about Jenny. She might have decided that he had too much baggage to even be friends with. He wouldn't blame her, but it still left a sour taste in his mouth.

After a few minutes of awkwardness between Hannah, her friend, and him, he'd excused himself and gone back to his table.

He'd looked up in time to watch Hannah and her friend leaving the restaurant, and the fact that she hadn't even waved good-bye disturbed him. What the hell had he done to piss her off?

He slowed to a jog as he exited the trail, and when he got to his car in the Dale's Diner parking lot, he almost didn't go in. He'd brought a change of clothes in case he wanted breakfast, but there was no point in going in if it was just going to make Hannah uncomfortable.

It could also have nothing to do with me. Maybe I just caught her on a bad day?

After another minute of deliberating with himself, he changed his shirt, grabbed his wallet, and climbed the steps to Dale's door.

He entered the diner, and Hannah glanced up from the coffee she was pouring, a definite frown on her face.

Nope, it wasn't just his imagination. He was the problem.

"Good morning, Hannah." He walked over to his booth and slid in without waiting for her answer.

Not that she bothered to. Nope, she didn't say a word, just came over with the pot of coffee and a cup.

She set the cup in front of him with a clank and poured the coffee. "What can I get you?"

His eyebrows rose in surprise. Now she was being downright hostile.

"Did I do something to piss you off?" he asked.

"Nope. Just real busy."

Blake turned his head to look around the empty diner. "Really?"

"Yes, so give me your order so I can get back to it."

Anger pricked along Blake's skin. "Just my usual."

"Fine, I'll put that in for you."

She spun on her heels away from him and sashayed behind the counter, that yellow skirt twitching with a definite attitude.

"Kenny, I'm taking a break," she said.

He watched as she stuck his ticket up in the window and disappeared toward the back.

Blake's eyes narrowed as he stood up from the table. She wanted to give him attitude with no provocation and walk away, no explanation? Fuck that.

It was time for Hannah and him to have a talk.

HANNAH ESCAPED OUT the back door, taking a deep, calming breath.

Damn, why couldn't she keep a handle on her emotions? What was it about him and his casual "Good morning, Hannah" that had set her off?

Last night, she'd let her imagination get the best of her and, unable to sleep, had written a pretty violent fight scene for her midgrade book. She knew she was going to have to tone it down when she did her final read through, but it had been therapeutic. Okay, so she didn't actually know if Blake had been talking about her negatively, but the way Megan had said "I've heard so much about you" had flown through her mind so much, she was convinced there had been a sneer to it.

She climbed down the stairs and sat in one of the plastic chairs, cupping her face in her hands. She should go back in and apologize. Taking the imagined insult out on Blake wasn't right, especially when there was nothing to be mad at him for. He'd tried to be a good guy and spare her feelings when he said he wasn't ready to date. There was no proof that he was mocking her behind her back.

Except that he's been avoiding me like I am the crazy stalker girl he'd make fun of with his friends.

"Hannah?"

She groaned as she heard his voice behind her on the step. "Usually, when someone takes a break outside, away from people, it means she wants to be alone."

"Well, tough. 'Cause I want to know what is wrong with you."

Hannah heard his steps approach, and she lifted her face to look up at him. As he stood over her, she noticed his arms were crossed and his face was locked in a scowl. He wasn't going anywhere.

"It's nothing. Don't worry about it," she said.

"There's something going on. You act as if you suddenly can't stand me."

Just the opposite, I'm afraid.

She sighed. "It's not you."

He stared mutinously at her, and it grated on her nerves.

"Fine." She stood up, too, hating that he still towered over her. "You wanted to be friends, right? Well, friends don't lie to each other."

"What are you talking about?" He seemed genuinely bewildered, and that really ticked her off.

"You said you weren't interested in me because you weren't ready to date yet. That's fine. Except now, I find out you've been talking to your coworkers about me! Were you laughing at me? It's not as if I haven't been rejected before, but you were discussing me like some silly girl with a crush. Plus, you've been avoiding me, and

I don't care if you were just trying to spare my feelings, I know you said she was just a coworker, but she is so pretty and the way she put her hand on your—"

"Whoa, whoa, *whoa*! Let's slow this down so I can get a word in here," he said.

Hannah, breathing hard, waved her hand. "You want a word? Have a whole sentence."

His mouth twitched, and Hannah decided if he had the balls to laugh at her, she was going to walk away again.

He managed to control himself. "Thank you. Now, first of all, Megan is a pain in the ass. She's a friend, but that is all, and I didn't talk about you to her. Best probably told her about you, because he is a gossiping asshole." His hand came up, and his fingers grazed the side of her face, leaving trails of heat in their wake. "But I would never hurt you, Hannah. Not on purpose, at least. As to avoiding Dale's, it was just so I could have some time to figure out what I wanted. Believe me, I wanted to see you. I drove by here almost every morning hoping to catch a glimpse of you but was too afraid to come inside."

Hannah could feel the blood leave her face. She'd acted like a crazy, insecure freak, and there was no reason for it. God, why couldn't she just stuff her emotions down like a normal person?

Sheepishly, she tucked a loose strand of hair behind her ear and stared down at her feet. "So, yeah…I'm crazy, don't mind me."

She tried to make a joke, but it fell flat, especially when she could feel his eyes on her. She looked up finally to find him staring at her in the weirdest way. It wasn't scared, and he hadn't taken off running to get a restraining order, so…was that a good thing?

"You were jealous." His statement jerked her gaze up to his, and she could have sworn he'd looked pleased. Excited, even.

There was no use denying that she'd been jealous. She'd acted like an insane stalker.

"Yes, I was."

Did he step closer? His hand caught her under the chin, and he tilted her face up. "You know you could have asked me instead of being passive-aggressive."

Now she was flushed with embarrassment. "I really didn't think it was any of my business, and I was trying really, really hard not to let it bother me, but I…I like you, Blake. I can't help it."

What the hell was wrong with her? In a million years, she'd never thought she'd be spilling her guts in the back of Dale's Diner, especially not to Blake.

For a second, his thumb smoothed across her lower lip, and she thought he was going to kiss her. Her breath caught in her chest as she waited, longing to feel the press of his mouth on hers, the caress of his fingers against her skin.

But he stopped, dropping his hand from her, and it fell back to his side.

"I like you, Hannah. I do. I just needed some time and space to think, and I didn't want to hurt you in the process." His hazel eyes bored into hers, and she was frozen to the spot, unable to escape. "Which is the last thing I want to do. Believe me, I want you more than I can put into words. I just need more time to sort through what that means."

Hannah's heart hammered at his words. He wanted her? Like really wanted her?

He pulled his wallet out of his pocket and held out a twenty-dollar bill. "This is for breakfast. I'm not really hungry anymore."

Hannah took it, unsure of what else to say. She didn't even turn around as he walked away; what was the point? He'd been perfectly clear about how he felt, and she had her answer. He liked her.

Just not enough.

BLAKE CURSED A blue streak as he got onto the freeway and hit bumper-to-bumper traffic. The last thing he wanted was be stuck in a car, with only himself for company. Everything he'd said to Hannah had been the truth…

But he'd also been lying.

He more than liked her. He wanted her. She'd woken him up and made him realize that he was still alive. That he could still feel, but he wasn't sure how much. And Hannah deserved someone who could give her all of himself.

Sometimes he felt as though his soul had been buried with Jenny.

Blake closed his eyes, trying to remember Jenny's laughter, but the sound had faded over time to just a faint echo. He could still see her smile, her bright blue eyes, and the delight on her face the morning she'd told him she was pregnant.

Just a week before the shooting.

If the ache of losing the love of his life hadn't been enough, the fact that she had died carrying his child had been brutal. He'd spent the better part of eight months with his face in a bottle at home, and when he was at work, he was getting in trouble for being hungover. His temper was short, he'd alienated most of his friends, and if he was being completely honest, he hadn't even liked himself then.

He'd eventually ended up in the base drunk tank after starting a fight, and his CO, Captain Marshal, had come to see him. He'd been the one to suggest he transfer somewhere else, that he would handle everything, including therapy to help Blake move past it. At first he'd resisted, not wanting to leave everything that reminded him of Jenny, but then he'd taken a hard look at himself in the mirror. At the bloodshot eyes and sallow skin. He was no longer the man Jenny had loved, and he hated himself for failing her again.

So he'd let his CO organize his transfer to California, and his first day in group therapy, he'd met Best, Sparks, and Martinez. They'd bonded over their reluctance to talk in front of the others and struck up a friendship that felt more like family. It had been an amazing feeling, one he'd never shared with any of his other friends or even the members of his squad.

Which is why he trusted Sparks's advice. He was right.

But, God, he was lonely. He'd tried to deny that he wasn't, but it had hit him hardest over the holidays, when all of his friends had been celebrating with their girlfriends and their families, and he'd been alone. He hadn't even bothered to get a Christmas tree, just sat in his apartment drinking beer and watching Christmas specials on TV and trying not to think about Jenny and their child. About how it would have been his or her second Christmas and all the traditions they would have performed just to make the holiday special.

It had been too depressing imagining what might have been.

The only thing that had eased the loneliness over the last year had been the guys and Hannah. Maybe that was why he'd come into Dale's every day until he'd finally figured out her schedule. It seemed a little stalkerish, but he could finally acknowledge that she'd made him feel something sooner than last week, even if he couldn't admit it to himself before. Walking in and seeing that shy, sunny smile had warmed him to his core, and he'd started craving it. Craving the way she slowly opened up, started to tease him and talk to him. About anything from the weather to the way the River Cats were playing. She'd been the thing that had helped pull him out of the dark, and he was afraid that if he took that step, if he took things to the next level with her—and ruined it—he'd lose that light.

And he didn't think he could give it up.

"THAT IS A total cop-out, and you know it, Han!" Nicki was practically yelling through the phone as Hannah walked out to her car after work, her stomach still churning from the encounter with Blake. She knew he was in pain, she could read it in his eyes, even as he'd been about to kiss her.

If only she could help him realize that it was okay, that she wanted to take the chance and be with him, even if it didn't work out. But she hadn't been able to get the words out before he'd taken off.

"Men only use that bullshit excuse about needing time when they want to chase tail on the side! He is a total douche bag, and I'm just glad you know now, so you're not hung up on him for months as he strings you along like a puppet! Man, I'd like to sever his balls with a spork."

Hannah choked on a laugh. "A spork? That is a horrible visual, thanks. But honestly, Nic, I just think he's sad. He's lost a lot."

"Do not make excuses. If he wants to avoid dating someone new, then he shouldn't go around kissing women and giving them sultry looks!" Before Hannah could defend Blake again, Nicki continued, "Just forget about the chowderhead, Han. On Friday night, we'll be looking hot and shaking it with sexy military men. Screw him."

Hannah grimaced at the mention of the ball again. "You're forgetting that he will be there."

"Good. We'll make him regret every word. Then we'll see who the jealous one is."

Hannah wanted to hop onto Nicki's happy, cheer-up train, but she just wasn't there yet.

"Seriously, Hannah, we will do whatever we need to in order to cleanse this man from your system. You are not going to pine. I will not allow it. Say it with me. 'I shall not pine.' "

Hannah rolled her eyes and muttered, "I shall not pine."

"Louder."

"No, I'm sitting in my car in front of Dale's—"

"Louder, woman! Let me hear the conviction!"

"I shall not pine!" She had to admit, it felt really good to yell out her frustrations.

"Good. Now, put him from your mind and think about all the cute guys we're going to have drooling after us on Friday."

That was easier said than done.

Chapter Sixteen

BLAKE SAT IN Dr. Stabler's office that afternoon, waiting for her to call him back to her office to begin their session. He'd left Alpha Dog a little early to make it in time and ended up getting there a good fifteen minutes before his appointment. As he scrolled through his phone, his thumb hovered over the Kindle app, thinking of the books Hannah had recommended.

He still couldn't believe he'd almost kissed her again, but in his defense, her plump lower lip had been almost too tempting to resist. He could still remember the way it softened under his mouth, her tongue gliding along his as they'd gotten lost in each other.

Knowing it would only ingrain Hannah further into his thoughts, he opened the Kindle app and tapped on the cover of one of the books she'd recommended. It was a contemporary sports romance, and the cover had a smiling couple who appeared to not be able to get enough of each other.

Blake started reading chapter one, his eyes scanning each line as the author introduced the heroine, and pretty soon, he found himself on chapter two. By the time Dr. Stabler came out to tap him on the shoulder, he was fully engrossed in chapter three.

"Blake," she called loudly, making him jump in his seat.

"What?"

"I called your name several times, but you weren't paying attention. What were you looking at?"

Blake stood up, tucking his phone into his pocket. "Sorry, I was reading."

"Oh? What's the book about?"

Blake could feel his neck and ears warm with a blush. He could lie and tell her it was a thriller or horror novel, but he was here to be honest.

"It's one of the romance novels that Hannah recommended." He sat in the chair across from her, waiting for her to raise an eyebrow or at least appear a little surprised, but instead, she just nodded.

"I see. And how are you enjoying it so far?"

"Well, to be honest, it isn't as bad as I thought. Granted, I'm only a few chapters in, but so far it's good."

"And you're showing an interest in something that Hannah enjoys. Does this mean that you're planning on taking things to a new level with her?"

Blake shook his head. "I just decided to read it. It doesn't mean anything more for me and Hannah."

Dr. Stabler seemed disappointed. "I see. So, you aren't even going to text or call her to let her know you are enjoying the book she recommended?"

"I...I hadn't really thought about it."

Dr. Stabler smiled, picking up her notepad and pen. "You should. Women are usually pleased when a man takes an interest in something they enjoy."

"Yeah, well, I'm not sure how much she cares about my opinion," he mumbled, but she'd heard him.

"What makes you say that?"

"She's pretty mad at me, and I can't blame her. On one hand, every time I'm near her, I have this overwhelming need to touch her, but then I have the voice in my head screaming that it isn't fair."

"Is the other voice Jenny's?" she asked.

"No. I don't think so, at least. It's just me." Running his hands over his face, he groaned. "God, I am so fucked up. You must think I am crazy, right?"

"I don't think that at all, but sometimes people imagine what their loved one might say if they were still alive, if only so they can still remember the sound of their voice." Dr. Stabler gave him a rather pointed look. "What do you think Jenny would say to you?"

Her question caught him off guard. The only time they'd discussed death was at his parents' funeral. Blake racked his brain to remember the conversation, closing his eyes as he pulled the memory up.

They'd gone out to dinner once the funeral was over, and after, they'd headed back to the hotel room they'd booked. Blake had been unzipping the back of Jenny's dress, and she'd blurted out, "I hope when I go, it's quick."

Blake had stilled, hating the conversation already. "I don't want to think about this."

"I'm just saying that I hope it's quick, and you better not let Courtney Mitchell through the door of my funeral."

Despite the morbidity of the conversation, Blake had laughed. "Fine, as long as you promise to have me cremated and dump me somewhere really cool. Don't keep me around in some urn as a reminder to your next husband that I'm always watching."

Jenny grabbed his hand and brought it to her lips. "I could never imagine being with anyone but you."

He'd kissed her softly on the side of the neck. "I feel exactly the same way."

"Blake?" Dr. Stabler called, bringing him out of the past. "You didn't answer my question."

"What would Jenny say to me about Hannah?"

"Yes, that is what I mean," she said patiently.

"I think she'd ask how I could move on so quickly." Even as he spoke the words aloud, they sliced through him like a razor blade. Jenny's face twisted up in a hurt expression was something he could easily imagine, and it pained him to think about.

"Really? Or is that just your guilt?"

Blake hated that she continued to turn these feelings back around on him, rather than believe him when he said that this is how he truly believed Jenny would feel.

"I was just remembering the only time we'd discussed if one of us died, and Jenny had basically said she couldn't imagine being with anyone but me."

Dr. Stabler frowned at him. "And that means she'd want you to be alone for the rest of your life? I think you don't give her enough credit. If she's dead, and she isn't coming back, I can't imagine her being so selfish."

Blake tensed. "Jenny wasn't selfish. She was warm, generous, and kind."

"I want you to repeat what you just said in your head and ask yourself why you think that Jenny would be disappointed in you. Especially when you yourself just admitted she wasn't a selfish person."

Swallowing hard, Blake imagined Jenny. If she had been the one to survive, he'd have wanted her to move on and be happy. And he really couldn't imagine that she wouldn't. Jenny had been too bright not to shine, and she deserved to find someone else who appreciated that.

"She would have wanted me to move on. To be happy."

"So, the question is, is Hannah the person you want to do that with?"

Blake left the office, and as he drove home, he tried to picture his future, one where he never remarried, never had kids or was happy. Where he was still living in a one-bedroom apartment, and while all of his friends were going to events with their families, he was alone, drinking.

He didn't want that future for himself, and neither would Jenny.

Somehow, he was going to get up the nerve to ask Hannah out, but it had been so long, he had no idea what to suggest. In a movie they couldn't talk, and he was afraid if he actually called, he might choke on the words.

Was texting a viable option?

HANNAH TAPPED AWAY at her computer later that night, trying not to check her phone every five minutes. After waitressing and teaching, she needed the downtime getting lost in her manuscript gave her, only she was distracted.

By Blake.

Despite what Nicki said about forgetting him, she just couldn't push him from her mind and found herself expecting him to call, which was just ridiculous.

It is the twenty-first century. I could text him.

Hannah set her phone down and walked away, temptation too great. Milo chased her heels, trying to capture them with his tiny teeth and paws, and Hannah finally scooped the puppy up and squeezed him.

"Hey, mister, we've talked about those razor blades in your mouth! No more biting!"

The puppy's long wet tongue caught her on the nose, and she laughed.

Until she heard the ding of her phone.

Setting Milo back on his feet, she picked up her phone and pressed the little message icon.

Hey, Hannah, it's Blake. Guess what I'm reading?

Tapping on the keyboard, she wrote out a long, roundabout question, then erased it, settling for short and sweet.

What?

Several minutes ticked by before it beeped again.

Blitzing Emily.

Hannah smiled. He'd actually bought one of the books she'd recommended and was reading it? She couldn't help melting a little as she responded.

And how do you like it?

She sat back down at the table, ignoring Milo's attempts to sharpen his teeth on her feet as she waited. Beep.

I am over halfway done. Just can't put it down. So, thank you for the recommendation.

Oh, yeah, it was going to be really easy to get over this guy. She snorted.

You are very welcome. Maybe we could talk about it over coffee sometime?

She sent the text before she thought of how he might react to it. He'd asked for time, and here she was, pressing him to see her. Her phone beeped, and she held her breath as she looked.

I'd like that.

She stilled, staring at the screen in shock. And then...

Damn him.

Here she was, trying not to get attached, and he went and said incredibly sweet things, even reading a romance novel she'd suggested.

Has it given you a new appreciation for romance?

Would he take that the wrong way?

I really think it has. In fact, I've got the next book you recommended ready to go when I finish this one.

Hannah squealed and did a little dance in her chair, laughing.

Well, please let me know when you finish. I'd love to hear your final thoughts.

Two seconds later, another beep.

And her heart stopped.

Anything for you.

What the hell did *that* mean? And what the heck did she say to that?

That's nice of you.

She wanted to bang her head against something the minute she hit send, but there was no taking it back.

BLAKE STARED AT his phone screen, reading too much into her last response. After he'd sent *anything for you*, he'd realized how it would come across, but it was too late to take it back. He'd figured it would just be easier to keep the conversation going so she wouldn't dwell on it, but it almost seemed as if it had pissed her off, if the formal response was any indication.

Text message tones are hard to interpret. I need to chill.

His fingers tapped the side of the phone as he contemplated what to do next.

Do you have an e-reader?

He knew the question had come out of the blue, but he'd actually been thinking about getting a tablet for a while, and if it kept her talking...

I am such a lonely, pathetic asshole.

His phone chirped, and he read her response.

I have a NOOK. Why?

Why was he asking her about e-readers? It wasn't just that he wanted one. It was also because he was bored and wanted to get out of the apartment. Maybe head over to Barnes & Noble and grab a coffee and look around…

But the thought of wandering around alone just didn't appeal to him.

I was thinking of getting one, but wasn't sure what to get. Was thinking about heading out and grabbing a coffee, maybe stopping by Best Buy or Barnes & Noble to check them out. Would you want to go with me?

Blake held his breath, panic setting in and churning in his stomach. But the excitement at her response seemed to override everything else.

Sure. Want me to meet you?

It didn't make sense to take two cars, but having Hannah alone, two feet from him in a small area, left his mouth dry.

I'll pick you up. What's your address?

HANNAH THREW EVERYTHING out of her closet and was still convinced she had nothing to wear that didn't look absolutely horrible. She'd finally settled on a light blue cowl-necked sweater and a pair of blue jeans when he knocked on the door.

Milo stood in front of the door barking like crazy while Hannah shushed at him.

"Stop it." She opened the door, and Milo tried to push past her to get to Blake. Picking him up, she smiled out at

Blake, who stood on the porch in a baseball cap, sweat-shirt, and jeans.

She'd never been into men in hats before, but there was something about Blake in one that definitely got her motor running.

"Sorry, let me just put him in his kennel."

"No problem."

Hannah ran Milo into the kitchen, giving him a puppy Milk-Bone and filling up his water dish before locking him inside.

"Nice place," Blake said behind her.

She stood up and looked around at her small white kitchen; she'd always thought it was a little sterile look-ing, but it was cozy and all she needed.

"Thanks." Standing in the doorway of her kitchen made Blake seem bigger, his shoulders taking up half the space and his head just nearly touching the top of the frame. "Shall we go?"

Blake nodded but didn't move, and as she drew closer, he stepped aside to let her pass and followed behind her out the door. She was completely aware of his presence at her back, and she felt awkward and clunky as she walked.

She locked her front door and could almost feel the warmth of his breath on her neck. "I like you in blue."

Her head jerked up in surprise. "Thank you."

"Is blue your favorite color?"

No, it's green with little flecks of gray, like your eyes.

"It is."

"Mine, too."

They headed for the car, and Hannah twisted her hand around her purse strap, unsure of how to keep things going. At the diner, she never had any trouble talking to him, but now that they were completely alone, she wasn't sure what to say. Especially since they'd said they were just going to be friends. There was all of this tension between them. It was hard to just be friends with a guy when you knew exactly how his lips felt against yours.

Blake got her door, and Hannah stepped inside with a quiet thank-you.

Hannah watched him run around the front of the car to the driver's side and took a deep breath.

Okay, I can do this. Just ask him questions about the e-reader. About the therapy dogs.

As he climbed inside, Hannah said, "So, what made you decide to go looking for an e-reader tonight?"

"I've been toying with the idea of getting a tablet for a while, but I actually just needed to get out of my apartment. Been thinking of buying a house, too, someplace bigger with a yard so I can have a dog."

He started the car, and Hannah's heart skipped. "So, you're planning on staying here permanently, then?"

"Yeah, I think so. I like my job and the area. I'm getting used to the way you Californians talk"—she caught his wink in the darkened car and laughed—"and I think I can make a home here."

Without thinking, she reached out a hand and covered his on the steering wheel. "That's fantastic, Blake."

The warmth of his skin blazed through her palm, and she jerked her hand back. This was all too confusing.

They were supposed to be friends. She touched her friends without wanting to glide her fingers across their skin.

Not Blake, though. She wanted to test the fine hairs on his arms and see if they were as soft as she thought.

She leaned back in the seat, hoping that eventually, she'd be able to be friends with Blake without the ache for more.

BLAKE PULLED THROUGH the drive-through of Starbucks and bought Hannah's coffee, his fingers tingling when their hands brushed as he passed her the cup. In the quiet, one question from therapy continued to haunt him.

If he had been the one to die, would he want Jenny to be alone and miserable for years?

The answer was no. He would want Jenny to be happy. To find someone else and live her life.

So why was he so worried about how Jenny would feel if he moved on? Two years did seem like a short amount of time, but just because he started dating someone new didn't mean he'd just forget about her. Jenny was a part of him. She'd been his world, and she would always have his heart.

That didn't mean he had to be miserable and alone. He could date, have a good time, enjoy sex…

But love? He didn't know if he could do that again.

Which was why he couldn't seem to understand the self-destructive habit of seeking out Hannah. At her work, on the phone…She was made for happily ever after, for romance and marriage and a half a dozen kids.

He wasn't sure he could give any of that to her, but he couldn't seem to stay away.

Live for today. Take it a day at a time, and go at my own pace. She'll understand.

They got out of the car at Barnes & Noble, and as they started to cross the parking lot, Blake slid his hand over the small of her back, leading her to the entrance.

She jumped but didn't say anything about the touch. Once they were inside, Blake let his hand fall back to his side.

"So, where should we start?" he asked.

Hannah nodded to the front display, which had three e-readers and tablets. "There are the NOOKs."

Blake looked them over. "Which one do you have?"

Hannah pointed to one with just a white screen and words on it. "I have the GlowLight, which is great for reading, especially in the dark, but the tablets are nice if you're in the market for that."

"What's the difference?"

Hannah stepped closer, her floral perfume drawing him in until his head was bent next to hers. Damn, she smelled good.

"Well, this one is just for reading and doesn't get that glare when the sun hits it. The tablet does everything, but you can't use it to read in direct sunlight."

Her shoulder brushed his arm, and he was tempted to reach out and draw her closer, to feel all of those soft curves pressed against his side.

"Hi, can I help you?" a cheerful voice asked.

Blake hadn't even been aware that a salesgirl had come up alongside them, he was so caught up with Hannah. "No, we're fine."

"Actually, can you explain the differences between the NOOKs and how they compare to a Kindle? I need to find the restroom."

Blake watched her take off for the back of the store, wondering if Hannah actually needed to use the bathroom or if she'd sensed he was about to pull her into one of the aisles to kiss her and bolted.

"Sir, if you're looking for just a basic e-reader, the NOOK…"

Blake listened with half an ear as the store clerk went over all of the descriptions and features, while all he could think about was Hannah.

What else was new?

Chapter Seventeen

HANNAH DABBED A damp paper towel on her face and neck, noting her flushed cheeks and wishing she could will away the high color. She hadn't meant to run away like a coward, but Blake's body so close to hers, the feeling that he was about to touch her, had sent her senses into overdrive. She'd closed her eyes, waiting for the press of his mouth on her neck or the brush of his fingers on the skin of her neck...

Instead, the store clerk had shown up, and Hannah had run away like a coward.

But honestly, how much more could she take? He was driving her wild one minute and dousing her hopes the next.

If he was about to kiss me, then I pretty much screwed myself.

But he'd been the one to say he had no interest in anything more than friendship, so why had this whole night felt a little like a...well, a date?

Knowing she couldn't hide any longer, she walked out the door and found him right around the corner.

In the romance section.

He turned and grinned at her. "There you are."

Hannah smoothed a hand over her hair nervously. "Here I am. What did you decide?"

"I don't know yet. Still thinking about it, and thought I'd come back here to browse while I waited for you." Blake picked up a book off the shelf and held it up to her. "Have you read this one?"

It was a Maya Banks novel and very steamy. She'd read it last year, after finishing the first two books in the series and becoming obsessed with it.

"Yes, but I don't think it's your style."

"Because it has flowers on the front." Blake waggled his eyebrows and gave her a lecherous grin. "Does that mean this is an erotic romance?"

Hannah crossed her arms and pursed her lips. "I thought you weren't going to tease me anymore?"

"I said I wouldn't tease you about regular romance, but erotic romance…Now I'm curious."

He started thumbing through the book and opened his mouth as if he was going to start reading it aloud.

In the middle of Barnes & Noble.

Hannah flew across the space between them and covered his mouth. "Don't you dare."

His eyes crinkled up, and something wet brushed her palm. She jerked her hand back and wiped it on his sweatshirt. "Gross, did you just lick me?"

"Yes, you interrupted my performance art."

"Seriously, Blake, don't."

Blake closed the book and gave her a sheepish smile. "Fine. I'll just buy it to see what all the fuss is about."

Oh, Hannah couldn't wait to see the salesgirl's face when tall, manly Blake went through the checkout with an erotic romance.

"Oh, please. I cannot wait for this."

"What, you don't think I'll do it?" There was a challenge in his hazel eyes that gave her a little thrill.

"No, I think you'll chicken out."

Blake lowered his head and his voice, his hushed tone running deliciously across her skin. "Are you double dog daring me?"

This time, she burst out laughing. "I've never seen this side of you."

"What side is that?"

"Like a naughty little boy."

"Oh, you want to see naughty? I can show you naughty." He grabbed her hand unexpectedly and started pulling her toward the register.

"What are you doing?"

"If you don't witness it, then it didn't happen."

A bolt of joy shot through her as Blake actually laced his fingers with hers. She liked this side of Blake. It wasn't the glowering, sad man she'd come to know or even the softly teasing one. This side of him was unfettered by doubt and grief.

Once they reached the checkout line, she pulled away reluctantly.

"It only works if I'm not around. Otherwise, they're going to think you're just buying it for me."

Blake nodded, and when he stepped up to the register, Hannah heard him say loudly, "This book is for me. It's not for her."

Hannah rolled her eyes with a laugh.

The clerk smiled politely, obviously not believing him, and when Blake finished, she was startled again when he took her hand.

"I thought you wanted a NOOK."

"We're going to Best Buy first to look at the Kindles, and then I'll decide."

They left the store and walked across the parking lot to his car, her hand still grasped in his. As Blake got her door and released her hand to close it, he dropped the book in her lap.

"Hold that for me, will ya?"

Hannah had no idea why holding a Barnes & Noble bag thrilled her so much, but as she watched Blake climb inside, she couldn't help thinking that tonight sure felt like a date.

And she would have been happy to live in the moment a little while longer.

AT BEST BUY, Blake kept ahold of Hannah's hand. Not because he was helping her across the street or trying to prove something to himself.

No, Blake held her hand because he just liked the way it felt in his.

They stood in front of the Kindles, studying the features.

"So, do you prefer e-books?" Blake asked.

"Actually, I like to read paperbacks. Something about the smell is comforting. E-readers do save space on my bookshelf, though."

Blake glanced over at her, a smile tugging at his lips. "What do they smell like?"

"Hmm…a little musty, maybe. Like paper, I don't know. It's nice."

He squeezed her hand and found himself twirling her down the aisle toward the iPads. "Oh yeah, it sounds nice. Just what I want to sniff, a musty pile of books."

Hannah was giggling now, letting him continue to spin her. "Don't knock it till you try it." Finally, she grabbed onto his arm with her free hand, weaving a bit. "Whew, I'm a little dizzy."

"Okay, no more spinning. Wouldn't want you to hurl on the DVDs."

She made a face at him. "Classy imagery."

Blake chuckled, having more fun bantering with Hannah than he'd had in…well, years probably.

As they started walking again, Blake had to admit that he liked the way his hand linked with Hannah's; Jenny had been barely five one, so it had actually been more comfortable for her to just slip her arm through his, but Hannah was probably five five or five six, so the height difference wasn't so major.

They just seemed to fit together. To complement each other.

Whoa, I'm getting a little ahead of myself on this.

They stopped in front of the white tablets, and Blake grimaced a bit at the price. It wasn't that he couldn't afford it, but that was more than he'd spent on his laptop.

"Can I help you?" a young guy in glasses and a blue Best Buy shirt asked.

"No thank you, we're just browsing," Hannah said.

Blake picked up the iPad, weighing it in his free hand.

"It's not ideal for reading. The sun glares off the screen like a laptop."

He set the tablet back down and wished that he could nibble the spot just below her ear. It was so bare, and pink, and tempting. "That's okay, if I'm outside, I'm doing something."

"What about the beach?" she asked.

"I've actually never been to the beach," Blake said.

Hannah looked so surprised, he laughed. "Is that bad?"

"No, it's just…Didn't they have beaches in Texas?"

"Yeah, we had the gulf, but I grew up closer to Dallas."

"Well, California has some pretty spots. I'm going to make it my mission to get you to the beach."

Blake really liked the sound of that and decided he wouldn't mind taking a trip where he lay in the sand all day with Hannah. Of course, in his daydream, she'd be wearing a tiny little bikini.

Or nothing at all.

When they walked out of Best Buy, Blake had a new iPad and case and was almost a thousand dollars poorer, but he decided that it was the most fun he'd had in a while, so it was money well spent.

He drove Hannah back to her place, and when he found himself in front of her door, he debated on what to do. He'd held her hand, which he'd figured was the clearest way to let her know he was interested in being more than just friends, but if this was considered their first date, did he kiss her?

If I'm going to take this slow, then I need to actually think with my head and not my dick.

"Thanks for going with me," he said.

"You're welcome, I had fun."

She seemed to be watching him expectantly, and he dipped his head, kissing her on the cheek softly.

"Good night."

He walked back to his car without looking back, fighting the urge to back her up against her front door and give her a real, toe-curling kiss.

But if he was going to do this with Hannah, he was going to do it right.

Chapter Eighteen

ON FRIDAY AFTERNOON, Blake walked out onto the field with Charge to find his guys already working with their dogs. He'd spent the morning decorating the ballroom of the Hilton and listening to his friends and their girlfriends make sugary-sweet love talk to each other.

It had left him feeling nauseated and wistful at the same time.

Jeffrey Tillman's freckled face split into a wide grin. "Yo, Sarge, is it true you're going to some dance tonight to be man meat for a bunch of desperate chicks?"

Jeff had been with Blake for three months and was one of his favorite kids. He was in for shoplifting—his second arrest—and the judge had hoped their program would help him. So far, the kid seemed to be responding well.

His boundaries left much to be desired, though.

"I'm going to a fundraiser, Tillman. And women don't usually like being called chicks."

"Yeah, yeah, but is it like a stripper thing? Are you going to get up on stage and make those dollar bills?"

Tillman did a dance, shaking his hips and thrusting his pelvis, and the other boys laughed.

Blake, still not happy about the fundraiser, shot Tillman a fierce look. "No one is stripping, and if you wanna keep it up, I'll have you doing burpees until your knees give out."

"Sorry, Sarge." Tillman's grin told Blake he wanted to say more but was refraining.

Blake made them do laps while practicing keeping their dogs in the heel position, giving him a chance to check his phone. No new messages.

"Yo, Kline!" Best called from the edge of the training field. "Phone call."

Blake nodded and started jogging toward him. "You got my hoodlums?"

"Yeah, I'll watch the little monsters."

Blake hurried inside to his office, and after he shut the door, he picked up the phone.

"This is Sergeant Blake Kline."

"Sergeant, this is Charles Gunn, returning your call."

Blake wanted to whoop. Charles was the friend of General Reynolds's who was selling his house in Orangevale, and although the address was in a nice neighborhood, Blake had been a little leery about a for-sale-by-owner deal.

Until Charles had e-mailed him pictures yesterday. The place was perfect, with a big backyard, four bedrooms, and two baths. He'd gone to see it yesterday after work and told Charles he wanted to think about it, but there was no reason to hesitate. He wanted that house.

So, he'd called Charles back this morning to discuss terms and left a message for him to call him back.

Now, it was go time.

"Hey, Charles. You can just call me Blake. I am really interested in your house, but I was hoping you'd take forty thousand dollars less if I gave you cash up front."

It was a bold move, and he knew it. He had the forty thousand if Charles wouldn't agree, but he thought it was a fair price with the updates the house needed.

Charles was silent on the line. "That's a pretty steep reduction in price. Most people ask for a couple thousand off."

"I realize that, sir, but the house needs quite a bit of updating, and it's been sitting on the market a year at the price you're asking, which should be indication enough that the price is on the high side. The good thing about this is you can take the money and no longer have this property wearing you down. You can fully retire in Florida with no worries."

Charles seemed to be chewing over his words. "I'm gonna need some time to consider before I make my final decision."

"I can respect that, and I'll wait for your call."

Charles's phone disconnected, and Blake breathed out a big, weighty sigh.

He wanted this house, bad. He only hoped that old Charles came through so he'd have a place to take Charge.

And maybe a home to bring Hannah back to without worrying for her safety?

It was true that Hannah had been factoring into his thoughts the last few days, and he actually couldn't wait to see her tonight at the ball. It was stupid, and he'd never admit it to the other guys, but for the first time in a long while, he had something to look forward to.

HANNAH DROVE MILO over to her parents' place that afternoon, carrying him up to the door. His nose and legs were healing nicely, and the fur was even starting to come back. She'd bought him a blue paisley harness and matching leash, but it was just easier to haul him around.

Besides, she loved to snuggle his warm body against her, and pretty soon, he would be too big to lift.

Hannah rang the bell, and her mom answered the door, pushing her glasses up the bridge of her nose as she smiled brightly.

"Ah, my little grand puppy. Are you ready to play with Grandma, Papa, and Uncle Miggons?"

Uncle Miggons apparently adored Milo and whined when he left. Her mother stepped back and Hannah said dryly, "Nice to see you, too, Mom."

"I was going to greet you," her mom assured her, giving her and Milo a squeeze as they passed. Hannah put Milo down and unclipped his leash just as Miggons skidded around the corner, looking very dapper in his recent lion cut and festive Valentine's Day sweater.

Excited barks erupted from the tiny fluff ball, and Milo lifted a huge yellow paw in greeting as the Pom attacked and ran away, encouraging the pup to give chase with several high-pitched yips.

Milo took off, and she heard her dad shouting about noise and chaos from the living room.

"Well, come in and say hi to your father. What time is your dance?" her mom asked.

"It starts at eight. Nicki hired a limo to drop us off and pick us up."

"Is it just the two of you going then? A limo is awfully expensive for just two people."

Hannah had thought so, too, but then she'd found out that they were part of a larger group sharing the limo. "Actually, there are about seven of us sharing it, so it won't be so bad."

Her mother frowned, her gaze lit with obvious concern. "Just be sure not to drink too much. Even in a group of friends, it's not safe to be impaired. I was watching ID network last night—"

"No, no ID network. Please! Please!"

Her mother huffed, but her lips twitched at the corners. "Fine, don't listen to your mother."

"Believe me, Mom, I'm familiar with rape culture. Never accept a drink from anyone, except the bartender. Never walk alone after dark, and always be aware of my surroundings. Plus, I took a self-defense class and I learned—"

"Oh, I've been wanting to take one of those! How was it?"

Good until the rejection and friend speech.

"Really good. I'll have to show you a few things sometime."

"Are you two hens going to just stay in the hallway clucking, or are you going to say hi to your old man?" her dad hollered.

Hannah laughed as she followed the sound of her dad's booming voice. She found him sitting in his favorite chair, his large frame folded over. Her father was six foot six with glasses, and she could still remember riding on those shoulders as a child and feeling as if she was on top of the world.

"Hey, Daddy." She bent over and gave him a kiss. "Did you miss me?"

"Always, Princess." His bushy brows lowered over his eyes, and he grunted. "I did not miss the chaos little Milo brings, however."

As if on cue, Miggins raced into the living room and bounded onto her father's lap, barking furiously at Milo, who tried to jump up, too, and ended up falling onto his back, his paws up in the air. Seeing an opening, Miggins pounced onto Milo's exposed stomach, nipping and retreating as Milo wiggled on his back and lazily tried to bite the other dog.

"See? Troublemaker." Her dad bent over and picked Milo up, holding the puppy's forehead to his. "Who's a bad puppy?"

Listening to her father's booming voice become a high-pitched baby voice sent Hannah into hysterical giggles. "You love him."

"Nope. He is an ugly little monster."

Hannah didn't believe him for a minute. "Well, I'll pick up the little monster in the morning, since the ball isn't over until late."

"Ball, ha. You just be careful, Cinderella. I don't know if your mother told you, but last night on ID network—"

"She doesn't want to hear about it, Gil," her mom said.

Her father grunted. "Fine." He patted her hand softly. "Be a good girl, Hannah Banana."

"Always, Dad."

As Hannah left, her thoughts returned to her last night with Blake, and she wondered what the hell it all meant. The hand holding, the coffee, the kiss on the cheek.

Her hands gripped the steering wheel angrily. It wasn't fair. He'd told her he wasn't ready, just wanted to be friends, but everything Tuesday night had been very un-friend-like. Whatever game he was playing, she didn't like it, and it was going to stop.

She'd tell him that, too, as soon as she saw him at the ball tonight.

Chapter Nineteen

BLAKE STOOD BY the bar, watching as the ball attendees trickled in, telling himself he wasn't looking for Hannah in the crowd of women. Although they'd exchanged texts and phone calls after their date, he hadn't had a chance to text or call today with all the hoops Eve had them jumping through, and he just hoped she hadn't assumed the worst. He was also hoping they wouldn't need to have a talk, but if they did, he had a speech prepared.

How fucking romantic.

"And here they come," Martinez said beside him. The crowd of women in the ballroom was growing thicker by the second, like a cluster of colorful butterflies.

"I'm surprised your girlfriend made you come tonight."

Martinez shrugged. "She trusts me, and besides, she knew that Sparks and Best would bitch and moan if I didn't come. She put the three of us on drink duty."

"Drink duty?" Eve had told him to pick a woman and make her feel special, and he already had her picked out.

"We're walking around with trays of specialty drinks. Didn't she give you a job?"

"Yeah, to cater to one of the guests' every whim." Blake downed his Jack and Coke. "I guess only the guys with girlfriends got the cool gig."

"Or she thought we'd try to escape if we didn't have something to do."

Blake didn't believe that for a second. Eve, Dani, and Violet, Sparks's girlfriend, had probably come up with the drink work detail so they wouldn't have to watch their boyfriends dancing with other women. They were all here tonight—Violet helping with serving food, and Dani taking tickets at the door. Devious.

"What's up, playas?" Bryce asked, popping up beside them.

Blake's eyes bugged out of his head in surprise. He hadn't even known Bryce owned a dress, let alone something so...so...

"What the hell are you wearing?" Martinez asked, reading Blake's mind.

The blue dress was tight, and Blake found himself staring up at the ceiling so she wouldn't think he was checking her out.

"I'm wearing a sombrero. What the fuck does it look like, asswipe?"

Blake grinned, relaxing. "There's the Bryce we know."

"Whatever, you both are dicks. Have you seen Slater?" she asked, craning her neck.

"Bryce, if something's going on between you and Slater, Sparks isn't going to like it," Martinez said, frowning.

"Sparks doesn't need to know." A satisfied smile spread across her glossy lips. "There he is. Later, boys."

Martinez shook his head. "Should we say something? They work together, and shit can get awkward fast."

"I've experienced annoying Bryce and friend Bryce...I don't think I want to meet pissed-off Bryce."

"You're right." Martinez picked up a tray of glasses with raspberries and mint leaves inside. "Duty calls."

"Have fun." Blake ordered another Jack and Coke from the bartender and continued watching the door. The ballroom was starting to fill up, and the DJ was playing a Madonna song. Women had begun making their way toward the four bar stations around the room, and he moved as a herd crowded around him.

Blake watched as the men who had been drafted to entertain started mingling, smiling and chatting with the women. There were two photo areas set up with props that people could pay five dollars to get their pictures taken in. Guests had received two drink tickets and ten complimentary raffle tickets for several large prizes and could purchase more raffle tickets at the door. The gift bags they received upon leaving were filled with "a single woman's dream," as Eve put it. All in all, Blake had to admit she had done an amazing job of creating an awesome event that would appeal to many women.

"You!" Eve stalked toward him and pointed to the dance floor. "Go make some girl's dream come true and dance with her."

Blake sighed loudly and set his drink down on the nearest table. "You realize this is incredibly sexist and you're objectifying me?"

"Yes, but it is for a good cause." When Blake crossed his arms and gave her what he hoped was his stubborn look, Eve threw up her hands. "I give up. You want to take off, fine, we've got plenty of guys to handle the crowd. I just thought maybe you might like to meet someone or, at the very least, not wallow alone in your apartment."

Blake scowled at her. "We are not close enough for you to give me life tips."

Eve huffed, tossing her black hair over her shoulder. "Well, someone has to, because your friends won't. Everyone is worried about you but won't say anything because they don't want to push. If you haven't noticed, I'm pretty pushy, and I'm not going to coddle you. You need to decide whether you are going to let one tragedy shape your life or if you're going to move on and try to be happy again. But stop making everyone around you miserable."

Then, she spun on incredibly high heels and walked away from him.

Blake stood there for a minute or two, shock, anger, and confusion warring inside him. He was making his friends miserable? He hadn't even realized he was doing it, but looking back, he could see it. They were all moving on from the things that had landed them in group, and each one had found happiness, while he...

Well, he was still holding on.

A flash of caramel hair in the crowd caught his eye, and he took a step toward it, trying to see if it was Hannah.

"Well, hello, handsome."

Blake looked down at a forty-something woman in a black dress, her red lips smiling at him seductively.

"Hello, ma'am. How are you this evening?"

"It's Kimberly, darling, and I'd be better if you dance with me."

Blake wouldn't catch another glimpse of Hannah unless he got closer, and he'd have to enter the dance floor to do so.

"May I have this dance, Kimberly?"

The woman appeared relieved, and he warmed toward her, realizing how nervous she'd actually been approaching him. He led her onto the dance floor, maneuvering them into the crowd so he could get a better look.

And his stomach dropped out when he got a look at Hannah.

Her hair was shimmering in the lights, pulled back from her face but erupting into a mass of curls down her back. Her glasses were missing, and her face was tastefully made-up. The purple dress hugged her curves as lovingly as a glove, and that neckline...

Blake's mouth went dry at the view.

His awe was derailed, however, as he watched a young guy in dress blues come up behind her and slide a proprietary arm around her waist. He whispered something in Hannah's ear, and Blake could see her cheeks turn pink in the low, flashing lights.

His jaw tightened as his gut churned. For the first time in their acquaintance, Blake didn't find that blush charming. It filled him with bitter jealousy.

"Do you know that girl?" Kimberly asked, bringing his attention back to the woman he was supposed to be dancing with.

Blake realized he'd dropped his arms from her waist and had been ready to cross the dance floor and yank the little turd away from Hannah. Kimberly was watching him with curiosity, and he cleared his throat, trying to speak past the dusty feel in his mouth. "Yes, she's a friend of mine."

She turned toward Hannah again, studying her before she said, "She's very pretty for being so heavy."

Blake had been about to pull her back and continue dancing, but he stopped, staring aghast at the woman's audacity. "She's not heavy."

Blake had no idea what expression was on his face, but she paled. "I didn't mean anything by it—"

Luckily the song ended and Blake didn't have to listen to her excuse for the thoughtless comment.

"Have a wonderful night, Kimberly. Thank you for the dance."

He walked back to his place at the edge of the dance floor, his vantage point finally cleared enough that he could see Hannah and the young Marine dancing. He fumed, playing over their date in his mind. He'd held her hand, for fuck's sake! Didn't girls know what that meant?

I told her I didn't want to start anything with her. Maybe she thought it was just two friends running errands.

She threw her head back, laughing, and he could hear the husky sound in his head.

Maybe she hadn't seen him or needed rescuing.

The Marine dipped her and spun her around, that beautiful smile he loved glued to her lips.

Or maybe she got tired of waiting on me.

HANNAH LAUGHED AT herself as she did the moves for "YMCA" with Nicki, her dance partner, Eric, and Caleb. When Caleb had first come up behind her and slipped his arm around her waist, her heart had lodged in her throat. She'd imagined turning and finding Blake behind her, but when he'd whispered, "I'm Caleb, and you're beautiful," she'd been both excited and disappointed.

Now, however, she had been dancing for an hour with him and thoroughly enjoying herself. Caleb was a twenty-five-year-old Marine with blue eyes and brown hair cut close to his head. He was sweet and funny, and she was having a great time.

Still, she couldn't stop her gaze from wandering occasionally, hoping to catch a glimpse of Blake.

She was still angry with him, but she'd secretly hoped that he'd be waiting for her tonight, ready to sweep her out on the dance floor and tell her he only wanted to be with her.

When the song ended, Caleb took her hand and leaned in. "You wanna get a drink?"

"Yes, please." She turned to Nicki and asked, "Want to get a drink with us?"

"Nah, I'm good," Nicki said, wrapping her arms around Eric's shoulders.

Hannah let Caleb lead her out of the crowd toward one of the bars, taking careful steps so her ankle didn't roll in her new heels. She'd practiced in the shoes all week, even dancing in them around her apartment, but she still wasn't completely used to wedges.

"What will you have?" Caleb asked as they stood in line.

"A water and one of those pink drinks with the heart-shaped watermelon slice." She'd had one earlier, and it had been to die for. She reached for her little clutch and her second drink ticket, but he waved her off.

"It's my treat."

"Thank you."

Caleb smiled warmly at her and wrapped his arm around her waist in a too-familiar way that made Hannah a little uncomfortable, especially since she could feel his hand resting on the top of her bottom through the dress. He wasn't acting gross about it, so maybe he didn't think anything of it.

As casually as she could, she reached around and moved Caleb's hand up a bit.

"Sorry, did I cross a line?"

He looked worried, and she wanted to reassure him. "It's fine, your hand just traveled a little below the equator."

It was their turn to order, and when Caleb didn't tip their bartender, she reached into her clutch and gave him a couple of bucks.

Caleb gave her a disgruntled look. "I told you it was on me."

"It's okay, I've got the tip."

He seemed irritated for a moment and shrugged. She picked up her drink and followed him over to a table.

"So, what do you do, Hannah?" he asked.

"I work as a waitress in the morning and teach kindergarten in the afternoon."

"That's hot. I wish I'd had a teacher that looked like you when I was in school."

Hannah shifted her feet and frowned a little. She didn't like Caleb's overly familiar touch or his suggestive comments.

"Even if you'd had an attractive teacher, it would have been inappropriate."

"Not if I was legal."

"Still…"

His arm snaked out around her waist once more, and he leaned down as if he was going to kiss her. "I'd love to play naughty student and dirty teacher with you."

As his lips descended on hers, she put her hands up and pushed against his chest. "Let me go."

"What's the matter? I thought you liked me." His lips fell on her cheek when she turned her face away, and she smelled the alcohol on his breath.

"I just met you!"

"So? What better way to get to know me than to—argh!"

Hannah had dropped one of her hands and grabbed his dick through his uniform, crushing it, just like Blake had told her to do. Caleb released her and fell back a few steps, cupping his groin as he curled onto himself.

"What the fuck? You stupid bit—"

Caleb was gripped around his neck from behind, and Hannah trembled when she saw Blake standing behind him, his expression thunderous.

"You're going to walk away now, or I'm going to throw your ass out and you'll crawl home. Your choice."

Blake released Caleb, who still couldn't quite stand up straight. He glared at Hannah and rasped, "I'm gone."

Hannah realized people around them were staring, and she bit her lip, trying not to burst into tears.

Without warning, Blake took her hand and led her out of the hotel ballroom. They weaved through the couples until they reached a door at the far end. He opened it, pushing her gently inside, and shut the door after them. Hannah took a few steps back, fighting the tears that had been gathering.

Once he locked the door, Blake walked up to her and smoothed his thumb across her cheek. "Come on, Hannah, don't cry. You'll mess up your makeup if you cry."

She gave a watery laugh at his joke. "I'm so stupid."

"No, I was watching every move that guy made, and he was a jerk. You were right to twist and pull his dick." Hannah could see the twinkle in his hazel eyes through the layer of tears. "I was so proud of my pupil."

His words gave her pause, and she caught his hands against her cheek. "You were watching him? Or me?"

His hands opened up under hers, framing her face gently.

"You."

Before Hannah could respond, his mouth covered hers, sending shock waves through her body that liquefied every nerve. She'd tried reliving the one kiss they'd shared, but it was never as good as the real thing.

Reality was better. So much better.

His mouth slanted over hers, his tongue pressing at the seam of her lips until she opened for him. The kiss deepened, and Blake held onto her hands as he pulled them down and wrapped his arms around her waist. Hannah's heart fluttered like a caged bird as Blake pressed the front of their bodies together from chest to groin.

She tugged her hands away from his and embraced him, snuggling as close as she could get as she lost herself in Blake.

One of his hands came up and cradled the back of her neck, tugging gently at the strands of her hair. Their lips broke briefly, and Blake whispered her name, his breath caressing her wet, swollen lips, and a quiver between her legs made her squeeze them together.

He pulled back, his gaze devouring her face. She wanted to bring him back to her, afraid reality would set in and he'd walk away from her again.

"God, Hannah, you taste so fucking good."

And this time when his lips came down on hers, they were desperate, powerful. He slid his hands down, gripping her ass through the poof of her dress, and she didn't protest or tell him to keep it above the equator. She wanted Blake to touch her, hold her…

Love her.

Chapter Twenty

BLAKE WASN'T THINKING of anything else but Hannah as he kissed her, memorizing the contours of her lips. He'd been halfway across the room when that little douche bag had tried to kiss her, and when he'd seen her use the move he'd taught her, he'd wanted to whoop in celebration.

Having Hannah in his arms felt so good, so right. He wanted to strip her slowly out of her incredibly poofy gown and kiss every surface of her body until she came, slipping into her when she was still warm and throbbing from her release.

God, just thinking about it was getting him close.

Slow, remember? What the hell happened to slow? Fucking Hannah in the storeroom is the opposite of slow...

Which meant he needed to put some distance between them before he forgot all about his good intentions.

Pulling back from the kiss, he pressed his lips to each of her cheeks, her nose, the spot on her neck just below her jawline. She sighed, and he felt it against his mouth as it vibrated in her throat.

"Blake…"

It was so hard to break away from her, but he did, leaning his forehead against hers, taking deep shuddering breaths to calm his libido.

"I don't want to stop."

"Then don't."

Her answer surprised him, and as he gazed down into her dreamy hazel eyes, he almost did it. Almost pushed it all aside and took what he needed so desperately. What Hannah was offering.

But he wasn't that guy. He wasn't going to hook up for the first time with a woman he liked in a storeroom. Hell, he'd rented an expensive hotel for Jenny the first time they'd…

Blake closed his eyes, pushing that thought away.

No, you aren't going to think about that. Not now.

Smoothing his hands up her body and over her hair, careful not to mush it, he said, "I am this close to pulling your dress up and making you come against the wall."

"Oh." Her mouth opened in a little O of surprise, and then her hand came up and she ran her thumb across his lips. Unconsciously, he flicked his tongue out against the pad, and the look on her face was almost his undoing.

"Okay, I'm going to step away from you, because if I don't, all my good intentions are going out the window."

She let him go, and he turned away, needing to adjust himself as his cock strained painfully against the front of his pants.

"I thought…" Her voice trailed off, and he turned, the sight of her leaning against the wall, her breaths still coming fast and deep, giving him a whole new understanding of the term *heaving bosom*.

"You thought what?"

A shadow fell over her expression, and she seemed to be thinking about what she was going to say.

"Was the other night a date?"

Blake's jaw dropped. Okay, maybe it hadn't exactly started date-like, but by the end, he had thought it was clear…

"Yeah, it was a date."

"But you said you weren't ready for anything serious."

"I know I did, but I—"

Her gaze narrowed, and she took a step toward him. "You said you weren't over your wife's death and you just wanted to be friends."

"But then—"

"No. No *but then*. You said those things, and then you ask me for coffee, and I'm trying so hard not to think about the way you smell or your hand on my back, and now you're telling me that you took me out and I didn't even *know* about it?"

Blake ran his hands through his hair, clearing his throat. "Are you going to let me get a word in?"

"Possibly, but it better be a good one."

Blake waited a moment, just to be sure she wasn't going to interrupt, and said, "I am still figuring things out, but I do know that I missed you. I like seeing you, and if you're okay with it, I would like to take things slow and see where we end up."

Hannah watched him, her expression pensive, as if she was searching his face for some catch. "What does that mean? 'Where we end up'?"

Not yet ready to have *that* discussion, he held out his hand to her.

"Mostly, that I would love to dance with you. And after that, we'll see how the night goes."

Hannah took his hand, and he led her out of the storage room, trying to be as inconspicuous as possible. Best caught his eye as he passed them carrying a tray of drinks, giving him a sly wink. The music was a slow Rascal Flats song, and as soon as they reached the dance floor, he pulled Hannah into his arms. She laid her cheek against his chest, and the two of them swayed to the melody. His fingers played with the curls of her hair and grazed the bare skin of her shoulders while his other arm wound around her waist, holding her close to his body.

"I imagined this moment a thousand times this week."

He smiled, kissing the top of her head. One of the things he liked about Hannah was how open and honest she was. She would blurt out her emotions as if she just couldn't help herself.

Jenny hadn't been like that. She would hold in her anger or irritation with him until it exploded, and they'd get into a big fight. He could tell when Hannah was upset with him; it was all over her face.

I need to stop comparing everything to the way it was with Jenny.

Trying to pull himself back into the moment, he kissed the top of her head, breathing in the sweet, floral scent. "How is this measuring up?"

"Better. Much better."

He brushed her hair back and dropped his mouth to the top of her shoulders, pressing sweet kisses up her neck until his lips reached the shell of her ear.

"I think so, too."

As they turned, he saw his friends standing in the corner, watching him. They all held their hands up and clapped like a bunch of idiots, and Blake wanted to walk over and lay all three of them out.

Hannah, as if sensing his tension, pulled away and looked up at him with those gorgeous amber-flecked eyes.

"Is something wrong?" she asked.

Ignoring his friends, he smoothed her hair back and smiled. "Nope. Everything is perfect."

"OH GOD, MY feet are killing me," Hannah groaned as they finally left the dance floor just after midnight. The last three hours had been a whirlwind of dancing, laughter, and joy, as she'd never been far from Blake's arms. All the anger she'd felt at the beginning of the night had melted after he'd told her he wanted to be with her.

*To see how things go. I still need to know exactly what
we are and what slow means. Are we exclusive?*

Determined to just enjoy tonight and worry about
the rest tomorrow, she kicked off her shoes with a sigh.
"That's better."

"Does that mean you're ready to go?" he asked.

She paused, studying him and trying to decipher what
he was asking. "Nicki ordered a limo that is supposed to
take us all back to where we left our cars."

"I can drop you at your car."

Hannah's heart fluttered. "I actually rode with Nicki,
so I need a ride back to my apartment."

His lips brushed over hers, and she shivered.

"Even better. I can make sure you get inside your
place safely."

Hannah liked the sound of that, especially since there
was no way she could dance another second, but she
wasn't ready to say good night to Blake, either.

"I just have to let Nicki know, and then I'll be good
to go."

"Okay, I'll wait right here."

Hannah limped back out to the dance floor, where she
found Nicki dirty dancing with another guy.

"Hey, Blake is going to take me home," Hannah said.

"The jerk? I thought we were over him." Nicki never
broke rhythm.

"No, *we* are not. Are you going to be okay?"

Nicki laughed as the guy did something to her neck.
"Oh, yeah, I'm good. You go and have fun. Love you."

HOLDING OUT FOR A HERO 223

"Love you, too."

Hannah turned and hobbled back to Blake, the strap of her clutch over her shoulder and her shoes in her hand.

"Did you check your raffle ticket?" Blake asked.

"No, I never win anything."

"Where is it?"

She opened her purse and handed it to him. Blake walked over to the winner's board with her raffle ticket and he whooped. "Check it out, oh ye of little faith. You're a winner."

Hannah couldn't believe it. She hadn't even bought any extras.

"What did I win?"

"Let's go see." He took her free hand and led her over to the table, where a pretty blonde and a red-haired woman sat talking, bags stacked behind them.

"Hey, Violet, Dani," Blake said warmly. "We have a winner."

The redhead smiled warmly at her, and then her gaze dropped to Blake's hand clasped with hers, and her eyes widened.

"Blake, what's our winner's name?"

"Hannah."

The redhead turned, checking bag numbers, and when she found what she was looking for, handed it to Blake, since Hannah's hands were full. "Here you go. The guys at the next table will give you your goody bag. Thank you for coming."

"Thank you," Hannah said.

Blake led her away from the curious stares of the two women, and they stopped off where Blake's friends Tyler and Oliver had been assigned.

"Give her the gift bag so we can get the hell out of here," Blake said.

"Hello, again, Hannah. You look beautiful," Tyler said.

"Thank you. Can I have my bag please"—she dropped her voice to a playful stage whisper—"before my ride gets too impatient?"

Oliver laughed. "He can wait."

"It's not too late to screw up that pretty face of yours, Martinez." Blake's voice didn't hold any real bite, and when Hannah gave him a stern look, he was grinning.

Hannah squeezed his hand. "Be nice."

"Yeah, Kline, be nice." Tyler handed her a pink glittery bag and grinned. "Enjoy, and have a good night."

Blake pulled her away before she could say thanks again, and she winced at the pain in her feet.

"Blake, I can't walk that fast. I think I have blisters."

He stopped and knelt, dropping her prizes next to him. He lifted the hem of her skirt up and examined her feet. Whatever he saw, it wasn't good, if his curse was any indication.

Before she could blink, he was on his feet and picked her up in his arms, bags, shoes, and all, and carried her through the lobby of the hotel.

"Put me down! I just need to walk slower, that's all."

"It's easier if I carry you. Then you'll have no pain at all."

"Except the pain in your back. I'm too heavy for you to carry."

He paused long enough to give her a hard kiss on the lips that would have had her toes curling if they didn't hurt so bad.

When he pulled away, he scoffed, "Please, I can curl two of you. Now, shut up, lay your head on my shoulder, and just enjoy the ride."

She did as he ordered with a small smile. "If you trip and drop me, I'll sue."

"I'm petrified."

Chapter Twenty-One

BLAKE PULLED INTO her apartment complex twenty minutes later and put his car in park. The drive from the Hilton to her place had taken just under twenty minutes, and he could tell by the expression on her face that she was tired.

He hopped out and went around to her side to open her door. She already had her feet out and on the ground when he growled at her.

"There might be glass on the ground. Just hang tight."

Gathering her up, he carried her up the walkway toward her apartment, waiting patiently for her to unlock it.

He didn't ask to come in, just strode over the threshold and sat her on the couch.

"Where's your first-aid kit?" he asked.

"Why?" she asked.

He gave her a sardonic look. "Because I am going to doctor up those feet before I take off."

"You don't have to do that—"

"I know, but I want to. So where?"

She sighed, settling back on the couch. "Under the bathroom sink. Around the corner on the right."

Blake made his way down the hallway, taking in the simple, homey feel to her apartment. The furniture was well worn and comfortable looking; maybe something that had been handed down or that she'd picked up at a thrift store. Pictures covered the walls, and three large bookshelves crossed the opposite wall.

He walked into the bathroom and grabbed the first-aid kit. Her towels were hung over the bar neatly, except for one that had been dropped right outside the shower.

For some reason, that out-of-place towel made him smile.

He came back out into the living room and sat down next to her. "Where's your puppy?"

"He's with my parents for the night. I'm still potty training him, and I hate to leave him alone too long."

"That's nice of them to watch him. Are you close?"

"Very. Nicki says we're freaks because we get along so well."

Blake opened the first-aid kit and pulled out alcohol wipes, Neosporin, and Band-Aids. "That's a weird thing to say. My parents died when I was twenty, and we were very close."

Hannah's hand covered his as he opened up one of the wipes, and he met her kind eyes. "I'm so sorry."

Blake's heart squeezed as he thought about his tall, dark-haired mom and goofball of a dad. "It's okay, it's been almost nine years, but I still miss them."

He picked up her right foot and brought it up to his chest. "This is going to sting, but I promise to make it all better."

She smiled a little at his teasing, but he watched that smile disappear as he started to clean the three blisters that had busted open on her foot. He blew on each one softly and then applied the ointment and bandages.

When the right foot was done, he hissed as he saw the big open, bloody blister on the back of her left ankle.

"Why would you wear such uncomfortable shoes?"

"Because they were perfect with the dress?"

He shook his head, and when he finished the other side, he set both her feet on his lap and gave her a level, serious look. "I am going to burn those shoes."

"But I just broke them in!" she protested.

"You women are crazy. You would rather tear up your feet and be in pain than wear comfortable shoes."

"It's just because they're new. Once I wear them a few times, no more blisters."

"Hmm."

Silence spread over the room as he realized he was stroking the tops of her feet gently.

"I should probably get going. It's pretty late."

"Yeah, it is. Do you want some coffee?" she asked.

"Nah, I'll never get to sleep if I have some now."

"Okay." She moved her feet off his lap and cleared her throat. "Do you mind, before you go, loosening the back of my dress? I can't do it on my own."

Blake tried to be casual, but his heart was tapping a heavy tempo against his breastbone. "Sure, turn around."

She did as he asked, moving her hair out of the way, and his fingers went to the tie, undoing the ribbon slowly. As he loosened one loop at a time, he couldn't resist brushing her bare shoulder with his lips.

Hannah turned, looking up at him, and he kissed her. Her mouth opened under his, welcoming his tongue as he continued working her stays loose. She twisted and wrapped her arm around his neck, and he touched the straps of her dress, pushing them down her arms slowly.

She pulled away abruptly, grabbing at her straps. "I'm sorry."

Blake almost groaned but bit it back. "No, I'm sorry. I'll go."

"You don't have to—"

"Yeah, I kind of do. But if it's okay with you, I'd like to take you out tomorrow night."

Hannah's smile was brighter than the sun. "I would love that."

"Good. Can I pick you up about seven?"

"Yes."

His hand cupped her jawline, his thumb playing across her lips before he gave her a soft peck. "Good night."

Standing up, he headed toward the door; he heard Hannah's soft "good night" just before the door shut.

He climbed into his car and took a deep, shaky breath, ignoring the hard-on he'd been sporting most of the night.

Whatever happened from then on out, it was too late to turn back now. Not that he really wanted to, but to start a new life, he needed to believe Jenny would be happy for him.

Blake turned on his phone before pulling out of the parking lot, and it erupted with notifications, mostly texts from his friends, asking about Hannah, but there was also a voicemail from Charles about the house.

"Blake, this is Charles. I've thought your offer over, and if you can give me cash, no payments, I'll accept."

Blake sat at the edge of Hannah's parking lot, staring at his phone.

He'd gotten the house. He was finally going to have a real home in California.

And he couldn't wait to tell her.

HANNAH GOT UP and locked the door behind Blake before shimmying out of the dress. Picking it up and laying it over her arm, she hummed as she danced her way back to her bedroom.

"I could have danced all night!" she sang out, twirling as she turned on the bedroom light. She hung up the dress and zipped it back into the plastic garment bag, still singing softly.

She had experienced the most magical, amazing night, and the best part was, he wanted to see her again.

Her phone rang, surprising her when she realized it was Blake's ringtone. Rushing out to her clutch, she answered breathlessly, "Hi."

"Hey. I just wanted to say that I might be getting that house."

Butterflies erupted in her stomach. She'd just said good night to him, which meant he'd gotten the message and immediately called her.

"Really? That's fantastic! When do you know for sure?"

"I'm going to talk to him tomorrow and iron out the details, but I couldn't wait to tell you."

She was so giddy about his admission, she almost squealed. He'd gotten amazing, life-changing news, and she'd been the first one he wanted to share it with.

"Well, we'll have to celebrate," she said.

"We will, tomorrow. I better get off the phone, so I don't get pulled over. I just wanted to tell you that, and I had a great time tonight."

"Me too, Blake. Good night."

Hannah clicked off the phone and, despite the pain in her feet, did a hopping, happy dance, full of high-pitched cries of excitement. She'd kissed Blake. She was *dating* Blake.

At least, she thought that was what was happening.

Afraid of waking her neighbors, she finally stopped and went back into her bedroom. Hannah took off the bustier and stockings and pulled on her gray flannel pajamas. She was too keyed up to sleep, so she went out to the living room and flipped on the TV as she sat back down on the couch.

Turning on Netflix, she picked up the first gift bag from the ball and started going through it. Bath & Body Works lotion, a 25 percent off coupon for a massage at a local spa. A bag of See's Candy hearts. Yum.

She put everything back and picked up the prize she'd won. It was a red wine bag, and she didn't remember it being this heavy when she'd grabbed it. Reaching in, she found a bottle of champagne with an envelope attached. She opened the envelope and pulled out the info and brochures inside.

Free two-night stay at The Landing in beautiful South Lake Tahoe. Must make reservation before April 1st. Weekend getaway includes two ski lift tickets for Heavenly Ski Resort.

Hannah stared at the script, unable to believe her eyes. She'd won a romantic getaway. She'd never won a contest in her life.

It was as if the universe was trying to tell her something. Maybe Blake was her happily ever after.

Forgetting about Netflix, she got up and went to her laptop. She was too hyper to sleep. She needed to write, but tonight, she wasn't in the mood for a kid's fantasy.

She started typing the first sentence in a brand-new document, and soon she'd written three whole chapters of a Cinderella remake.

Only in this version, Cinderella let the prince do some pretty naughty things in the royal storage room.

Chapter Twenty-Two

THE NEXT DAY, Blake found himself facing off against his greatest challenge; training Charge was beginning to seem like an impossible task. The dog was strong, determined, and had nearly no discipline to speak of.

But staring down at Charge as the dog seemed to smile wickedly back at him, Blake refused to give up.

"Best says you are trainable, but I think he's full of shit."

The dog's tail whipped around like a windmill, spinning with excitement.

He held onto Charge's leash but was so winded he could hardly breathe. He'd been running the dog for nearly an hour, and the son of a bitch just kept going. He was like the energizer bunny.

"How's it going out here?"

Charge leaped forward when he heard Best's voice, and the motion nearly jerked Blake's arm out of the socket. Charge strained against the leash as Blake tried to bring him back to heel.

"You've given me a robot for a dog! This thing doesn't tire, he is as strong as an ox, and I'm pretty sure he's got the mind of an evil genius."

"So, you're saying it's working out. Perfect."

Blake grunted, digging in his heels. "Damn it, Charge, heel!"

The dog stopped pulling and came back to Blake's side as pretty as you please, sitting. He stared up at Blake adoringly.

Blake blinked down at the dog.

"What the hell?"

Best shrugged. "Guess he likes the way you yell."

Blake knelt by the dog's side and lifted both his ears. "Did you check his hearing?"

"Of course I checked his hearing." Best sounded offended, but Blake didn't care. There was something going on with this dog.

"Maybe he's not deaf, but hard of hearing. Do we have any of those training whistles still?"

"I might have one or two in my office," Best said.

"I'm going to schedule him another veterinary appointment and, depending on what they say, try the whistle on Monday."

"Does that mean you're taking off?"

"Yeah, I've got a date tonight." Blake didn't really want to get into it with Best, especially after the razzing they'd all given him.

"Where're you taking her?" Best asked casually.

"I'm not sure yet. Dinner, I guess."

"But where, man? This is a first date, if we're not counting last night. You want to wow her."

"It's actually our second date, not counting last night." *Although since she didn't exactly know that was a date, Best might have a point.*

"Where did you take Dani on your first date?" Blake asked.

"The Cheesecake Factory and a movie."

Blake rolled his eyes. "Yeah, big wow factor there."

"Touché."

Thoughts of his first date with Jenny creeped in. Blake had taken her for dinner at Sonic, and they'd gone for a walk through town. Nothing fancy, but it had been nice.

"I'm already stressin' without you telling me what I'm doing wrong, so if it's all the same, just shut up, okay?" Geez, he hadn't dated in almost a decade, and his one attempt earlier in the week had failed miserably. At least he had nowhere to go but up.

Best saluted him. "You got it. It will be fine, anyway. I've seen the way that girl looks at you. You could take her to McDonald's, and she'd still think the moon rose and set on your ass."

"That's not shuttin' up."

"Fine, have fun tonight, and don't do anything I wouldn't do."

"There is nothing *you* wouldn't do."

"True."

Best walked away, and Blake turned his attention back to Charge.

"Don't worry, dude. We'll figure out what's up with you."

BLAKE STOOD ON Hannah's porch at two minutes to seven, taking a deep breath before he knocked. He'd gone casual with a pair of jeans, a collared shirt, and a jacket, leaving off a hat.

The door swung open, and Hannah smiled at him.

"Come on in, I'm just getting on my shoes."

Blake followed her inside, his gaze traveling over her. She was wearing a low-cut black wrap dress with gray leggings, and as she bent over to pull her boot on, he got a great view of her breasts overflowing the black lacy cups of her bra.

She straightened up, brushing her loose hair over her shoulder. "I just need my jacket, scarf, and to find Milo."

"I'll get the dog, you finish up." Blake gently touched her arm, and she stilled, looking up at him questioningly. He kissed her lips softly and whispered, "You look beautiful, by the way."

She melted against him, and her hands slid up his chest, playing with the collar of his shirt. "You look nice, too."

Disengaging himself from her before things heated up, he went in search of the puppy.

"Milo?" he called. The distinct sound of a puppy growl drew his attention, and he found the golden brat at the end of the hallway, his hackles straight up.

"Come on, dude, we're going to be friends."

Hannah came up behind him, her voice stern. "Milo, stop that. I don't know why he's being that way. He never growls."

"He's a puppy, and he's used to being the man of the house." Blake bent over and scooped the pup up, looking him in the eye. "He'll get used to me."

The sound of liquid hitting fabric reached his ears before Blake realized the damn dog was pissing on him.

"Shit!"

He could have sworn the little runt smirked at him, as if saying, *You wanna bet, asshole?*

"Oh my God, please tell me he didn't just pee on you," Hannah asked behind him.

"I hate to break it to you, but…he did."

"Crap! That is so weird, I just took him out! Let me put him in his crate, and while I'm doing that, take off your shirt, and I'll throw everything in the washing machine."

Blake felt a jolt at her command and slowly started peeling off his jacket, shirt, and undershirt. He wadded them up in his hands just as Hannah came back.

She opened up the hall closet and the washer on a small, stackable unit, tossing his clothes in. Once it was all started, she looked him over, biting her lip. "Do you want to take a shower? I imagine it soaked through your shirt."

"If you just have a wet washcloth or something to clean up with."

"Sure, hang on." She squeezed past him and knelt down under the bathroom sink. Milo started whining and rattling his cage, and Blake glanced toward where the dog was watching him through the bars.

He stuck his tongue out at the dog, who barked and growled back.

"Here we go." Before he knew what she was going to do, Hannah was running a hot, wet washcloth over his chest and stomach, the wet warmth raising gooseflesh across his skin. "I don't know where he got you, but let me know if I miss a spot. Are you cold?"

"No, I'm fine." In fact, his skin grew hot with every pass of that rough material, the only thing separating her hands from his bare skin. His heart pounded as he imagined her dropping the rag to the ground and running her hands over him, the soft brush of her fingers on him, touching every inch of him.

"I think that's it. I'll get you a towel."

She walked away, the washcloth in her hand, and he couldn't believe it. Here he was, sweating buckets and trying not to yank her against him, and she was acting as if she was just helping him out.

She could not be that innocent. She had to know what every sweep of that wet, rough fabric did to me.

Hannah came back with a dry, soft towel and started dabbing at his skin. Her motions slowed, and she glanced up at him, as if she was suddenly aware that he was half naked in her living room and she was cleaning him up.

Her hazel eyes wide, she started to step back. "I guess I could have let you do this."

His hand covered hers, and he squeezed. "I like it when you do it better."

He could practically see her pulse fluttering under the skin and had the urge to find it with his mouth, running his tongue along the column of her throat.

"Oh, boy."

Her sweet little exclamation made him smile as he followed his instincts. His mouth covered that spot that had been teasing him, and he kissed his way down her neck until his mouth rested in the valley between her breasts, her chest heaving against his lips.

"I fucking love this dress." He brushed his mouth against the mound of her breast, and she gasped.

"Maybe we should skip going out to dinner and just order a pizza," she whispered.

Blake took a deep breath, trying to get ahold of himself as he brought his mouth back up to hers.

"No, I promised you a real date, and we will have one. It will just be a little later."

"I might have something you can wear."

Blake arched a brow at her.

"One of my dad's T-shirts. Hang on."

He reluctantly let her go, and she went into her bedroom. He was curious enough to follow her, looking around at the white four-poster bed and matching dresser. A cedar chest sat at the end of the bed, and several paintings graced the wall. One was of a little girl with the same coloring as Hannah cuddling an orange tabby kitten.

"My mom painted that when I was four." Hannah held out a T-shirt. "Sorry, it's all I could find."

Blake held up the T-shirt, reading the front of the shirt with a grin. "Does your dad like Pomeranians?"

"It was a gag gift my mom got him when he brought home a Pomeranian puppy for my mom. He ended up taking Miggins over, and she bought him the shirt as a joke."

Blake pulled it over his head, surprised at how long it was on his six-two frame. As he looked down at the panting Pomeranian picture on his chest, he shook his head. "Yeah, I can't wear this out in public."

"Then pizza it is."

Blake had a feeling she didn't mind staying in.

HANNAH WAS VERY aware of Blake and the fact that she'd been rubbing down his bare chest less than a half hour ago. What the hell had possessed her to do that? Especially when it had led to his mouth doing those delicious things...

God, her palms were sweating. She'd messed around with guys in the past, but it had never gone too far, mostly just because she hadn't been that into it. She was always afraid of a parent walking in, and after that, she'd just never gotten that passionate, *oh-my-God-I-want-him-so-bad* feeling her friends had described, so she'd always pulled the plug before it got beyond third base.

But she definitely felt that for Blake.

She grabbed two Cokes from the kitchen and let Milo out of his cage, shooting him a dirty look. "Be nice."

He gave her those soft, innocent brown eyes, and she melted.

When she came into the living room, Blake was looking over her bookshelf, his back to her.

"I hope Coke is okay."

He turned, and she bit her lip to keep from laughing at the large picture of a Pomeranian on the front of the shirt and the words *I LOVE MY POM-POM* underneath.

"Go ahead, laugh it up." He was smiling as he reached for the can she held out to him.

"I'm sorry. I use it as a sleep shirt mostly, and I've just never imagined a man actually wearing it."

"You sleep in this?" Blake's tone had taken on a gravelly note, and she swallowed.

"Sometimes, if it's hot."

Speaking of hot, had she turned up the heat, or was the air between them just charged?

"Wanna watch a movie?" she asked.

"Sure, I'm good with that."

They sat down on the couch, and Hannah took off her boots. She grabbed the remote and turned on Amazon, searching through the new releases.

"Here, you pick something. I'm good with anything."

Blake scrolled through and stopped on a comedy. "How about this?"

Hannah wasn't a fan of one of the actors but just shrugged. "Sure."

He clicked play and settled back into the couch, his arm stretched along the back behind her. She wasn't sure what to do, so she sat a little away from him, her feet planted firmly on the ground.

She felt him move before the warmth of his breath brushed her ear and neck. "You can relax."

His arm wrapped around her shoulders and snuggled her into his side. Hannah tucked her legs up onto the couch and leaned her head on Blake's shoulder.

As the movie played, Hannah was very aware of Blake's fingers stroking her arm through the thin fabric of her dress.

There was a sound from the porch, and Blake stood up, waving her back down.

"I've got it. Besides, you look too good right now. Don't want to have the pizza guy drooling all over the pizza when he sees you."

Hannah's cheeks heated up as she watched Blake open up the front door and pause.

"Um, Hannah? It's not the pizza guy."

Hannah jumped up and came to stand behind Blake.

On the front porch were her mom and dad, holding on to a plastic bag and staring at Blake as if he was an alien.

"Mom. Dad. What are you doing here?"

Her mom at least appeared sheepish.

"We tried to call your cell phone and figured if you weren't home, we'd just drop these things off to you. They were having a sale at Target, and I just thought they would look so pretty on you."

Hannah took the bag and looked inside. Three or four brightly colored wool scarves intertwined, and Hannah smiled at her mom.

"Thanks, Mom. I love them."

"Aren't you going to introduce us to the guy wearing my shirt?" her dad said gruffly.

Hannah cleared her throat and glanced up at Blake, whose expression was friendly.

"Blake Kline, these are my parents, Gilbert and Patty York."

"How do you do, sir?" Blake took her dad's hand first and then her mom's. "Ma'am."

"Oh! You're the man who saved Hannah's life," her mother said excitedly. "What are you to up to?"

Her father was still scowling at Blake, and Hannah sighed, knowing there was no way out of the situation.

"Blake is my date."

Chapter Twenty-Three

HANNAH WANTED TO bang her head against the wood of her kitchen table, cursing her weirdly close relationship with her parents. Considering how rarely she dated or even mentioned having a date to them, it was no wonder they expected her to be home alone, doing nothing on a Saturday night. Of course, they didn't have to make it any more awkward by inviting themselves in, but they had. Her dad had actually grabbed the pizza that arrived moments later and bulldozed his way past all of them, camping out on the couch.

Hannah leaned to the side, trying to see Blake, who was sitting on the couch adjacent to her dad, looking incredibly uncomfortable.

"Hannah?" her mother whispered.

Hannah turned her attention back to her mother, who was watching her with one of those worried expressions she always got when she thought Hannah wasn't eating right or wasn't studying hard enough.

"What?"

"Well, we came by to drop off a present—"

"Unannounced," Hannah muttered.

"We tried to call, but you've never minded us dropping by before."

"I've also never had a guy over when you've dropped by."

Her mom grimaced, as if she'd tasted something foul. "Do you…have men over often?"

"God, Mom! No, but even if I did, I am an adult, and this is humiliating. How would you feel in my place? You meet this great guy—"

"Is he great? I know he saved your life, but you never said you were interested in him. Why didn't you tell us about him?"

"Because I wasn't sure there was anything to tell, and there probably won't be anything ever if you don't get Dad and *go*!"

Hannah could tell she'd hurt her mom's feelings, but honestly, at some point they had to treat her like a grown-up and respect her boundaries.

"You know I love you guys, but next time, if I don't answer, please don't just drop by."

"But what if there was something wrong? On ID—"

"Mom…"

Her mom huffed. "Oh, all right, we won't just drop by anymore, but if you're killed by a sadistic serial killer who eats livers, don't come crying to me."

Hannah refrained from explaining if she was killed, she wouldn't be crying at all.

Now she just had to get her parents out of there before Blake bolted.

BLAKE SAT IN the living room with Hannah's dad, eating a slice of pizza silently. The pizza guy had shown up several minutes after Hannah's parents, and when her dad had snatched the pizza and settled into the big easy chair, Blake's plans for the rest of the night had seemed to go up in smoke.

To top it off, Milo sat at the older man's feet, mean mugging Blake as only a little twerp pup could.

"So you're army?"

Her dad's voice was loud and booming, like he imagined a giant's would be.

"Yes, sir. I train dogs at Alpha Dog Training Program."

"I saw that on the news broadcast. I've heard good things about it." Her dad took a bite of pizza, chewing slowly. "I guess I should thank you for saving my daughter's life."

Blake swallowed, his own bite almost lodged in his throat. He didn't know what was worse; having her dad resent him or admire him.

"Although, I should point out that it takes a special kind of man to have more guts than brains. You took on an armed assailant with my daughter in the crosshairs. She could have been killed during your rescue."

Well, the admiration was short-lived, at least.

"I had the situation under control, sir, and would never put Hannah in harm's way. She's really special."

"I know she's special." Her dad pinned Blake with another piercing stare. "What I want to know is, *how* special is she to you?"

"I'm not sure what you mean, sir." Blake knew exactly what he meant, but he wasn't going there.

"I mean, how long have you been seeing each other?"

"Since last night. I made sure Hannah got home from the ball okay and asked her out on our first date for tonight." There was no point in mentioning the other night with the bookstore, as Blake was trying for a redo.

Her dad shot him a pointed look. "When I used to ask a girl on a date, we always left the house."

"Yes, sir, that was the plan, but Milo peed on my shirt before we could leave, and Hannah offered to toss it into the washer. We were just waiting for it to finish."

Her dad stroked Milo's head, as if rewarding the dog for pissing on him. "Wouldn't it have just been easier to go home and get another shirt?"

"Yes, sir, I suppose it would have been," he said, silently praying for Hannah to rescue him.

Hannah and her mom came back into the room, and Blake stood up, grateful.

"Come on, Gilbert, we're leaving," Hannah's mom said briskly.

"I haven't finished my pizza yet."

"Gilbert York, stop torturing this young man, and get your wrinkly old ass out of that chair."

Hannah covered her mouth, and Blake glanced at her. Yep, she was laughing behind her hand.

Hannah's dad stood up slowly, giving him one last warning look before he kissed his daughter on the top of her head. "Behave yourself."

"Shut up, Gilbert," her mom said.

"Woman, I'm getting tired of the way you talk to me."

"Then stop being an old fool and embarrassing your daughter."

The two walked out, and Hannah locked the door with a groan.

"I am so sorry."

"It's okay." The buzzer for the washer went off, and Hannah beat him to it, transferring his clothes to the dryer.

"No, it's not, but I love them. We're just really close, and there's never been a reason to tell them they couldn't stop by—"

"Really, Hannah, I get it. I've got to say, your dad is pretty intimidating."

"Oh God." She spun around and looked at him with wide-eyed panic. "Did he ask you one question after another, as if he was a CIA interrogator?"

"Yes, pretty much."

"Damn it." She leaned over the back of the couch, her hair falling down over her face.

Blake took a few steps closer, lifting her hair with a grin. "Hey, it's not exactly the first date I had planned, but we're both still here. Wanna finish the movie?"

Hannah stood up and came around to flop on the couch. "I would love that."

This time he didn't have to say anything, she just snuggled into his side.

WHEN THE MOVIE finished, Hannah went to pull Blake's shirt out of the dryer while he used the bathroom. She laid the shirt and jacket over the back of the couch and went into the kitchen to chew on a leftover candy cane can she had from Christmas, trying to freshen her breath after the pizza.

She heard him come out of the bathroom and chewed faster.

"Hey, thanks for washing these for me." She turned to find him pulling his collared shirt into place. "I love warm clothes right from the dryer."

"Me, too. I actually heat my blanket up every night before bed just so it's warm when I snuggle into it."

"That's pretty smart," he said.

As he drew closer, her heart kicked into high gear. He brushed her hair back behind her ear and asked, "So, should we call it a night? Or can I take you out for ice cream?"

"Ice cream sounds amazing."

"Good. I think for my shirt's sake, though, you should put your dog in the crate."

She laughed. "Let me take him out to go potty first."

Getting Milo's harness and leash, she took him out front to do his business and brought him back inside, locking him in his cage.

"I'll be home soon, love."

Milo whimpered, and Hannah waved Blake out the door quickly, flipping off the light before she shut it behind her.

"I'm hoping he isn't making too much noise when I leave him for short periods of time. He stays with my parents when I'm at work, but sometimes I have to run an errand. My landlord is okay with dogs as long as they aren't noisy."

"I'm hoping this house goes through, so I can have a hundred-and-eighty-pound hound," Blake said, holding the door open for her.

"I didn't know you had a dog."

He came around the front of the car and slid into the driver's side. "I didn't until Best sprung him on me. If I want to stay at Alpha Dog, I have to train Charge."

"The dog's name is Charge?"

"Yeah, 'cause he likes to Charge everywhere." Blake started the car and backed up.

Hannah laughed. "That is funny. I would love to own a house someday, but even if I get a full-time teaching job, all the places I'd want to live are pretty expensive. I want to live comfortably without paying out the nose."

"Well, I was lucky to talk him down a bit by offering him cash. I have to call and get some things moved around to make it happen, but I love this place. It's in Orangevale, almost a quarter of an acre, four bedrooms, two bathrooms with a decent-size kitchen."

"Wow. Sounds amazing."

"Yeah, and with no payments, I won't have to have a roommate," he said.

"I had a roommate for several years, trying to save money but still live on my own, but it wasn't worth it. I'd rather pay more for rent and have my own space. If I ever live with anyone again, it will be my husband."

She noticed him stiffen before she realized what she said.

"Relax, I wasn't proposing."

Blake gave a stiff laugh, and it hurt—she couldn't deny it. She knew this was only their first date and that he was still working through his issues, but in her mind, a husband, house, and babies were all a part of her future, and if she couldn't talk about that stuff, how were they going to give this a real shot?

"Out of curiosity, why did you want such a big house for just you and a dog?"

Blake shot her a quick glance, and she stared back mildly. He must have decided there was no hidden agenda with the question, and he finally answered, "I don't know. I guess I figured, if I'm going to buy a house, I want it to be one I can grow in."

She stayed quiet until they reached Cold Stone Creamery, thinking about that answer. She took it as Blake might get married and have a family someday, and he wanted the room to do it. She wasn't going to come out and ask, though, at least not after the whole parent fiasco.

She climbed out of her side of the car before he could get her door and headed toward the sidewalk.

"Hey, hey, hang on a second." Blake reached out and grabbed her arm, gently bringing her in against him. "Did I say something wrong?"

Screw holding back. If he's going to run, it's better he does it now.

"I just don't want to walk on eggshells around you. I know you want to take this slow, but I have an idea of what I want already. I want a full-time teaching job, maybe a little house, and I definitely want a husband and kids. We can take it slow, but I don't want you freaking out every time I talk about what I imagine for my future. Believe me, it's too early to picture you in it yet."

Hannah waited for him to say something, never expecting it to be an apology.

"I'm sorry. This is new for me, believe it or not. I've only ever dated one woman, and she was…"

Blake didn't finish the sentence, and she wanted him to so badly. Maybe if he could talk about her, he would really start to move forward.

"Anyway, I'll try not to be so damaged." He reached out to tuck a strand of hair behind her ears. "So, are we good?"

She caught his hand and held it to her cheek. "Believe me, Blake, we're good."

He held on to her hand and grabbed the door with his other, leading her into the empty ice cream shop. He ordered a Love It of mint chip and Hannah got a Like It of peanut butter and chocolate. While he paid, she sat down, staring out the window at the busy street.

She shouldn't be so sensitive. Blake had lost his wife only two years ago, and if he was just starting to date, she needed to be patient. It wasn't as if she was in any rush.

"You know, I'd love to watch you train Charge sometime. Maybe you could help me with Milo."

"I think that little demon is a lost cause."

Hannah laughed, waving her spoon at him like she'd wag a finger. "You be nice. He just needs to get used to you."

"That puppy has a mean streak a mile long. You wait. When he's eighty pounds, he's going to tear my throat out."

Hannah tried not to react to his comment, just silently celebrated that even if he didn't know it, he was thinking of a future with her.

Chapter Twenty-Four

BLAKE WALKED HANNAH to her door after ice cream, holding her hand in his. Compared to his first date with Jenny, this one was a lot more interesting, but it was still nice. Better in some ways, because even though he was a little nervous about what would happen next, he wasn't pumped up with teenaged hormones and insecurities. And Hannah had been honest about what she wanted, had called him out on his bullshit, and he liked it. He didn't have time for games, and he appreciated Hannah's candor. He could tell at the time she hesitated saying anything, but he was glad she had.

"So, what are your days off this week?" she asked.

"Well, we're not exactly on a military schedule, but my days vary. Most of the time, I get Sundays off."

"That's it?"

"Being in the military is not like a normal job. I'm lucky at Alpha Dog because we do shifts, usually ten hours for six days, but if I was doing guard duty or any other job, it could be twelve hours or even twenty-four and nine days on."

"That is crazy."

Hannah leaned her back against the door and gazed up at him. The way the porch light shone down on her, brightening her hazel eyes, distracted him until he just repeated, "Yeah, crazy."

He should walk away and leave her with just a peck on the lips. That would be the smart thing.

At least, he'd intended to kiss her chastely.

Instead, he'd put his hand on the wall above Hannah and leaned in. His body pressed her back into the door, and his mouth covered hers, his tongue sweeping inside her already parted lips, tasting the sweet mix of chocolate and Hannah.

Hannah's hands cupped the back of his neck as he kissed her. He was dying to slide his hands around to cup her ass but, leery of someone coming up or driving by, he kept them at her waist.

She was the one to break the kiss, pressing a hand to his cheek. "I should go inside."

He released a breathless chuckle. "Yeah, you probably should."

Hannah kissed him again and whispered, "Text me."

"When?"

That sweet smile was all Hannah flashed. "Anytime."

As she slipped inside and out of his reach, he laid his burning forehead against the cool wood of her door and breathed deeply. He felt like he should congratulate himself for making it through such a crazy first date.

When he climbed back in his car, he called Best.

"Yo, man, what's up?"

"What are you up to?" he asked.

"Dani and I are watching Netflix. Your date over already? How was it?"

"Her dog pissed on me, so I had to wash my clothes at her place. We ordered a pizza, and then her parents showed up, and I had to sit through an awkward interrogation from her dad. We watched a movie and went for ice cream after—where I freaked over an off-the-cuff remark she made and she put me in my place—and finally, I kissed her good night and she went to bed."

"Well, that sounds like a fucking nightmare," Best said.

Blake thought back to when Hannah had wiped his chest, to the adorable horror on her face when her parents walked through the door, and that last look of longing right before she closed the door.

"Actually, parts of it were kind of nice."

"Well, all right," Best drawled like Matthew McConaughey. "When are you going to see her again?"

"Not sure. She said to text her anytime."

"Ho! You know what that means? You got an open-ended invite to get freaky over text message. Ow! Babe, I'm talking about him. No, I don't talk about our sex life." His voice grew muffled as he spoke to his girlfriend. Finally, Best came back on the line, his voice hushed, "I'm in trouble. Got to go."

Best hung up the phone, and Blake grinned, contemplating his friend's assessment.

Was it too soon to send a text?

When he pulled into his parking spot at his apartment complex, he texted her.

Had an amazing time. Can't wait to take you out again.

Shoving his phone in his pocket, he whistled all the way up the stairs…

Until he saw his front door hanging off the hinges.

Stepping inside cautiously, he looked around at the destruction and cursed. Everything was gone. His TV, his laptop. Even his fucking microwave. At least his iPad had been in his duffle in the trunk of his car.

Then a thought occurred to him, and he raced inside to his bedroom.

They had ripped up his mattress and tossed his bed, which made no sense. What the hell had they been looking for?

His gun safe, which was at the back of his closet, was unharmed. They hadn't gotten to his guns.

Dialing 911 on his phone, he waited until the dispatcher answered before he spoke. "Yes, my name is Sergeant Blake Kline of the United States Army, and I need to report a break-in at my apartment."

"All right, Sergeant, what is your address? Is there anything missing?"

He rattled off his address and kept looking around, searching for anything else missing. "Yeah, they took all the electronics and tore apart my bedroom. Looks like I've got a couple pairs of shoes missing."

"Okay, have you searched the house to see if there is anyone left inside?"

"Yeah, they're long gone."

"Good. Sergeant, I've dispatched officers to your home. They should be there in approximately thirty minutes."

"Thanks, appreciate it."

Blake hung up the phone, looking around the place in disgust. His phone beeped, and it was Hannah.

I can't wait either.

Blake took a picture of his bedroom and typed, *What a way to end a night, huh?*

His phone started ringing a few minutes later, Hannah's name flashing across his screen.

"Pretty sight, isn't it?"

"Oh my God, I can't believe that! Are you okay?"

Blake laughed bitterly. "Besides being pissed off, yeah, I'm good. Glad to be getting out of this hellhole. Just waiting on the police and then going to get comfy on my shredded bed."

There was quiet on the line for a half a second, and then she spoke rather softly. "If you need a place to crash, I've got a pull-out bed in my couch."

Blake knew the offer was just Hannah being kind, but he couldn't help thinking about staying over with Hannah, imagining sleeping on the couch and having her come out in something sexy, inviting him to share her bed.

God, he really needed to stop with these crazy fantasies.

"No, it's okay. I'll call Best, and he'll put me up if I need it. Thanks, though."

"Okay, well, if you need anything, just call."

"Thanks, Han. You're too good to me."

"Good night, Blake."

He ended the call, a little bit elated despite current circumstances.

Blake was pretty sure Hannah had been disappointed he hadn't taken her up on her offer.

HANNAH WOKE UP the next morning to Blake's ringtone and smiled sleepily as she answered. "Hey, you okay?"

"Tired, but yeah. Had to call my landlord in the middle of the night to fix the door, which was fun. Did I wake you?"

She squinted her eyes and looked at the clock. It was almost ten. "Nope, I was awake."

"Liar. I was going to see if you wanted to go with me today to pick out a new mattress and appliances."

Hannah sat up a little at that. He wanted to see her again? Flopping onto her back, she said, "I'd love to."

"Good. I'll give you forty-five minutes, and I'll even bring breakfast and caffeine."

"Grande nonfat, single-shot caramel macchiato, hot."

His deep chuckle radiated through the phone and sent a shiver down her spine.

"Anything for you."

He hung up the phone, and Hannah lay there for a minute or two before she dragged her butt out of bed and let Milo out to go potty. Then, she hopped in the shower and pulled on her clothes, finishing the outfit off with one of the scarves her mom had brought her last night.

She twisted her wet hair into a bun and dialed her parents.

"Hello?" her mother answered.

"Hey, Mom."

"Well, good morning."

Hannah rolled her eyes at her mom's sarcastic tone. "All right, are you going to be a brat, or do you want to hear about my date?"

"Are you sure you want to tell me?"

"Going to hang up."

"Oh, fine. I suppose we should have called."

Hannah let the rest go. "Thank you."

"You were saying?"

Hannah told her mother about most of the date— some things just weren't fit for a mother's ears—and then about the break-in at Blake's.

"So, we're going shopping for some of the things that were ruined or stolen from his apartment."

"Well, I am glad he's okay, but you make sure you don't go over to his apartment if it's that dangerous."

There was a knock on her door, and Milo went wild, barking up a storm.

"Hey, Mom, he's here, so I gotta go. Give Dad my love."

"I will. Tell Blake hi for us."

Hannah hung up the phone and snorted. Yeah, she'd skip that.

She opened the door to find Blake holding a white pastry bag and a drink carrier. He was in his usual casual clothing and hat.

"Morning."

Blake gave her a kiss as he stepped inside. "Morning, beautiful."

Hannah blushed as she shut the door behind him. "What did you get to eat?"

"Cheese Danish."

"Yum." Hannah shushed Milo, who was still having a hissy fit. "Hey, stop it!"

"I got something for demon spawn, too." Blake pulled out a package of foil and revealed four bacon strips.

Holding the meat above Milo's head, he said, "Want some?"

He broke off a piece, and as he held it over the pup's head, he pressed down on his butt until he sat.

Hannah watched him work with the puppy, and he was so filled with patience and quiet delight when Milo sat. Despite her assurance that she wasn't thinking of a future with him, she could easily see Blake showing the same care for a child while teaching him how to ride a bike or fish.

"Have you read any more of *Blitzing Emily*?" she asked.

"Not really. I guess I've been a little distracted."

His pointed smile made her blush. "Me, too. I've hardly read a thing."

He pulled her hand up to his mouth, kissing her fingers. "Don't get me wrong, I like the distraction."

"Good, 'cause I like being distracting."

Blake let out that surprised laugh, the one she'd heard only a few times at the diner, but now, his mirth had become more common.

"You seem lighter."

Blake lost his smile. "What do you mean?"

"Just that you didn't used to laugh, not the way you do now. It's as if a weight's been lifted."

Blake fed Milo another piece of bacon, quiet so long that she almost apologized for upsetting him.

"I've been seeing a therapist, and it's been…helpful, I think."

Hannah was shocked. Although they were still learning new things about each other, she never imagined Blake actively seeking professional help.

"That's great. When did you start that?"

"Couple of weeks ago. It was a requirement if I wanted to stay at Alpha Dog."

Ah, that made more sense.

"So, is that why you changed your mind about me?"

Blake's hazel eyes blazed at her for a moment. "I already liked you, but I had…reservations."

Hannah's heart ached at his words. "Because of your wife?"

"No, because of me. Not everything is about her."

Hannah jerked at his rough tone. "I didn't mean anything by it."

Blake sighed, running his hands over his head. "I'm sorry. I didn't mean to lash out at you."

Hannah got up from the table and pulled her drink from the carrier. Just as she set it on the table and reached out to free his, she was yanked back into his lap.

"Eek," she squealed.

Blake's arms wrapped loosely around her waist, holding her. "I am. I'm just trying to put the past to rest and don't want it dragged up all the time."

His lips found the skin of her neck, just below her chin, and she released an involuntary shiver.

"Hmm, you like that? How about here?"

He lifted her hair, and his mouth moved farther back, nipping lightly.

Hannah clenched her thighs together as a shock shot her straight between her legs.

Blake's hand came up to cup the back of her neck, then he pulled her down, and she opened her lips as his covered hers. Hannah wrapped her arms around his neck and kissed him back, running her hands along his nape and over his shoulders. She didn't want to be mad at Blake, not when she knew he was going through a lot and trying. Trying for her.

Blake's hand crept up to cover her breast, and she gasped into his mouth, pressing closer into his touch. As he squeezed and played with her, she wiggled on top of him, pressing her butt against the hard bulge of his dick. She could feel her panties dampen, and a heavy throb started pounding as she longed to get closer, seeking relief.

Blake broke the kiss, pressing his mouth against hers once, a brief, chaste peck before laying his head on her chest. Hannah's hands slid down his back, and she leaned her cheek against the top of his head, trying to slow her racing heart and raging hormones.

"I'll try to keep my temper in check from now on."

Hannah ran a hand over the top of his head. "Okay."

Chapter Twenty-Five

WHEN HANNAH WALKED into her apartment on Thursday evening, all she wanted to do was see to Milo's needs and bury herself in her bed. It had been an exhausting week, between Dale's and school. Plus, she was already grouchy that she hadn't gotten to spend time with Blake since Sunday. He was busy with Charge and preparing to move, and although he'd come into the diner and they'd talked on the phone every night before bed, she'd wanted longer than a few stolen moments behind Dale's, making out.

Hannah had just finished taking Milo out when her phone started ringing. When she saw that it was Blake, she slid her finger across the screen and answered in what she'd hoped was a semi-awake voice.

"Hey, Blake."

"Hey, what are you doing right now?" he asked.

"I just got home. I grabbed some Mexican food on the way and was going to eat dinner, then go to bed."

"Man, are you really tired? Because I have something I really want to show you, but if you're exhausted—"

"No, I'm fine," she lied.

"Fantastic. Do you mind if I swing by and get you in a half hour?"

"Well, sure, but what—"

"It's a surprise. See you soon."

Hannah got off the phone and proceeded to scarf down her burrito like a Hoover vacuum. When she finished, she hopped up and raced to her room, Milo hot on her heels, barking excitedly.

She reapplied deodorant and pulled off her comfy teacher sweater, searching for something else to wear. She finally settled on a scoop-necked red T-shirt and a black open sweater. Spraying herself down with her body spray, she barely had time to brush her teeth before there was a knock at her door.

Milo barked and growled at the door, and Hannah scooted him back with her foot so she could open it.

Blake stood on the other side, holding a bouquet of assorted roses, that knee-weakening smile on his face.

"Hey, Han. Ready to go?"

"Yeah, just let me put Milo in his crate."

Blake walked inside and closed the door while she pulled out a puppy Milk-Bone and led Milo into his cage. When she turned around, Blake held the roses out to her.

"These are for you. I'm sorry that it's been mostly phone contact and me coming into the diner to see you. I've missed you."

"I missed you, too." Hannah took the flowers, her chest warming as she inhaled their sweet scent. "Thank you, but you didn't have to. It's been a busy week for both of us."

"Yes, but I couldn't stop thinking about you." He cupped the side of her face and covered her mouth with his, giving her a deep, bone-melting kiss.

"I thought about you a lot, too."

"Good. So, put those in water and come on. I want to get there before it's too late."

Hannah put the roses in a vase of water and grabbed her coat before following him out the door. After he helped her into the car, they drove up the freeway and got off on Madison Avenue, heading past Sunrise Boulevard and into Orangevale.

"Where are you taking me?" Then it clicked. "Are you taking me to see the house you're buying?"

"Just hang on, we're almost there."

Hannah settled back in the seat, laughing. "I hate surprises."

"I'd never guess."

"Secrets, too. They always make me feel skeezy."

He made a left and then a right into a quiet neighborhood, pulling up in front of a house with the sign FOR SALE BY OWNER.

Blake held up a set of keys. "Wanna see the inside?"

"Yes, but…How did you get it so fast?"

He climbed out of the car before answering, and she jumped out, coming around the front to stand next to him. Even at night, the street was well lit, and the only sounds were that of a dog barking in the distance. The house itself appeared to be light gray or maybe blue with white trim. It was hard to tell for sure in the yellow streetlight. The yard was well kept, and the driveway didn't have any cracks.

"This is the one I talked about."

"But...this is a pretty nice neighborhood. How can you afford this?" Hannah realized too late it was really none of her business, but Blake didn't seem to mind.

"When my parents died, I put my inheritance into an interest-bearing account and never touched it. It grew from there, and when I saw this place, I just knew."

Blake unlocked the door, and Hannah stepped in. He flipped on the light, and Hannah looked around at the open living room. "This is so great, Blake! I am so happy for you." She turned around and hugged him hard, elated that he'd wanted to share such a momentous occasion with her.

He squeezed her back, kicking the door shut behind him. "Come on, there's more to see."

As he excitedly took her through every room, pointing out all the things he wanted to update and fix, Hannah couldn't help thinking of his wife. Wondering if they'd had a house together before she died. Was this bittersweet for him?

She hadn't mentioned her at all since Sunday, figuring when he was ready to share more with her, he would.

"And this is the master bedroom."

Wow, the room was huge, and the attached bathroom had a deep Jacuzzi tub. Hannah almost started drooling just staring at that jetted paradise.

"Oh, I am so jealous! I would kill for a tub like this."

Blake's arms snaked around her from behind, and his mouth pressed against the side of her neck. "You'll have to come over and try it out with me."

Hannah shivered at the images his words elicited, and she reached up to rub the back of his neck. "Nice of you to offer to share."

"Sharing is caring."

"Oh, is it?"

"Hmm."

Hannah closed her eyes as Blake's hands smoothed over her abdomen. "What are you doing?"

"Touching you. I missed you."

Hannah pulled away from him reluctantly and headed back into the bedroom. "So, when are you going to move your stuff in?"

"I roped a bunch of the guys into helping me out this weekend. Wanna join in? I've promised pizza and beer."

Okay, so he was inviting her to hang with him and his friends this weekend. That was pretty sweet, even if it did mean manual labor.

"Would it be okay to bring Milo? Is your backyard fenced in?"

"Yeah, you can bring that devil dog."

Hannah smacked Blake's arm playfully. "He is sweet! Don't call him that."

"He is sweet to you because he loves you. He hates my guts."

"Well, maybe you can keep giving him treats and change his way of thinking."

Blake tucked her hair back with a grin. "Maybe I will."

BLAKE STOOD IN the hallway, watching Hannah gaze around the house in awe. Despite his resolve to stop comparing moments with Hannah with his past with Jenny, he couldn't help but think of her in this moment. They had never owned their own home, choosing to live on base since he was gone on tour and he wanted her to have a support system. Jenny had tried to turn their base house into a home, but it hadn't been the same as if it had been theirs.

Jenny would have loved this, although she wouldn't have cared about the tub.

He'd liked the way Hannah's eyes had lit up when she'd seen it, and even though it was his house, he wanted her to like it.

For a guy who said he wanted to move slow, I sure am jumping into this with both feet.

Blake wasn't going to feel guilty about being happy with Hannah, about wanting to share this with her. Every time something had reminded him of Jenny or he'd had a twinge of guilt over missing Hannah, he'd tried to remember that Jenny would want this for him. That it almost seemed sometimes as if Jenny had sent Hannah to him because he needed her.

Of course, when he'd talked to Dr. Stabler about the guilt he was still experiencing, she'd agreed that going slow was probably good. And he did want to do that, to take his time and be sure.

But he also couldn't seem to get enough of Hannah.

"The only problem with this place is I don't have enough furniture to fill it up."

"Hmm, what's your style?" she asked.

"Casual comfortable."

"Do you mind used furniture?"

"As long as it isn't falling apart, I'm okay with it."

She gave him a look over her shoulder, and he grinned.

"What are you going to do with the other three rooms?"

"I'm not sure yet. Set up one as a guest room, maybe? A gym in the other. Not sure about the third room."

"It's a nice-size house. Maybe after we get all of your stuff moved in, we could check out some of the thrift shops next weekend. I found some great stuff in really good condition when I moved into my place."

Her enthusiasm was infectious, although Blake had a feeling Hannah was a power shopper. He usually only lasted a couple of hours before he was done.

"That sounds like fun," he said.

"Liar, I can hear it in your voice. You think it sounds like a fate worse than death." She stood on tiptoe and kissed his lips, and he decided that he'd do anything to keep that smile on Hannah's face. "I promise to make the whole experience painless and fun."

"I'll hold you to that when you drag me to twelve stores and I'm begging you to stop."

"Oh, you so get me."

The funny thing was, he felt like he did get the basic core of Hannah. She liked to make people happy and would never intentionally hurt someone. Hannah's openness brought out a protectiveness in him he'd never experienced with anyone.

Not even Jenny.

The thought was like a sock in the gut, and suddenly, all he wanted was to be alone.

"Well, I should probably get you home."

He turned away, but she caught his arm. "Hey, what happened? Where did you go just now?"

He tried to shake her off and grumbled irritably, "Nowhere. You said you were tired, so I'm taking you home where you can get some rest."

Hannah's lips pinched together. "Fine."

Hannah let him go and headed for the door, and for some reason, the sight of her walking away from him sent a cold shot through him.

He caught her at the door, his arms going around her from behind and his mouth pressing against her ear. "I just thought of something that upset me. It had nothing to do with you."

"Yet you have no problem letting it affect the way you treat me."

Blake sighed. "I know." He let her go, shaking his head. "I'm really trying, Han. I just get these bad thoughts and feelings, and I don't want to talk about them. Not yet, at least."

His admission seemed to soften him, and she turned around, slipping her arms around his waist and kissing his chest.

"Just know that when you are, I'm here, okay?"

Blake held her tight, the fear that he'd never get there forming a lump in his throat.

"I will."

Chapter Twenty-Six

SATURDAY BLAKE ARRANGED for his squad to do some charity work. Which meant he had them hauling his shit from the moving truck to inside his new house.

Sparks and Violet were helping out with the unpacking, since Sparks had agreed to accompany them on their charity field trip today. They had been out to the truck three or four times, hauling in box after box. Meanwhile, Blake hated to admit it, but he was slacking. He couldn't wait for Hannah to get there and was looking forward to having the whole day with her.

Her little car pulled up along the curb, and she got out, leading Milo by his leash. He watched her bend over to pull a pink pastry box and a plastic bag from the backseat.

"Damn, Sarge, who is that hot mama?" Pedro Gonzales asked next to him.

"Hey, watch it or I'll bury you in the backyard, Gonzales."

Pedro's eyes widened, and then he was shouting. "Yo, yo, check it out! Sarge has got a girlfriend. And she's smoking hot!"

Eight clomping teenaged feet rushed to the window, and comments started flying around. Several of them bordered on obscene, and Blake had to count down from ten to keep from telling them to run to the backyard and do burpees till they puked.

"If one of you says anything disrespectful to Miss York, I will make sure you run laps until you blow chunks. You got me?"

"Yes, Sarge," they chorused.

Shooting them one last warning look, Blake opened the door with a smile, taking in Hannah's funky leggings, long T-shirt, and sweatshirt. "You dressed for the occasion."

She gave him a mock scowl over the top of her glasses, which had slid down her nose. "I wasn't going to get any clothes I like dusty and gross."

"You calling my stuff gross?"

She stopped in front of him with a coy grin. "Not all of it."

Blake really wanted to kiss her but was aware of the ten curious eyes watching.

"Miss York, these boys are in my squad. Squad, this is Miss York. And Violet and Dean are helping out in the kitchen."

"Well, I brought donuts for everyone and drinks, so help yourselves, guys. Plus, the monster pup."

Blake gave Milo a dark look, which the pup returned with a bark. "Well, monster pup can go play in the backyard. Gonzales, you wanna handle that?"

Gonzales took the leash from Hannah with a cheeky grin. "Come on, pup, let's go play out back."

Blake took the bag and donuts from Hannah and bent over to kiss her cheek.

"Pick a room, any room."

Blake walked into the kitchen, where he caught Violet and Dean canoodling.

"Hannah brought donuts, and try to remember there are children present."

Sparks kissed Violet again before responding, "Shut up, Kline."

Hannah came up behind him and smiled at the couple. "Hi again."

"Hello, Hannah," Violet said. "It's nice to officially meet you."

"You, too." Hannah flipped open the box and snagged a donut. "Help yourself."

Blake was suddenly pushed out of the way as a horde of teenaged boys fell upon the box of donuts like ravenous wolves.

Eyeing the donut in her hand, Blake followed Hannah down the hallway until they reached the master suite. They had already moved Blake's bed in first, along with his dresser and other furniture, but his new mattress had stacks of boxes on top and alongside it.

"I don't suppose you want to share that, would you? I doubt there will be anything left once those kids get through."

Hannah held the donut out to him and jerked it back at the last minute to take a bite. "Mine. Go wrestle your own."

Blake grabbed her wrist and stole a bite anyway, laughing at her outraged squeal.

"Remember, sharing is caring."

"Oh fine, here." She ripped the donut in half and gave him one side.

"See, doesn't that make you feel good?"

"It makes me feel hungry," she grumbled as she bit into the donut. "Don't you need to watch the kids?"

"Yeah, but I wanted to say hi to you." He gave her a kiss, savoring the chocolate on her lips.

"Well, as much as I enjoy your 'hi,' we're about to have an audience."

The sound of footsteps coming down the hallway made Blake pull away.

"We'll finish this later."

"Can't wait," she whispered.

Blake left the room and called out several names. "Help me get the rest of the stuff from the truck. I've got to get you back to Alpha Dog by noon, so let's hustle."

HANNAH EMPTIED ONE box at a time, and so far, she'd been through his underwear, shirts, toiletries, and more.

"Hey, Han," Blake called from down the hall.

"Yeah?"

He came through the doorway, looking around his room with a smile. "Wow, you've gotten a lot done in here. Thank you. I'm going to take the boys back to Alpha Dog, and I won't be back until after six. Violet is going to stay for a while doing the kitchen, and I've promised to take her and Dean out to dinner as a thank-you for helping. Are you in?"

"Yeah, that would be great," she said.

"Okay." He leaned over and kissed her forehead. "See you in a bit."

Hannah listened to Dean and Blake holler at the kids as the front door opened and shut. She was down to one more box, and then she could move onto another room.

She opened the last box on the floor and realized it was filled with albums and photographs. Sitting down on the floor, she pulled out a newspaper-wrapped frame that had an old picture of a middle-aged couple smiling at the camera. The man looked enough like Blake that she figured it must be his parents, so she stood up to put the picture on his dresser.

The next photo was of Blake holding a pretty blonde woman in a wedding dress, and Hannah's stomach twisted in sadness. A younger Blake smiled into the camera, handsome in his dress blues, and her heart broke for these two young people who had loved each other so much.

She set that photo on the bed and pulled out one of the albums, thumbing through the pictures. Blake as a child, a teenager, and a young man. Hannah had no idea how long she sat there, going through Blake's past, but when Violet called her name from the doorway, she jumped.

"Hey, sorry, I was just thinking of grabbing some Chipotle and bringing it back. You want some?"

Hannah was crying silently, too choked up to speak.

"Hannah, what is it?" Violet came into the room and sat next to her. "Oh, I see."

Dabbing at the tears in her eyes, Hannah laughed. "Here I am snooping through Blake's life and crying over everything he lost. You must think I'm a freak."

"No, I know all about being with someone who has a past. It's tough."

"Was it hard?" Hannah asked.

"For Dean, I'm sure it sucked." Hannah gave Violet a confused look, and she elaborated. "Dean had been through a lot when we met, but compared to me, he was the poster child for stability. I was convinced that we shouldn't be together and did everything I could to keep him at arm's length. I know I'm laying all my personal shit at your feet, but I thought maybe it would make you feel better to know that even some of the heaviest crap can be overcome."

"Thanks, I appreciate it. Do you think I should put the albums out or leave them in the box for him?"

"I'd leave the picture of Jenny and the albums in the box and let him decide where to put them."

Hannah took her advice and set the box on his bed.

"Have you found his sheets and blankets yet?" she asked Violet.

"Not yet."

"I was thinking I could make his bed so he wouldn't have to."

"You can check in one of the spare rooms. The kitchen has been completely unloaded."

"Okay, let me get you money for lunch."

"No, really, it's fine. It's on me," Violet said. "You bought donuts for everyone. I'll grab lunch."

"Thank you, that's really nice."

"Well, I figure that we'll be seeing a lot of you, and I want to get to know you. These guys are all really close, almost like brothers, so it's important that us girls all get along, as well."

Hannah appreciated Violet's straightforwardness and honesty. "I'm all for it."

"Good, then I'll see you in a bit."

Violet left the house, and Hannah wandered into the rooms, looking through boxes to find Blake's sheets. Was it weird that she was here? Even though they'd been friends for at least a year and they were now seeing each other, it felt like an invasion of privacy for her to be unpacking Blake's things.

Stop analyzing everything. I'm here, and things are great. Don't wreck it by overthinking.

Chapter Twenty-Seven

ON TUESDAY, BLAKE and Charge jogged along the trail, and Blake had to admit, he kind of liked having a partner. He'd been working hard with Charge since taking him to the vet the week before, and so far, things were great. Dr. Standen had determined that Charge had only about 50 percent hearing left, and by the way his teeth were filed, he thought the cause was most likely because Charge had been used as a hunting dog. Having a gun blast in his ears over and over for several years was bound to have some ill effects.

Dr. Standen assured him he could still work in search and rescue and thought the whistle was a fantastic idea. Once they'd diagnosed Charge's issue, Blake had been more confident about his ability to train the giant dog.

Even though it was out of the way, Blake had still been coming down to Dale's for breakfast, if only for those ten minutes he got to snag with Hannah during her break.

Once he'd slipped Charge into the car, he'd headed toward the front steps of Dale's and heard a horn honk.

"Blake! You got a minute?"

Blake turned and found Bryce in her little car.

"What's up? Not crashing my jogs anymore?"

"No, you were hostile. But I do need a favor."

Blake moved closer without saying anything.

"Aren't you going to ask what it is?"

"Figured you'd just tell me."

"You are such a pain in the ass."

Blake shrugged and started to turn away.

"Wait! I'm sorry. Please, just hear me out."

Blake sighed and leaned into the passenger-side window. "What?"

"I was wondering if you could cover for me on Friday night."

"I'm busy Friday."

"So am I, which is why I need you to cover for me!"

Blake took a deep soothing breath. "Fine. Must be nice not to be in the armed forces anymore and actually have a choice on taking a day off."

She stuck her tongue out at him before calling, "You're the best!"

Blake shook his head as he went around to the back of Dale's. He knew exactly when Hannah took her break and didn't even bother going inside until after he got her kisses.

Blake saw her sitting in one of the plastic chairs, and when she saw him, her face brightened. "Hey." She stood up and gave him a hug. "I didn't think you'd be coming by anymore now that you live in Orangevale."

"I packed my clothes, and I'm going to shower when I get to work. I just wanted to see you." He tried to kiss her but she pulled back, wrinkling her nose.

"You're all sweaty."

"So?" He kissed her hard and fast before she could get away, and he kept kissing her all over her face until she was squealing with laughter.

"You taste all salty."

"And now so do you." He kissed her below her ear, his tongue snaking out to lick at her skin, and he felt her relax against him.

"When you do that, I'm powerless against you."

"Hmm, so I'm your kryptonite?" he said teasingly.

"Yes, you are." Her soft tone made him pause, and he pulled back to study her.

"You say that like it's a bad thing."

"No, it's not. Sorry, I'm just tired. Plus, I should get back inside and take your order."

"In a minute. I've got Charge in the car, so I'll have to cut your sugar time short."

She snorted. "My sugar time?"

"Hell yeah, you complain, but you know you like it."

"So why do you have Charge with you?" she asked, ignoring his comment.

"I took him for a run, and he absolutely loved it."

"That's great."

"In fact, he's doing so well, I was thinking of celebrating early. Could we move our dinner on Friday up to tonight?"

"Yes, of course. What do you have going on Friday?"

"Going to work a few extra hours to cover for Bryce." One last kiss, and he murmured, "I'll see you inside."

He jogged out of the alley, the grin on his face actually hurting his cheeks. He felt this way every time he saw Hannah, and he had to admit, the way she could brighten his day was becoming addicting.

IT WAS JUST before seven that evening, and Hannah was getting ready for Blake to pick her up. She'd taken a shower when she got home and pulled on a pink skater dress, pairing it with a floral shrug from Torrid. She slipped on her black heels and finished her hair, her makeup already in place.

She was really nervous, mostly because things had been more intense and intimate each time they were together. She'd been trying to prepare herself for having the talk with Blake about sex and her lack of experience, but there never seemed to be a right time.

Especially when he was kissing her and she couldn't keep a thought in her head.

Her doorbell rang, and she placed a barking Milo in his cage with a Milk-Bone before answering.

She pulled the door open, and Blake stood on the porch, wearing a sports jacket over a collared shirt, no tie.

"Hi, you look handsome."

"And you're beautiful." He placed a long lingering kiss on her lips that made her shiver all the way down to her curling toes.

"Thank you."

He led her down the walkway and opened her door like he always did. "How does Thai food sound?"

"Amazing. I haven't had it in a long time."

Once he pulled out of the parking lot, his hand fell on her bare knee, and the muscles between her legs clenched and throbbed from just the mere touch. When his thumb slid across her skin, she shivered.

"Are you cold?"

"No," she said.

Blake's hand squeezed her knee before slowly sliding up under her skirt. Hannah held her breath, her heart pounding so hard she was sure it was going to bust wide open.

"Blake…"

His fingers brushed her inner thigh, and against her will, her legs spread wider to give him better access. As they caressed the outside of her lacy pink panties, Hannah let out a moan of frustration. She wanted those fingers touching her, inside her, not just teasing.

Without warning, Blake withdrew his hand with a heavy, shuddering breath, placing both hands on the wheel.

"I'm sorry. I don't know what came over me."

She turned and gave him a little smile. "I didn't mind."

"Maybe we can pick it up after dinner."

Here it was, the perfect chance for her to be honest.

"Sure, but just so we're clear, there are some things I want to take slow, too."

Blake glanced toward her for a second, then returned his focus to the road. "Such as?"

"Well, the…intimate stuff. I'm not terribly experienced, and I just want you to know that even though

I'm not ready for sex, that doesn't mean I don't like you."

Blake didn't say anything for the longest time, and Hannah was sure she'd spooked him.

Finally, he asked, "Are you telling me this because you feel like I'm pushing you? Because I never meant to—"

"No! God, no, I don't feel pressured. Believe me, I like it when you touch me. I just don't want to get in over my head before I'm actually ready to take that step."

"Okay, sure. We can take our time. I don't mind."

Hannah breathed a sigh of relief. "Thank God. I was a little nervous telling you, especially because it's a little embarrassing being almost twenty-five and a virgin, but it was my choice—*Blake*!"

Blake had swerved into the other lane, coughing.

"Are you okay?" she asked.

"Yeah, I just…Did you say you were a virgin? As in, you've never had sex with anyone?"

"Well, yeah, that was what I was trying to explain. Is that a problem?"

He hesitated. He *freaking* hesitated. "No, no, it was just a surprise."

But Hannah didn't believe him.

"It wasn't for religious reasons, and I'm not holding out until marriage. I was holding out until I found someone I could really love."

Someone like you.

Even though she hadn't said the words aloud, the car filled with tension, and she could have sworn Blake was sweating.

"Are you panicking?" she asked.

"No, I'm fine. Just hungry."

Hannah turned to look out the window, her stomach sinking in disappointment.

Why did the fact that I've never been with anyone else send Blake into a full-force meltdown?

BLAKE DIDN'T KNOW what the hell to say about the bomb Hannah had just dropped on him. He'd figured she'd probably been with one, maybe two other guys, but he didn't think she was very experienced.

Turned out she was even more innocent than him.

Blake hadn't meant to let on how much the news affected him. Losing your virginity was a big deal—at least, it had been when he'd been eighteen and Jenny had been seventeen.

Fuck, how the hell did this happen?

It happened because he wanted Hannah. She made him happy, and he'd liked the way that had felt. It had been nice to let things progress, to enjoy getting to know her on a whole new level.

But now he knew she was a virgin, and a thousand what-if scenarios went through his mind. What if they had sex and things didn't work out? What if she resented him for hurting her, or he disappointed her?

"Blake? You sound as if you're hyperventilating over there."

"No, I'm fine."

But he wasn't. He was crazy. He was fucking losing his mind.

Chapter Twenty-Eight

DINNER WAS A quiet, awkward affair, and for the first time since Blake had stepped foot in Dale's, Hannah wanted to get away from him.

She'd hated the way he'd looked when she'd told him she'd never been with anyone. Why had that sent him into a full-blown panic attack? Because he'd been trying to keep things fun and light and he thought virginity somehow made sex more complicated? She'd saved it so when she fell in love, even if it didn't last, it meant something, instead of randomly hooking up and regretting it later.

Then he'd had to act like an idiot and made her regret even mentioning it.

"So, maybe we could do this again on Saturday?"

Hannah shrugged, too irritated with him to hide it. "Maybe, I'll let you know."

"Hannah, come on—"

She climbed out of the car and shut the door on whatever else he was going to say, wondering if she'd made a mistake telling Blake at all. Maybe she would be better off dating someone else. There were any number of guys who were cute, smart, and completely uncomplicated...

But none of those guys ever made her feel the way Blake did.

Hannah walked into the apartment and let Milo out of his cage, taking him into the front yard to relieve himself. She noticed Blake was still sitting in the parking spot and tried to ignore him.

Calling Milo back inside, she locked the door, ready for bed and the new romance she'd picked up at Walmart. Romance novels had flawed, tortured heroes, but they only drove her crazy for a page or two.

Unlike real men.

BLAKE SAT IN his car, trying to decide whether he wanted to call up the guys to meet him at Mick's Bar or bang on Hannah's door and try to explain himself.

How did he explain that he was a big, fat pussy who couldn't handle the responsibility of being her first?

She'd been waiting for someone she could love. Did that mean she thought she could love him?

He wasn't there yet and didn't know if he could ever be in love again, but he cared about her. He needed her.

Blake climbed out of his car and jogged up to Hannah's door, knocking loudly. Once he explained why he'd freaked out, everything would be back to normal.

It flew open, and both Hannah and Milo stared out at him.

"Blake, what—"

Before he even knew what he was doing, he'd cut her off with his mouth, backing her into her apartment and slamming the door behind him. He tried to tell himself to slow down, to seduce her slowly and listen to that little sigh of surrender she gave when he kissed her neck just right.

But he was overwhelmed with the need to prove he wasn't scared without actually saying the words. That what they had between them was real and that he hadn't meant to freak out, that he'd be happy to be her first, if it ever came to that.

Blake eased the pressure of his mouth, teasing her lips as he maneuvered her back toward the bedroom. He ignored Milo nipping at his ankles as he ran his hands all over Hannah, lovingly caressing every curve beneath the sheath of her dress.

Her hands gripped his shoulders, kneading the muscles, and he almost groaned, it felt so good.

When they reached the bedroom, he lowered her onto the bed, following her down until he hovered over her. He pulled away from her lips reluctantly and tucked her hair back behind her ear, studying her beautifully flushed face with a caressing gaze.

"I know that I am a whole bucket of fucked, but I wanted to make sure we ended the night with you knowing how much I like you. How wonderful I think you are and especially"—he pressed his mouth against the shell of her ear—"how much I want you."

"But in the car and at dinner—"

He kissed her again, cutting off her reminder. "I was an idiot. I am an idiot. And I want to make it up to you."

He trailed his lips down the length of her neck, his fingers inching up the hem of her dress.

"What are you doing?" she whispered.

Blake paused, his mouth hovering over the tops of her breasts. "I plan to make you very, very happy. But first we need to get this dress off you."

Hannah didn't protest as Blake helped her sit up and found the zipper on the back of her dress. Once it was over her head and on the floor, Blake's gaze ate up every inch of her, from the pink lacy panties to the gray bra pushing her breasts up into creamy, round offerings.

"Now, I want you to feel free to tell me everything you like and anything you don't. And if you want me to stop for any reason, I will."

Hannah stared up at him, her eyes wide, and Blake didn't wait for her to agree.

His hands slid over her breasts, squeezing them gently as he kissed down her stomach, his teeth lightly nipping her. When he reached her navel, his tongue dipped in, sliding out and down to the edge of her panties.

He could feel the rise and fall of her breasts in his hands, and he looked up at her from just above the scrap of lace covering her. Blake's hands left her breasts, sliding over her ribs until they teased the sides of her panties.

"If you're a screamer, you might want to grab that pillow." He slowly slid the underwear down and off her feet before kissing his way back up. "Just in case you don't want your neighbors to hear."

He didn't give her a chance to respond as his lips moved over the soft skin of her inner thigh and settled between her legs.

Hannah gasped and arched off the bed, panting, "Blake!"

"Remember to use the pillow."

OH MY GOD. Oh my God. OH MY FREAKING GOD.

Hannah couldn't speak, she was too busy moaning as Blake dragged his rough tongue up her seam in slow measure until he found her clit. Pressing his mouth around it like a vacuum, he flicked it in rapid succession, and Hannah couldn't breathe.

It wasn't as though she'd never had a guy use his mouth on her, but it had been a long time, and she remembered being a little bored. She'd even tried a vibrator she'd bought at a Pure Romance party a few years back, and that had felt good.

But nothing had prepared her for Blake's mouth working her into a stiff, feverish frenzy. Sweat beaded across her skin, and her head fell back, tossing and turning on the pillow as she tried to find some relief from the sweet torture he was inflicting.

"Blake...please..."

He sucked her nub between his lips hard, and she flew, lights exploding between her eyelids as she came in great, racking shakes. Her cries mingled with gulping breaths, and she slowly came back to herself to find Blake still there, still pressing his mouth against her softly, lovingly, and she quivered again.

In a daze, she reached out and rubbed the top of his head. "Why?"

He came up over her body, his hazel eyes on fire in the dim light.

"Because I want you to know that I'm here. That I'm in this. Even when I freak out, I want to be with you."

Hannah stared up at him in surprise. Blake had given her an amazing orgasm, expecting nothing in return, just to prove that he cared for her?

A smile curved across her lips, and she cupped his cheek in her hand.

"You really are a hero."

BLAKE SAT UP on the bed and kicked his shoes off while Hannah put on some flannel pajamas. He had every intension of staying with Hannah, of curling his body around hers and snuggling with her for a while. It was something he'd been thinking about, what it would be like to cuddle with someone again, and it scared the hell out of him.

But despite his fear and the tiny niggle of guilt for wanting to replace Jenny in his bed, he needed Hannah to know that he wasn't just going to run every time he got scared.

"Do you mind if I stay with you until you fall asleep?" he asked.

Hannah looked up from straightening her clothes, and that warm, welcoming smile was almost his undoing.

"You can stay the whole night if you want."

Blake didn't respond right away, mostly because cuddling with Hannah was one thing, but sleeping over was a step he needed to think harder about. Maybe go over with Dr. Stabler...

Blake almost laughed out loud. For a guy who had been so against therapy just a month ago, he sure had become dependent on it.

"Maybe another night. We've got plenty of time for you to get to know all my really bad sleeping habits."

"Oh, yeah? Like what?"

"Well, I'm a bit of a bed hog. I'll kick you right off this queen-size bed so I can stretch out."

Hannah laughed softly. "I snore."

As he settled in behind her and wrapped his arms around her waist, he breathed in the fruity scent. "Everybody snores, babe. It's not a deal breaker. I just figured we can continue to take his slow. Okay?"

Hannah stroked his forearm gently. "Okay."

The only sounds in the room were of their gentle breathing, and for a second, Blake thought she'd fallen asleep already.

"Thank you for knocking," she whispered.

Her words made him laugh, and he kissed her hair. "Thanks for opening up."

"Oh, come on. Like you really thought I was going to leave you standing out on the porch?"

"Hey, you were angry Hannah for a while, and I never know what to expect from her."

She turned and tilted her head to look up at him, her gaze soft. "I like less angry Blake."

Blake stiffened at her words, but when she reached up to cup his cheek, there was no judgement on her face. "I just mean that you used to come into Dale's so angry some days, like there was a black cloud following you around. Even when you smiled, there was such a sadness to it. And now I know why. I'm just glad that I get to hear you laugh, that's all I meant."

He relaxed, her words sinking in, and he brushed her lips with his. "If I've changed, it's because of you. You do things to me no one else can."

Hannah sighed against his mouth and turned to snuggle into his chest. Even when he heard her breathing slow down after she fell asleep, he was afraid to move. Realization dawned on him that it was true. No one had ever made him feel the way Hannah did, and he found himself pulling her tighter against him.

There was no way he could lose Hannah. He wouldn't survive it.

Chapter Twenty-Nine

"YOU ARE A freaking sadist!"

Blake laughed at Hannah's breathless shout as she jogged next to him, sweat rolling down her temples. In the last week, slow had pretty much been thrown out the window. Now that they were officially together and seeing each other every day, Blake's opinion on sleepovers had adjusted. Especially when things got pretty heated on the front porch of his or her place and they found themselves doing some heavy making out on the couch and migrating to the bedroom. They still hadn't had sex, although the foreplay was fantastic. It had been a week of touching, tasting, and pretty much driving each other crazy, so Blake had suggested that on this beautiful Sunday morning in March, Hannah go jogging with him to help blow off some of the sexual frustration.

At first, she'd been against it, citing that she hadn't run in a long time and she couldn't keep up, but he'd promised to stick with her, which he'd been doing, like any good boyfriend would.

Boyfriend. It was definitely going to take some getting used to, but things had been really good between them. No more confusion, just the two of them back to discovering new things about each other.

"You just need to get your muscles used to it, and it won't be so hard."

"Lies. You just want me to go with you again so you can mock my pain."

"Come on, you're doing great, and we're almost to the end of the trail."

She gave him the stare of death, and he slowed down and squatted in front of her. "Want me to give you a lift back to the car?"

"Yes."

"Then hop on, 'cause I don't have all day."

He heard her groan loudly before she ran past him, her pink workout shirt dark with sweat. When he caught up to her, he heard her chanting something and he bent closer to hear, but it was too soft to make out. "What's that?"

"I am saying, 'I hate you. I hate you.' "

"That's not nice. I offered to carry you."

"It was a test to see if I would crack under pressure, but you will not break me, sir!" She sped up, her feet flying, and never one to turn down a challenge, Blake caught up, teasing her by keeping pace for a second or two.

Then he took off, loving the rush of the wind in his face.

A sharp cry behind him made his heart and feet skid to a stop. When he turned, Hannah was on the ground, holding her leg with pain-filled sobs.

Blake was by her side in seconds. "Fuck, Hannah, what happened?"

She didn't open her eyes, but he could see the tear tracks on her cheeks. Blake reached for her leg to see what had happened, and she yelled, "Don't touch it!"

"Is it your leg or your ankle?"

"Ankle," she choked. "It turned, and I heard a snap before I went crashing into the pavement."

Blake grimaced and moved her hands away. Her ankle sock was already stretching around the swelling, and as he started to roll it down gently, she whimpered.

"It's okay, I'll take you back to the car, and we'll go have it looked at." He lifted her into his arms and started walking down the trail to where he'd parked the car. Several moms pushing strollers slowed, watching them curiously. Hannah continued to sniffle against his chest, every once in a while releasing a moan when he had to readjust her and her ankle got jostled.

They made it back to the car, and Blake helped her in. "Is there somewhere specific we need to go?"

She shook her head, her skin a pale green shade that reminded him of a dead fish. "Any urgent care."

He shut the door and got into the driver's side. If the foot was broken, she might have to have surgery on it, but if it was a sprain, she'd just be in pain for several weeks and moving around in one of those plastic boots.

Blake searched for the closest hospital on his smartphone and set it up to give him turn-by-turn directions. He tried to drive gently, but when he took a turn too fast, he heard Hannah suck in a painful breath.

"Sorry, we're almost there. Still hate me?"

Blake saw her shake her head out of the corner of his eye, a small smile on her lips. "Not at the moment. I can't hate beyond the pain."

Blake reached across with one hand and took hers in his, giving it a gentle squeeze. "I'm sorry, baby."

"Not your fault. I wanted to go. I just got these weak ankles that turn without any warning."

"This has happened before? I wish you had told me—"

"Not like this, but I've rolled them just by wearing heels. I should have wrapped them for extra support, but I didn't think about it." She squeezed his hand back. "I appreciate all the care and concern, though."

"Hey, I don't like how pale you are. I might need to take extra good care of you."

"I like the sound of that."

HANNAH SAT IN the hospital bed with her foot elevated on a pillow, waiting for the ER doctor to come back. Blake had taken her to the hospital just in case it was broken, and she had been in so much pain, she hadn't argued. But when they'd put an IV in her arm, she'd told them that she didn't like strong pain meds, mostly because she knew her birth mom had been an addict, and she had always thought *why risk it?*

They hadn't listened to her, though, because she was definitely a little loopy. The room started spinning, and she closed her eyes against the swoony sensation.

"What did you give me?" she slurred.

"Just something for the pain. The doctor will be in after he looks at the X-rays."

"Thank you." Blake's deep voice sounded different under the crashing waves in her ears.

When she heard the door close, she turned toward where she thought Blake was and spoke in a loud stage whisper. "I think that nurse is trying to get me high."

"Baby, I think she already did."

Blake's chuckle wrapped around her like a soft blanket. "I like it when you laugh. You don't do it nearly often enough."

He paused, and while she wanted to open her eyes and see the look on his face, she couldn't pry her lids apart.

"I've laughed more with you than I have the last two years," he said softly.

He sounds so sad.

She didn't want sad Blake. She wanted happy, laughing Blake.

"Your laugh makes me all warm inside, like cinnamon rolls baking in the oven."

"How do you know how cinnamon rolls feel?" At least the smile was back in his voice.

"I can imagine it."

A knock on the door interrupted the absurd conversation, and another male voice called, "Hello? Hi, Hannah, I'm Dr. Gould."

Hannah turned her head lazily toward him but still couldn't open her eyes. "Give it to me straight, Doc...Is my ankle busted?"

"No, but it is sprained. I'm going to suggest you stay off it as much as possible for a week and make sure you ice and elevate it. Eight hundred milligrams of ibuprofen and you should be good as new."

Hannah tried to sit up and fell back almost immediately, her stomach turning. "Well that sucks."

"I'll even get you a handy-dandy note to give your employers that says exactly that, if you need it. Do you have someone who can help you out for a few days?"

Before she opened her mouth to say her parents, she heard Blake's firm yes, and this time, her eyes did pop open. Her vision was blurry, but she squinted at Blake, trying to bring him into focus.

"You don't have to. I can call my mom or Nicki—"

"I can help you out if I want to, and there's nothing you can say to stop me."

Hannah had no desire to stop him. In fact, the only thing she wanted was to go to sleep.

Starting right...now.

BLAKE PICKED UP Hannah's prescription and a pair of crutches from the pharmacy, all while she snored lightly in his front seat. She definitely hadn't been lying when she'd said she couldn't handle strong pain meds. She'd been completely out of it since the nurse had dosed her up.

It was better than her being in immense pain, but damn, she was funny when her inhibitions were lowered. While he was wheeling her out, she'd started singing some song about living under the sea and broken out into giggles between verses. Even some of the nurses and patients they passed sang along with her, so the song must have been popular, but he had never heard it before.

He climbed back into the driver's side, and she opened one eye at him, completely dazed.

"Are you my sunshine?" she asked groggily.

Blake chuckled as he started the car. "First time I've ever been called that."

"Hmm." She went back to sleep, and as he drove back to his place, he kept glancing over at her, studying her when she was so vulnerable. The softness of her face and the full pout of her mouth, pink and open. Her black lashes fanned out over the delicate skin under her eyes.

Hannah had been the bright spot in his day for the longest time, and now that he'd finally given in and let her get close, she'd quickly become so much more. The way he felt when she was with him was indescribable. She had wiggled her way into a part of him he hadn't even known existed, and the happiness he felt at that made panic and acceptance fight for control.

When he pulled into his driveway a few minutes later, he lifted her from the passenger seat and laughed as her head flopped back over his arm, her ponytail flopping back and forth. He managed to unlock the door and carried her back to his bedroom. Once he'd laid her gently on top of his comforter, he went to the closet to grab his extra quilt, figuring he'd just lay that over her.

When he picked it up, he saw the white box underneath with the word *photos* scrawled on the lid. He hadn't even bothered to unpack any of the albums or the photos of Jenny and him in his apartment, the memories too painful to even look at. Now, he wondered if the reason he hesitated was because he was afraid he wouldn't still miss Jenny the way he had before...

Well, before Hannah.

He placed a lightweight quilt over her, and, after he retrieved the box, closed the door gently behind him. Blake set the box down on the coffee table and went out to grab her pain meds and crutches from the car. Finally, when everything was quiet, he sat down on the couch and lifted the lid.

The picture of Jenny and him from their wedding day sat on top, and he wondered if Hannah had been the one to pull out the picture of his parents. Had she seen this? Was it painful, or had she left it for him to go through on purpose?

He set the picture aside and opened the first album, memories assaulting him with every page he turned. His whole childhood—no, his whole life—was compiled into these albums, and as he made it through his early years, his eyes were already damp with tears.

Then he reached his high school years, and besides several pictures of him on family vacations or just out with his friends, nearly all the rest included Jenny.

Jenny holding up the fish she'd caught when they were seventeen and his parents had let her come camping with them as long as they slept in separate tents. His mom had even grounded him when she'd caught him trying to sneak in with Jenny, who'd been sound asleep and hadn't known anything was going on.

Their graduation ceremony, where he'd given her a promise ring he'd saved six months for. The picture was of the two of them kissing, the ring sparkling on her finger as she cradled his face.

When he'd made it through basic and Jenny had come down with his parents to watch him graduate. His mom had caught the moment Jenny had run to him and thrown herself in his arms, his face buried in her soft blonde hair and his arms squeezing her tight. He could almost smell the vanilla scent of her shampoo as he stared at the photo.

The last picture in the album was several months after he'd lost his parents, and when he'd been home on leave, Jenny had helped him go through their things. When he'd found their wedding picture, he'd hung it in the living room, and while he'd been adjusting the picture, Jenny had snapped one of her own. It was a haunting picture, beautiful with the afternoon light shining through the window behind him.

Blake ran his finger over Jenny's smiling face, and although it still hurt to think about, he didn't long for the past the way he had. Before Hannah had come into his life.

He closed the album and stuffed it in the box. He put it back in the spare bedroom and shut the closet door, leaving the room to check on the flesh-and-blood woman sleeping in his bed. The one who was slowly stealing his heart and slowly healing his soul.

Chapter Thirty

HANNAH HAD BEEN planning the day trip for the better part of two weeks, making sure that they both had the day off. She'd wanted everything to be perfect.

Blake was currently driving along the twisty, coastal highway, with Milo and Charge in the backseat and Hannah gripping the *oh, shit* handle for dear life. Her stomach churned at the jerky movements the car made with every curve.

"Do you think you could slow down just a bit, babe?"

Blake glanced her way with a frown. "I'm going the speed limit."

"I know, but I get carsick, and the way you're taking the curves…"

Suddenly, the sound of retching behind her and the unmistakable smell of vomit filled the car.

She turned around to find Milo looking a bit bleary-eyed and a puddle of doggie puke dripping down the front of his seat.

"Please tell me your dog didn't just ralph in my backseat."

"I can't tell you that."

Blake cursed a blue streak, and Hannah put her hand on his thigh, fighting a smile.

"Don't worry, I'll clean it up when we get there."

"We gotta get him some doggie Dramamine or something. Real dogs don't get carsick."

"Come on, he's just a puppy. Besides, I was on the verge of decorating your dash before you slowed down."

"Gross, Han. That's too vivid." One of his hands came off the wheel to cover hers, and he laced his fingers with hers.

"Sorry, but it's true. You drive like you're literally hugging the curves."

"It's how I learned, and I've never had any complaints before."

"I'm not complaining; I'm voicing some comfort concerns."

"Hmm."

Blake made a left into the parking lot, and once they got the dogs out of the back, Blake climbed in and cleaned up the puke, despite her protests from the front seat. She sat on her seat with the dogs' leashes in her hands.

"I said I would."

"And I told you I got it." He climbed out of the back of the car and kissed her briefly before taking the wad of paper towels over to the trash. When he came back, Blake grabbed the blanket, picnic basket, and her tote, groaning as if the weight was too much.

"Holy crap, what did you pack in here, woman?"

She stood up and put her free hand on her hip. "All kinds of good stuff."

"It feels like you cleaned out your whole refrigerator."

"Nah, just half of it."

Blake set the stuff down on the backseat and squatted in front of her. "Hop on, Princess. Your noble steed awaits."

"I don't know how I feel about you calling yourself my horse. Besides, I've been fine for nearly three weeks."

"Just climb up. I'm not having you injure your ankle again walking on sand."

Hannah climbed up, laughing as Blake boosted her higher.

They picked a spot in the middle of the beach, and Hannah was glad she'd worn her Sac State sweatshirt. Despite the sun shining above, the wind off the ocean was frigid.

Blake dropped Hannah off and headed back to the car for the rest of their stuff. Hannah spread out the quilt, smiling to herself. She liked it when Blake hovered and was a little overprotective. It made her feel cherished.

Loved.

When he returned, she reached into the tote for two dental bones, a small one for Milo and the other for Charge.

"That ought to keep them busy while we eat."

Blake scooted next to her, taking Charge's and Milo's leashes and latching them to the hook he'd twisted into the ground. "Good, because I do not like sharing my food."

"Not even with me?" she teased as he pulled out a strawberry.

He held it toward her lips, giving her a wicked grin. When she moved forward to take a bite, he pulled it back and popped it in his mouth.

"Now, that was just mean."

He chuckled and leaned over, kissing her deeply, and she shivered as his tongue swept inside, the sweetly tart taste of the strawberry delicious.

He pulled back slightly, his mouth a whisper away. "I'm sorry."

"I don't think you are." Her lips twitched as he kissed the corner of them.

"Hmm, so, so sorry." He held up a strawberry between them, rubbing it against her bottom lip.

She bit into it, the juices running down her chin, and she shivered as he caught a droplet on her chin with his tongue.

Hannah blushed and looked around. A few families closer to the beach played and romped near the water, but no one seemed to be paying them any attention.

Hannah took the strawberry from his hand and popped it into her mouth. "Wanna see what else I brought?"

She moved around him, shattering the steamy atmosphere, and started pulling out Tupperwares of food.

"I've got sandwiches. Some sliced apples. More strawberries. Chocolate-chip cookies and bottled waters are at the bottom."

"Hmm, a feast. Are you trying to distract me with food so I'll stop kissing you?"

His direct question made her cheeks burn. "We're in public."

"So, I can't kiss you when other people are watching?" he asked, making little finger hearts on her jean-clad thigh.

"No, that's not what I'm saying." She grabbed his hand and set it back in his lap. "Behave."

"I can't help it. You bring out the naughty parts of me."

Hannah laughed. "Eat something, and maybe I'll let you kiss me some more."

"Maybe?" He tackled her back onto the blanket, and Hannah's breath whooshed out as he landed on top of her. "Maybe you'll let me?"

When his fingers found her ticklish ribs, she squealed and hollered, laughter erupting from her as she begged him to stop.

"Mercy, mercy!"

"I have no mercy!" He got her in the armpit, and she couldn't breathe, she was laughing so hard.

"Please, you... You can kiss me. Just...stop."

Blake stopped and hovered over her, his hazel eyes twinkling. "Victory."

This time as he kissed her, she was too lost in the warmth and feel of him to worry about anyone watching.

BLAKE LAY ON his back with his head in Hannah's lap, listening to her hum as she trailed her fingers through his hair. His eyes were closed against the bright sunlight, and he stroked the back of the hand she was drumming against his chest.

"Thank you for the day," he said suddenly.

Her hand stilled on his forehead. "I didn't do anything. You drove and carried me out here—"

He opened his eyes and reached up to cover her mouth with his hand. "But it was your idea. You said you wanted to show me the beach, and you made that delicious lunch. So, thank you for making this such a great day."

"It would have been better if you didn't have to break your back carrying me."

"I don't have to carry you. I just figured you'd be more comfortable if you didn't have to struggle across the sand. Besides, the sprain was kind of my fault, anyway."

"Stop it. It's my fault I'm a klutz."

He tangled their fingers together. "What else?"

"What?"

"I want to know more about who you are."

Hannah went back to playing with his hair. "I don't know. I'm an only child, as far as I know."

"What does that mean, as far as you know?"

"Well, I assume I'm an only child. I've never tried to find out anything about my birth mother. For all I know, I have enough siblings to make a football team."

Blake tilted his head so he could see her face better. With the sun shining almost directly behind her, it hurt his eyes. "Did you ever want to meet her?"

"Nope. I have a mother already, and as far as I'm concerned, there is nothing I'd gain from meeting her. I've read stories about people always feeling as if they were missing something, but I never did."

"That's good. Your parents seem like good people."

"Yeah, they're great, so long as the ID network doesn't convince them a new catastrophe is heading my way every second day."

"What got you excited about teaching?"

"I don't know, I've always loved kids. I used to babysit almost every weekend for kids in my neighborhood, and in high school, I'd tutor some of them."

"We should have you come out to Alpha Dog and help out some of the guys who are struggling."

"I'd love to help."

"When you aren't teaching, what else do you do?"

She hesitated—at least, that's what it felt like.

"I like to write."

"Write what?"

"Stories. Mostly midgrade or elementary school. My dream is to be published one day, but I just haven't found the time yet."

"How long are these stories?"

"About two hundred pages each. I've written four of them."

"What are they about?"

"Kids who've had hard lives becoming almost superheroes. They are just for fun."

"I think that's great. The only thing I was ever good at was running track and being a soldier."

Blake caught her smile. "What?"

"Nothing, I was just thinking that I know several things you're really good at."

Sitting up in front of her, he raised an eyebrow. "Oh, yeah?"

"Mmm-hmm." She gathered the front of his shirt in her hand, and he let her bring him toward her. "Like kissing, for instance. I happen to think you're really, really good at kissing."

Blake wasn't going to argue.

Chapter Thirty-One

THE NEXT MONTH passed quickly, between work and spending any free time with Hannah. After their day at the beach, Blake had been ready for them to take the next step in their relationship. Every time he left Hannah's place or she left his, he felt like a teenager fighting off crazy hormones.

It wasn't just about the sex, though. He wanted to move forward with her because he was so happy. When he was at work, Blake's friends had told him he was grossing them out with all of his jaunty whistling, but he wasn't taking it personally. He knew his friends were glad things were working out, and today, Blake had even more to be excited about.

It was Hannah's and his first weekend away, and they were going to spend a few days in Tahoe. And Blake was giddier than a kid on prom night with his very first hotel key. As he took the curvy road down the mountain and the lake came into view, Hannah looked out over the beautiful sight and sighed.

"It's so gorgeous."

Blake put his hand on her knee and squeezed. He loved the way she reacted to things with no pretense, no holding back.

In fact, he was really looking forward to watching that unfold this weekend. They still hadn't had sex, although they had done other things. Whenever a situation started to escalate to that point, Hannah usually pumped the brakes, and Blake didn't want to rush her, but his balls had to be the color navy by now.

But every time he touched her, it was as though he was teaching her something new, something that she found she liked, and he wanted to keep making her happy.

The sun was setting, and the orange and purple sky was reflected in the water below. When they finally hit the bottom of the mountain and drove through the forest, passing gas stations and hotels, Hannah reached over and put her hand on his knee.

"I can't wait to get there. I saw the pictures of this room, and it is amazing. Big spa tub and extra-large shower, a fireplace, a king-size bed, and a private terrace that looks out over the beach."

He took her hand and kissed her fingers. "I can't wait, either."

Hannah laced her fingers with his, and they drove the rest of the way to the hotel listening to the radio. Occasionally one of them would stroke their thumb across the other's palm or the back of their hand. The ease in their affection was relaxing to Blake.

He pulled into the hotel and went to the trunk to gather their luggage.

"Here, I can get my stuff."

"My woman does not carry her bag," Blake growled playfully.

"Your woman has been carrying bags for many moons," Hannah said mockingly. "Come on, you look like a pack mule lugging all that."

Without waiting for him to hand her anything, she just took one of her bags from him.

"Dork."

Blake wrapped his arms around her, his hands full of luggage, and held her back to his front. "It's not nice to call me names."

He nibbled the side of her neck, and he loved that she giggled and squirmed. "I'm so sorry."

"As you should be." He released her, and they walked into the hotel. While Hannah checked them in, he grabbed one of the luggage trollies. Honestly, Hannah packed as if they were taking a month's vacation.

She came skipping over to him with two keys and led the way down the hall. She unlocked the door to their suite, and when they stepped inside, Blake's jaw dropped.

"Wow, this is really nice."

"I told you!" she said, flopping back on the bed. "They even put a bottle of champagne on the table."

Blake didn't care about the champagne; he was too distracted by Hannah, who'd rolled up onto her side and was rubbing the bed suggestively.

"Wanna feel how soft it is?"

Blake grinned, and pounced on top of her, lying flat against her. "Oh yes, so soft."

Hannah was gasping with laughter and then crying, "Wait, I can't breathe."

Blake rolled off her, but before he could get too far, her arms snaked up around the back of his neck. "You don't have to go that far."

"I thought you wanted to get dinner. You told me after Pollock Pines that you were starving."

"I am." She kissed him and licked her lips. "You taste good, too."

Blake's cock stirred to life, and he shook his head. "If you keep that up, you're not getting anything to eat until Sunday at checkout."

"Hmm, is that a threat?"

"A promise."

"Then I guess we better get out of here." She escaped from his arms, and he leaned back on the bed with his arms folded behind his head, watching her.

"Has anyone ever told you you're a tease?"

"All in good time, my man." She picked up her tote and escaped into the bathroom, the lock clicking loudly.

Blake sighed and closed his eyes, listening to the sound of the water running and imagining Hannah's naked body twisting under the spray as she washed all those lush curves.

HANNAH CAME OUT of the bathroom all dressed for dinner, only to find Blake snoring on the bed. She thought about waking him, but considering he'd been up since five, had gone to work, and had just completed a two-hour drive, she didn't have the heart to disturb him.

Besides, considering what she had planned for him later, he would need his rest.

After their beach trip, and the realization that she was in love with him, Hannah had decided to use her trip to Tahoe for something special.

Being with Blake for the first time.

Yes, there were still times she caught him looking sad and wondered if he was thinking about his wife, but he had never given her a reason to doubt he cared for her. The way he spoke to her, laughed with her, touched her…They all compiled into a thousand reasons why she was sure that she was over the moon in love with Blake.

Quietly, she snuck out of the room and went down to the front desk. The woman behind the desk smiled at her and said, "May I help you?"

"Hi, I was wondering if the restaurant did to-go orders?"

"Yes, they do. There's also room service, ma'am."

Hannah didn't really want someone coming to the room and waking Blake up if he needed rest. "That's okay, I'll just grab it since I'm down here."

"If you want to go into the restaurant, it's through those doors. You can order at the bar, and they'll get you anything you want."

"Thank you."

Twenty-five minutes later, Hannah snuck back into the room and found Blake still passed out. She spread the tablecloth they had given her out in front of the fireplace and set up both meals.

Going to the bed, she put her hand on his shoulder lightly.

"Blake, come on. It's dinner time."

Blake woke up with a start, his gaze heavy lidded. "I fell asleep."

"Yeah, but it's okay. I just thought you might want to eat something now."

Blake sat up and looked over at her makeshift picnic with a smile. "Look at you, bringing home the bacon."

She turned on the fire and sat down, patting the ground. "There's no bacon down here; I'm way classier than that." Blake chuckled softly, and she sighed impatiently, "Come on, sleepy, I'm hungry."

Blake sat across from her and dug into his steak. She took a few bites of the chicken and groaned at the rich flavors. "Hmm."

"I didn't realize how hungry I was," he said.

"Or how tired," she quipped.

"Hey, maybe I got tired of waiting for you to primp."

"I wasn't primping. I was washing eight hours of paste and germs from my body."

"How is the job going?" he asked.

Hannah had cut back her hours at the diner in order to sub in the morning more and continue doing her job at Fairview Elementary. She was still hoping they kept her on for next year and bumped her up to full time, but after butting heads with the vice principal, she wasn't getting her hopes up.

"It's great. I wish it was something I could count on past the end of May, but I'll keep looking until I find something permanent."

"You'll find something. You're great with the kids at Alpha Dog, so I can only imagine that kindergarteners adore you."

Hannah had come by Alpha Dog a couple times and helped some of the kids with their schoolwork during study hall. The boys perked up when they saw her coming, although Blake had told her it wasn't for the reason she thought, which had made her too embarrassed to go back for a while.

"Yes, but according to you, they only like me for my assets."

"I didn't say that! I said they are teenaged boys and susceptible to pretty women."

"Toe-MAY-toe, toe-MAH-toe."

Blake inhaled the rest of his steak and tried to take her plate from her, but she protested. "Hey, I am not finished yet. Don't make me bite your hand."

"You have until I put these plates outside the door, and then I will be back to kiss your ass...sets."

Hannah tried not to laugh at his little joke and ate another few bites of her dinner before gathering up her plate and the tablecloth. Blake took it from her and set it outside, and while his back was turned, Hannah took a breath and pulled her simple cotton dress over her head, standing in front of the fireplace with just her matching bra and panty set.

When Blake saw her, he stopped dead in his tracks, his gaze traveling from her head all the way down to her toes.

"So," she cleared her throat, "what should we do now?"

Chapter Thirty-Two

BLAKE APPROACHED HANNAH slowly, his heart hammering harder than it ever had before. He took her glasses from the bridge of her nose and set them on the nightstand beside the bed. The teal blue bra and panty set was a beautiful contrast to her soft, white skin, and when he finally stood in front of her, he reached out to finger the strap of her bra.

"Well, I think the first thing we should do is get you out of these wet clothes."

She cocked her head to the side, her hair falling over one shoulder. "They aren't wet, though."

Blake's arm snaked around her waist, and he bent his head, taking the thin lacy bra and Hannah's nipple into his mouth. Hannah released a little "oh" of surprise as he sucked on her for another second or two and then released her.

"Now it is."

Hannah reached behind her, and he watched with rapt attention as she unsnapped it and slid the straps down her arms. Her breasts sprang free, the dusky pink nipples small, pert, and tempting as hell.

Blake knelt down and kissed her stomach right above the top of her panties and then moved over to her hip. Slowly, he pulled the scraps of lace down her legs and kissed his way down to her right knee and back up the other side.

He could have sworn she was shaking.

"Are you okay?" he asked softly, his lips floating across her abdomen.

"Mmm-hmm. Just a little nervous."

He stood up and pulled his shirt over his head, tossing it to the ground. "I don't want you to ever be scared of me." He wrapped his arms around her, bringing her naked breasts against his front, and it was incredible. "Trust me."

"I'm not scared, just a little apprehensive. I'd probably feel better if you lost the pants."

Blake's cock pressed hard against his zipper in agreement. "Happy to."

He stepped back from her and unbuckled his belt, making quick work of his jeans and boxers. With his clothes piled high on the floor, he laid her gently on the bed, coming over her and taking her lips with his.

His hands were everywhere, kneading her breasts, gliding over her waist and abdomen until one of them cupped her, his finger dipping within her lips. It glided up and down, pressing into the wet heat of her until she was murmuring and moaning against his mouth. God, his cock strained to be inside her, but he held back.

Blake pulled away and hovered over her, continuing to stroke her. "I promise I'm going to take care of you, but it's been a while, and I gotta say, I'm probably not going to last long."

"How long?" she whispered.

"Two years."

He thought her eyes looked a little shiny, but then she was wrapping her arms behind his neck and bringing him down for a kiss. "Let's fix that."

Sometimes it was like she could read his mind.

Blake's fingers stopped caressing and found the nub of her clitoris, rubbing it in short, circular motions. He continued to kiss her cheek, her neck and chest, listening to her cries of joy, her breaths coming faster, hitching with every stroke until he felt her body quiver and stiffen. Her nails dug into his shoulders, and he took her nipple into his mouth, rolling it with his tongue until her trembles subsided.

Blake released her breast and gave her a quick peck before leaning over the side of the bed and picking up his wallet. He found the condom tucked in there and opened it with his teeth, rolling it down his cock slowly.

Once he was sheathed, he covered her body with his and went back to kissing her. He lifted her legs up on either side of his hips and held his shaft, rubbing it up and down the slit of her opening. He wanted nothing more than to thrust in and slake his desire, but Hannah deserved to be treasured. For him to take his time and savor her.

He came up on his knees and pulled her onto his lap, holding her by the hips. He kissed her lips, nipping playfully until she opened for him, her arms encircling his shoulders as she straddled him.

Blake adjusted and pressed against her, pushing into her passage inch by glorious inch. God, she was so fucking tight, it was excruciatingly wonderful.

Tangling one of his hands in her hair, he kissed her, murmuring against her lips, "I'm sorry, baby."

And then he thrust up.

Hannah tensed against him, and he caught her soft cry in his mouth. He hadn't wanted to hurt her, but he figured it was better to get it over quickly than to drag it out.

Blake gave her a minute, kissing her cheeks and eyelids before finding her lips again. He eased back and pressed in slowly, his hand massaging the back of her neck as he rocked her on him gently, lovingly. After a few moments, he felt her hands relax on his shoulders and start to stroke him.

And when he glided out again, she actually sighed.

God, he wanted to wait. He wanted to make her come again, but he was already close. His hips picked up tempo, and he gritted his teeth and then groaned, a deep guttural sound of satisfaction that vibrated all the way down his body as he jerked inside her. Her lips pressed against the side of his neck as he tried to say something, to apologize for being too rough, but nothing came out.

Instead, she was the first one to speak.

"I love you."

OH SHIT.

Why had she said it aloud? It was too soon, and he was going to freak.

But it didn't make it any less true.

She knew that she loved Blake Kline. She'd loved him since the first time he'd coaxed a smile from her at Dale's, and that love had only deepened as she'd grown closer to him the last two months.

And she knew that Blake loved her, even if he wasn't ready to admit it. She wasn't afraid that her love was all one-sided.

No, Hannah was scared that he wouldn't be able to admit it. Ever. She knew Blake's hurt and his fears; he'd had one love ripped from him. He was protecting himself from losing another.

Blake's breathing evened, and he pulled away from her, his hands coming up to frame her face. "Are you okay?"

"Mmm…yeah, I'm good."

Blake rolled to his side with her, and when his dick slid out of her, she winced.

"Hey, I saw that. I'm sorry I was so rough—"

She kissed him, shutting him up. "I said I was fine, and I meant it. I think I'd like to get cleaned up, though."

"Hang on, let me go first."

"Okay, I'll just wait here."

Blake kissed her lips swiftly and got up from the bed. He shut the door to the bathroom, leaving Hannah alone on the big bed and lost in thought.

Hannah remembered all the years sitting around listening to her girlfriends complain and bitch about their first times and their boyfriends, how much both had sucked and that they had hated every minute of it, but it got better. Even with the pain, Hannah hadn't been disappointed with her first time. It had been tender and sweet and with someone she loved.

It was everything she'd ever wanted.

She heard the shower go on, and she closed her eyes, suddenly sleepy.

BLAKE STARED AT the blood on him with a grimace and felt like a selfish asshole for asking to clean up first. Dropping the condom into the wastebasket and stepping into the shower, he let the hot water run over him, scrubbing himself down as he tried not to panic.

Hannah had told him she loved him, as clear as day. And he hadn't known what in the hell to say back.

It wasn't that he didn't have strong feelings for her, he did. He just wasn't sure he could love again, let alone if he wanted to. Love had almost broken him once. Twice?

He didn't think he'd make it through.

He finished cleaning up and rubbed himself dry. His gaze landed on that deep tub, and he remembered Hannah's excitement over it.

Blake plugged the tub and ran the hot water, pouring some complimentary bubble bath into it. Taking care of Hannah and settling her in for a nice soak in the tub should make up for his dick move. He wrapped the towel around his waist and walked in to get Hannah.

He realized she'd fallen asleep as he watched the slow rise and fall of her chest, her face turned toward him.

Part of him wanted to just let her rest, but then he thought about the blood and imagined she'd feel better after a good soak.

Slowly, Blake bent over and picked her up off the bed, carrying her into the bathroom.

"Hmm, what're you doing?" she mumbled.

"Cleaning you up."

Hannah lifted her head from his chest and looked up at him with one eye squinted. "Did you run me a bath?"

"I ran us a bath." He stepped into the large tub and sank down with her. The tub had two seats, but he preferred her right where she was.

"Lean back against me."

She did as he asked, and he grabbed a washcloth from the stack of towels displayed artfully in the basket behind the tub.

Dunking it into the hot water, he ran the soft cloth over Hannah, starting at her chest and working his way down. As he took care of her, she relaxed back into him, and he heard her hum of pleasure.

"This is heaven."

Blake moved her hair out of the way so he could kiss her neck. "I don't know about that, but I'm trying to make things good for you."

"You did. Just being here with you is good for me." Hannah rolled over on top of him and kissed his mouth.

Blake's fingers threaded in her hair as he cradled the back of her head, his mouth opening against hers. Their tongues played together as Hannah rubbed her body against him.

Blake's dick stirred to life, stiff with excitement, and he grimaced. "We probably shouldn't yet."

Hannah lifted over him and smiled down at him. "I'm fine. Go get a condom."

There was no way he was going to argue. Blake laughed as he leaned up and kissed her before climbing out of the tub. He rummaged through his duffle and opened the box he'd brought.

When he came back into the bathroom, Hannah was leaning over the side.

"Can I try something before you climb in?"

Blake, curious, grinned. "Sure."

"Okay, stand right here."

He moved to where she'd pointed, and before he knew what she was going to do, her hand had reached out and circled his cock.

"Is this okay?" She squeezed him gently and slid her hand down.

"Um, yeah."

She leaned farther over the tub, and he watched as she licked along the head, her little pink tongue driving him wild.

"How about that?"

"Fuck, as long as you don't bite it, I'm gonna love everything."

Hannah laughed and stopped asking questions. Especially since her mouth was busy exploring him, her tongue teasing its way down his torso. He finally cupped the back of her head, just so he'd have something to hang onto as she went down on him. When she sucked him hard, he thought he was going to blow right then.

"God—fuck—Hannah. I'm gonna go if you keep that up."

In answer, she sucked again and slid her mouth all the way up until only the head of him remained in her mouth. Blake closed his eyes, losing himself in the rhythm of Hannah's mouth until he couldn't stop himself.

Lights exploded behind his eyelids, and when he finally caught his breath, he was hanging on the edge of the bathtub, sucking in air.

Hannah stood up in front of him, droplets of water running down her body as she reached for a towel. When she had it secured around her, she gave him a sly look.

"So, are we ready for bed yet?"

Chapter Thirty-Three

SOMETHING WAS STROKING Hannah between her legs lovingly, a warm, firm touch that brought her out of a sound sleep with a groan of desire.

Her hands sought the source of that intense pleasure and soon found herself cupping the back of Blake's head. His tongue and fingers were playing with her, teasing her into a frenzy.

"Blake…"

Suddenly, his finger curved up inside her, and the room started spinning as she broke apart, gasping as her orgasm tossed her over the edge and she came, screaming.

"Shhh, baby, you'll wake the neighbors," Blake teased from beneath the sheets.

Hannah was slowly aware that he was kissing his way up her body, her chest still heaving from the intensity. When he reached her breasts, he actually squeezed them both and covered first one nipple with his mouth, then the other. The pull on her sensitive flesh created a heavier pulsing between her legs, and she whimpered, caught somewhere between pain and pleasure.

Blake finally reached her lips with his, kissing her in a messy, deep way that was hot as hell.

Hannah realized that Blake was reaching for something right before she heard the crinkle of a wrapper.

She opened her eyes to watch him open the condom with one hand, and then it disappeared below the sheet.

"Are you good?" he asked.

Hannah nodded, her breath rushing out as he grabbed the outside of her thighs.

"Put your legs around me, baby."

Hannah did as he asked and felt the press of his cock between her legs before he sank into her. It pinched a little but faded swiftly as he hovered above her on his arms, pulling out and in, thrusting his dick into her slowly, like a wave rocking her gently. A shock of sensation built inside her as he moved, touching her in all the right places.

It didn't take long for Hannah to fall again, with Blake groaning her name seconds later, his cock twitching inside her.

He lowered himself down onto his forearms, and his chest smashed her breasts, but she didn't care. Having Blake make love to her first thing in the morning was definitely her favorite way to wake up.

He rolled to the side and pulled her against him, kissing her temple and running his hand over her back.

"Do you wanna go first this time?" he asked.

"Sure." She got up from the bed and went into the bathroom to clean up. When she came out again, Blake took her place behind the closed door and she crawled back into the big, comfy bed.

She must have drifted back to sleep, because when she woke up again, Blake was showered and dressed.

"I brought breakfast." He held out a travel mug and a paper Starbucks bag.

"Thank you." Hannah gripped the sheet to her chest as she sat up. "How long have you been up?"

"About an hour. I decided to walk across the street and let you sleep, since we're going to have a busy day today."

"I guess with the lack of snow, skiing's out." Hannah had been hoping to avoid it. She was not a fan of snow or high moving chairs with no safety belts.

"I wouldn't want to even if there was. I thought we'd give those tickets to the front desk and we'd go for a drive around the lake, explore. Whatever floats your boat."

"But what about you? What do you want to do?"

Blake tucked her hair behind her ear. "I want to make you happy."

"Well, you get a gold star in that so far."

"Good. Now eat your breakfast and get dressed. I'll go turn in the tickets."

Hannah took a sip of her latte and sighed. So far the weekend was almost perfect.

Only one thing would make it better, but Hannah wasn't holding her breath.

She could be patient. Eventually, Blake was going to admit that he loved her.

She was sure of it.

BLAKE PARKED IN front of a line of old shops, coming around to get Hannah's door. He took her hand in his, and they walked up to the first little store, a souvenir shop that made Blake want to run the other way. He really hated shopping.

But Hannah had wanted to explore the little lakeside town, so he'd figured he could handle a few hours of hopping from shop to shop.

Hannah grabbed the doorknob with her free hand and went inside. The first thing she picked up was a big floppy orange sun hat, and she set it on her head.

"What do you think?"

"Not a fan."

Hannah laughed and kept walking. Blake trailed behind, eyeing all the junk on the shelves.

"Oh, check this out!" Hannah held out a little license plate with his name on it.

"What am I going to use that for? It won't fit on my car."

Hannah huffed and continued on. When she stopped at the end of the aisle, she held up her hand. "Stop. Close your eyes."

"What?"

"I'm going to buy you something, and I want it to be a surprise."

Blake walked out of the store and waited, leaning against the wall and thinking that he'd rather be hiking.

When Hannah came out of the little store, she held out a bag to him with a grin.

"For your car."

Blake stuck his hand into the bag and pulled out a bloodhound figurine with a head that bobbed when you moved it.

"I know it doesn't look like Charge exactly, but I thought it would make your car just a little bit cooler."

Blake thought it was the ugliest thing he'd ever seen, but the joy in Hannah's face made him hold his tongue.

Wrapping his arm around her neck, he brought her closer for a kiss. "I love it."

"You do?"

"No, it's actually pretty fugly." He kissed her again, taking in her outraged gasp until she melted into him. When he pulled away, he smiled softly down at her. "But I love how it makes you smile."

"Aw, that was almost sweet," she murmured.

"No time for that," he teased, swatting her on the butt. "Now, you have two hours and twelve minutes."

"Then what?" she asked.

Blake wiggled his eyebrows. "Then we go back to the hotel."

"Oh…" She slipped her arms around his waist and kissed him back. "I'm good with that."

Chapter Thirty-Four

BLAKE LAY IN the king-size bed that night with Hannah curled against his side, her leg thrown across his lower body. It had been a good day playing tourist with Hannah and checking out all the towns and spots around the lake. Hannah had especially liked looking around the little shops, and while that part hadn't exactly been stimulating, he'd gone along with it for her.

They'd held hands, chased each other along the beach, and even made out against a tree.

And not once had Hannah repeated that she loved him.

He should be relieved that she hadn't said it again, since it saved him from looking like a jerk. But weirdly, he *wanted* her to say it again.

God, he was losing his mind.

"Tell me about you and Jenny."

Blake started at her question, partly because he'd thought she'd been asleep and mostly because it was something he really didn't want to get into, especially in bed with Hannah.

"You know about her."

"I only know that you were married and she was murdered. Oh, and I know what she looks like. But you've never told me how you met or what she was like."

"Hannah, I really don't want to talk about it."

Silence radiated through the room before she finally whispered, "Okay."

He could tell by her tone that it definitely wasn't okay, but what the hell did she expect? They were away on a romantic weekend, and she wanted to talk about his dead wife?

"I just thought that maybe if you talked about her, it might help you find some closure."

Blake stiffened. "You think I haven't talked about her? I have spent the last two months working through it with my therapist. I had to relive my life with Jenny and her death every time she asked me to speak. I've got closure."

"I'm sorry. I guess part of me was just curious. I figured she had to be pretty amazing for you to love her so much."

Blake moved away from her and got up from the bed, picking up his pants with a snap.

"Where are you going?" she asked.

"For a walk. I need some air."

Blake slammed out onto the private terrace and walked through the gate and down to the beach. Hannah's question swam through his mind as he stood under the full moon, looking out over the water.

What was she like?

How could he put into words that when he was fifteen, he'd been completely mesmerized by Jenny? That while he played JV football, she'd cheered from the sidelines, driving him to distraction. That they'd lost their virginity to each other on graduation night, and when he'd been deployed, he'd kept her letters in his jacket pocket. That it had taken almost a year to get pregnant, and Jenny had been making little announcement cards to send to their friends once she passed the first trimester.

Why would Hannah want to know any of that? Jenny was gone, and she was in his past. He didn't want to go back there; he wanted to move forward and be happy.

Be happy with Hannah.

Blake made his way back to the room and found it dark. The moonlight spilled through the glass door behind him and cast shadows across the room, highlighting Hannah's frame under the blankets.

Blake stripped down and crawled into the bed behind her, wrapping his arm around her waist. He pulled her into him and pressed his mouth against the back of her neck.

"I'm sorry for being such a dick."

She didn't say anything, but he knew she was awake.

"I just want to move on with my life. I don't want to hang onto the past anymore."

Hannah still didn't say anything, and Blake sighed.

"Good night, Hannah."

HANNAH LISTENED FOR Blake's breathing to even out before she relaxed, wiping at the hot tears trailing down her cheeks. She'd been hoping he'd be okay with talking about Jenny, finally sharing that part of himself with her, but she should have known that he wasn't ready.

The question was, would he ever be?

Chapter Thirty-Five

BLAKE WHOOPED AS Charge located Travis Johnson, one of his newest squad members. It was Wednesday, and the sun was shining down, hinting that in just a month, summer would be here. After working together so hard with Charge, Blake was extremely comfortable telling Best that the dog would be ready for the search and rescue competition in Montana.

Blake grabbed Charge gently by the ears and kissed him on top of his head. "That's a good boy."

Charge put his paws up on Blake's shoulders, and unprepared for the massive hound's weight, Blake lost his balance and fell back. Subjected to wet doggy kisses, Blake laughed.

"Hey, Kline! Stop making love to that dog, you've got a phone call."

Blake climbed to his feet and grabbed Charge's leash before addressing his squad.

"All right, guys, let's head in."

Once Blake got his squad situated in study hall, he took the call in his office.

"Sergeant Kline."

"Sergeant Kline, this is Colonel Major at Fort Hood."

Blake's heart slammed. Colonel Major had sent a letter a month ago, telling him about a memorial they had made to honor those they had lost and that Jenny would be included. The letter had been to invite him to the ceremony, but he'd never responded.

He still wasn't ready to go back to Texas.

"Hello, Sergeant Kline?"

"Yes, I'm here. What can I do for you, Colonel?

"Well, I am calling in regards to your late wife, Jennifer Kline. We sent you a letter last month about the monument to honor those who lost their lives in service and support for the US military, and we are inviting friends and family of the deceased to come down. We'll be opening it up on Memorial Day weekend. We've made several attempts to call you, but you haven't responded."

Because I've just been deleting your voicemails.

"I'm sorry, I can't."

"I'm sorry to hear that, but if you change your mind—"

"I won't," Blake said firmly.

"I understand. There is an information packet that has been mailed to you, just in case. I appreciate your time, and good luck, Sergeant."

Blake hung up the call, trying to breathe. Why was it that the harder he tried to move on, the more Jenny and the past seemed to come up? Thankfully, Hannah had stopped asking about her.

Speaking of Hannah, that was exactly who he needed to make his day better. Dialing her cell, he glanced at the clock. It was after four, so she should be home.

It went to her voicemail, and he left a message.

"Hey, Han, I just wanted to say hi and hear your voice. Give me a call, okay?"

I love you.

He hung up without saying it. No matter where they were or how close they'd become, those three little words still sent his stomach plummeting.

HANNAH CHEWED ON a cracker, trying to fight the nausea that had been plaguing her for three days. She'd thought she might be getting the flu the first day, but when it continued to come and go, she'd had a terrible feeling it was something else.

That's when she'd called Nicki.

Her door opened, and Nicki came through in a black tank top and red shorts, pushing her sunglasses up on top of her head as she looked at Hannah.

"Oh, sweetie. Come on, let's go." She held up a plastic bag. "You're going to take this test, and if it's negative, I have Pepto."

Hannah groaned as she got up, holding her hand out for the pregnancy test. She really didn't think she was. Blake had always used a condom, and she'd started the pill a couple weeks ago, as a backup. Nicki assured her it was probably just a bug but had gone to the store anyway.

Hannah went into the bathroom and a moment later set the pregnancy test on the counter, waiting. She stared at the wall, taking deep, even breaths.

Nicki knocked on the door. "Have you looked yet?"

"Not yet."

"It shouldn't take long to show up if you are."

Hannah looked over, and the blood rushed to her head, making the room spin a little.

The digital test's answer box had one word, not two.

Pregnant.

She was pregnant.

Putting her face in her hands, she groaned.

"Shit, that's not good." Nicki came into the bathroom and stood over Hannah for a few seconds before she knelt down in front of her. "Hey, it's okay. You have options. It's not the end of the world."

Hannah jerked her gaze up to Nicki's. "That's not it. It's Blake. How am I going to tell him?"

"You don't have to. Only if you decide to keep it, and even then, if you don't think he'd be good for you—"

"It's not that he's not good for me. He's wonderful. He's sweet, and loving, and wonderful, and I love him, but...but he doesn't love me. Not really."

The incredulous look on Nicki's face would have made her laugh if she wasn't so miserable. "What are you talking about? I've seen him with you. He can't keep his hands and eyes off you."

"I thought he might, I really convinced myself, but now, I think he's still hung up on his wife. I'm sure he cares, but I don't think there's any more room left in his heart for me."

Nicki frowned at her, shaking her head. "That is crazy talk. Guys are always a little standoffish when it comes to feelings and all that love stuff. You're just hormonal."

Hannah didn't argue. What was the point? She knew she was right. Blake might have put Jenny in a box in the closet, but she was still haunting him.

And if he couldn't let go, then where would that leave them?

Chapter Thirty-Six

On Sunday, Hannah fought down the urge to vomit as Blake cooked hamburgers and hot dogs on the grill. The smell of meat was turning her stomach horribly, but the last thing she wanted to do was explain to her boyfriend and a house full of his friends why she had a sour stomach.

Charge sat next to his master, staring at him hopefully, and Hannah shook her head as Blake tossed him a piece of hot dog. Charge's enthusiastic chomping just made the nausea worse.

"Han, baby, you okay? You look a little green." Blake put his arm around her and bent to look into her eyes. "Maybe you should go sit down."

"Thanks, I think I will."

He kissed her forehead lovingly, and Hannah went into the house. In the living room, Dani's son, Noah, was

giggling as Milo chased the plastic ball he kept throwing across the room, while Violet and Dani looked on.

The scene made Hannah's chest tighten. She could easily imagine a black-haired, green-eyed little boy doing the same thing, one who looked a lot like Blake.

"He's a cute little booger, huh?"

Hannah jumped at Bryce's question. "Crap, I didn't hear you come in."

The back door slid open, and Violet's teenaged brother, Casey, went to the fridge, his red head ducking inside. "Blake sent me in to find the cheese. I'm not interrupting, am I?"

"You're always interrupting, you little brat!" Bryce grabbed Casey in a headlock when he came back out and gave him a noogie, as if he was *her* kid brother.

"Bryce, you're going to mess up the do." He pulled away and smoothed it down dramatically.

"Oh, you trying to impress someone?"

Casey reached out and took Bryce's hand, dropping to one knee. "Bryce, you know you're the only girl for me."

Bryce rolled her eyes at Hannah, who smothered a grin.

"Yeah, see you in eight years, kid."

Casey jumped to his feet, looking appalled. "But I'll be eighteen in four."

"Keyword being *teen*. Now get out of here before I tell your sister."

"Tell his sister what?" Violet hollered from the other room.

"Nothing, sis!" Casey covered his heart with the package of sliced cheese. "I'll be thinking of you, my darling."

"Jesus." But Hannah saw the amusement in her eyes and the twitch at the curve of Bryce's lips.

When Casey closed the door behind him, Hannah couldn't stop smiling.

"I have to say, I've got friends, but you guys are on a whole nother level," Hannah said.

"How do you mean?" Bryce went into the fridge for a beer. "You want one?"

"No, thanks. I mean that my best friend Nicki and I are close the way all of you are, but our extended group are more like acquaintances. With you guys, it feels like I'm at a family barbeque, rather than just a bunch of friends hanging out."

Bryce nodded, seeming to understand where she was coming from. "Yeah, that's true. When Eve and Martinez first started dating, the guys would hang out three or four times a week at Mick's, and she didn't get it. They already spent all day together, what the hell could they talk about for another four hours, right? But I think it's more that they all went through shit and bonded over it. Things like that fuse, and you don't get between it. Of course, now that Sparks and Best are taken, the hangouts have become more family friendly, but yeah, if you're welcomed into this group, you're pretty damn lucky. These guys would put their lives on the line for people they love."

Hannah flinched. *For people they love.*

The sliding glass door opened, and Best stuck his head in. "Dani, I got Noah's hot dog."

Noah came running into the kitchen as fast as his two-year-old legs would carry him, Milo running beside him, and Best grabbed him, swinging Noah up into his arms.

"Are you hungry, dude?"

"Hungry Dude!"

Dani and Violet came into the kitchen, laughing.

"You got him?" Dani asked.

"Oh, yeah. We're going to go stuff our faces with watermelon, hot dogs, and potato chips." Best gave Dani a soft look before stepping back outside and shutting the door.

"God, I love that man," Dani sighed.

"Yeah, I never thought I'd see Tyler Best holding a kid." Violet walked over to the fridge, bumping Bryce with her hip. "Stop hogging the beer, wench."

"How's your little sister doing in college?" Bryce asked, no reaction to being called a wench.

"You mean besides dating her TA and driving me crazy? She's acing her classes. Coming home in the middle of June for a week, but apparently she is going to get an apartment off campus with some friend she met." Violet sounded more like an exasperated parent than a big sister.

Hannah smiled, although she felt a little awkward, since she didn't know any of them well.

"So, Hannah, tell us about how things are going with Blake," Bryce said.

Violet nodded next to her. "Yeah. Has he said the *L* word yet?"

Hannah's heart sank a bit. The love thing was definitely a sore spot, mostly because she was so sure he did, but he never said it. He'd tell her he missed her, that he loved all of these things about her, but never just a simple *I love you*.

"No, he hasn't yet."

Awkward silence stretched over the little group until Dani piped up.

"Well, he's probably just waiting for the right time. All the guys have been talking about how much he's changed since you two started dating."

"Absolutely!" Violet agreed, sticking her head back into the fridge. "Is anyone else starving?"

Hannah wasn't really, not with her stomach turning at every new smell. "No, I'm okay."

"Holy crap, have you seen these pickles?"

Violet pulled out a jar of jumbo pickles and popped the lid.

"I used to love these things. Hannah, if your boyfriend asks, Casey ate them."

"You got it," Hannah said.

The smell of the spicy dill was the catalyst, and she gagged. Racing down the hallway, she slammed the door and barely made it to the toilet before the contents of her meager breakfast erupted into the bowl.

A few minutes later, someone knocked softly on the door.

"Hannah, it's Dani. Can I come in?"

Hannah wiped her mouth with toilet paper and flushed the toilet with shaky hands. "Um, sure."

Dani slipped inside, and after staring at her for a few seconds, searched through the cupboards. She pulled out a wet washcloth, and a white packet fell to the floor.

"Whoops."

Hannah reached over and picked it up, turning it over to read the name and address. "Why would this be under there?"

Dani put the wet washcloth on her forehead with a shake of her head. "I don't know, but this should help. I was sensitive to heat and smells when I was pregnant with Noah."

Hannah didn't even try to deny it. "Do Bryce and Violet know?"

"They might suspect, but they won't say anything." Dani glanced down at the packet expectantly. "Are you going to put it back or read it?"

Hannah was torn. She knew it was an invasion of privacy, especially since Blake had obviously been hiding it. But on the other hand, it was addressed from Texas and looked official.

Unable to resist, she pulled out the papers inside and read the letter on top.

Dear Sergeant Kline,

 We would like to invite you to the unveiling of our "Gone But Not Forgotten" memorial, where we will be honoring your late wife and all of those who have lost their lives in service to the military and their families. If you could let us know whether you will be attending, we would be happy to set up accommodations for you and your family.

 With Regards...

Hannah's eyes blurred.

"Hannah, what is it?"

"The military is honoring Blake's wife."

Dani took the letter from her, a surprised expression on her face. "Why would he hide this away?"

"Because he's not going," she said bitterly.

Dani gave her a wary look. "Maybe it's too painful for him."

Hannah knew that was partly it, but how was not dealing with his past healthy? How could he not want to honor Jenny, a woman he had supposedly loved?

Because he isn't ready to let go.

Hannah stood up and took the letter from Dani when she held it out to her. Shoving the whole packet back under the sink, she stood with a shaky sigh.

"Does Blake know you're pregnant?"

Hannah shook her head, her hand on the doorknob. "No. I'm not ready to tell him yet."

Not until she knew whether or not he was ready to really put the past to bed.

"Just don't keep it from him. I think Blake is a good man and would be a really good father. Children need that."

Hannah opened the door, and they headed back out to the party, but Hannah was stuck inside her head. She wanted to tell Blake, of course she did. He would be a kind, loving father, and any child would be lucky to have him.

But if things weren't going to work out between them, did she really want to bring a child into this world?

BLAKE WAS RELIEVED when the last of his friends left. As much fun as it was to sit around and shoot the shit, he'd hardly seen Hannah all week, and he missed her. He wanted to get her alone, naked, and kiss her until they were both too exhausted to speak.

He walked into his kitchen and found her in front of the sink, washing dishes. Milo lay right behind her, his head lifting when Blake entered the room. The two of them had seemed to form a sort of truce, although he still didn't seek out affection from Blake.

Coming up behind her, Blake wrapped his arms around her waist and splayed his hands over her stomach. He took her earlobe into his mouth and sucked.

"I'm almost done," she said.

"Just leave them, and I'll finish later."

His mouth traveled down the side of her neck.

"I'm not in the mood, Blake."

Her snapping tone surprised him. He'd never heard her talk like that.

"Hey, what's up? Are you mad at me?"

She sighed, her shoulders rolling forward. "No, I'm not mad. I'm just...I'm tired."

"All the more reason for you to stop doing dishes and come to bed—"

"I'm tired of this."

Her words sliced through Blake like a sword, and he backed away, turning her to face him with a hand on her shoulder. "What do you mean? Of me? Of us?"

"No, Blake. I love you. I love us." It was the first time she'd said the words in a month, and his heart sped up. "But I don't want just a part of you. I want it all."

"What are you talking about? I'm not seeing anyone else, I've been completely devoted to you."

"I'm talking about your love. Do you love me, Blake?"

It was like he'd swallowed a meatball and it had lodged in his throat, making it impossible to speak and hard to draw breath.

"You can't say it. Which tells me that we've known each other for a while, spent the last three months building something, and you're still holding back from me. Keeping parts of yourself away because they already belong to someone else."

Finally, he croaked, "Are we back to Jenny, again? She's dead, Hannah. The only person here still obsessed with my wife is you."

"Really? Then why won't you go back to Texas? Why won't you go to the memorial unveiling?"

White-hot rage shot through him. "What, you're going through my stuff now?"

"I saw it when I was in your bathroom, and I was curious. You can hate me for that later, but the question remains: If you are really ready to move on and be here, in this, with me, then why can't you go say good-bye?"

"Because I said good-bye when I put her in the fucking ground!"

She jumped at his angry shout, and Milo started barking and growling, his hackles standing on end. Charge howled from the living room and came lumbering in, sniffing everyone, as if trying to detect where the problem was.

"I just...I think maybe we should take a break. Figure out what we both need and—"

Blake took her by the shoulders, wishing he could shake some sense into her. "I know what I need. I need your smile, and the way you talk to your stupid dog, and the curve of your cheek. I need the sweet sound of your voice. I need the way you say my name, and how you make my day better just by calling to check in."

Her hazel eyes filled with tears, and his anger dissolved into fear. He cupped her cheeks, kissing her tears, her lips, panic taking over as he realized she was serious. She wanted to leave him.

"Please, Han. Don't go. I need you."

Hannah trembled in his arms, and he picked her up, carrying her from the kitchen. He just needed to show her. Show her how much she meant to him. How much he cared.

They reached the bedroom, and Blake set her down, afraid to stop touching her. Scared that if he let her go for a single second, she'd be gone.

He undressed in a frenzy, his clothes flying across the room as he kissed her. Loved her. He slid his hand beneath her skirt and pulled her panties down, needing to feel her around him.

Blake helped her sit up and pulled her dress over her head, his face buried in the pillow of her breasts as he kissed first one and then the other.

Blake grabbed a condom from the drawer, and once he was sheathed, he sought entrance in her warmth. Her arms wrapped around him, and she sighed, her hands caressing his shoulders lovingly. He couldn't be gentle any longer. He was desperate. Desperate to make her see how much she meant to him. That what they had was special.

That he couldn't survive without her.

Hannah's cries broke through his thoughts, her voice rising with every thrust.

"Blake!"

"I need you, Hannah. God, I need you so much, baby."

She shook under him, her orgasm squeezing him tight inside her, and he came, blood pounding in his ears as he shouted his satisfaction.

He kissed her gently, lying there for a few moments as their breathing slowed. Blake got up without a word, and after disposing of the condom, he lifted the covers and slid her underneath before he joined her, spooning her as they lay on their sides, his arms wrapped around her.

"Never doubt what you mean to me, Han. I do need you."

Hannah didn't answer, just stroked his forearm until he dozed, falling into a deep sleep.

When he woke up the next morning, she was gone, and a piece of paper sat on the pillow she'd slept on almost every night for weeks.

I'm sorry, but I need more.

Chapter Thirty-Seven

"GET THE FUCKING lead out of your asses! What the hell is wrong with you this morning?" Blake had been yelling at his squad since he walked through the door. The little shits just wouldn't listen today for some reason, and he was not in the fucking mood. He still couldn't believe Hannah had left a fucking note and snuck out of his place like a damn cat burglar.

And taken his heart with her.

God, he wasn't sure if he wanted to be sick or put his fist through a wall. When he'd read those six little words, his stomach had dropped out and he'd started to sweat, sucking in air like it was running out.

Now, he was doing everything he could not to think about her, about how she'd ripped him up. How could she not see how much he cared, how he was trying?

Several of the boys faltered as they tried to do another push-up, and it sent Blake into a rage. "Jesus, you know, what? If you're going to act like sissies, then just run."

"Come on, Sarge, we're tired," Gonzales griped, bent over sweating.

Before Blake told him where he could take his weak-ass excuses and shove them, Sparks called from behind him. "You guys head in for class. I've got to talk to Sergeant Kline."

His squad filed past, shooting him mixed looks of anger, confusion, and hurt, and Blake hated himself for taking his frustrations out on them. Shit, he really shouldn't be around people today.

He turned around to face Sparks and crossed his arms. "What?"

Sparks's eyebrows shot up his forehead. "Dude, what is your issue this morning?"

"None of your business. Why does everyone feel like they have to get a tour inside my head? Can't a guy just be in a bad mood?"

"A bad mood is one thing, but you're torturing the kids and, frankly, scaring the shit out of me."

"I know." Blake leaned against the fence, gripping it until the metal bit into his skin.

"What's up?"

Blake laughed bitterly. "I'm fine. Free as a bird and doing fine."

Sparks appeared shocked. "What do you mean? Free from what? From Hannah?"

"It's just over," Blake said.

Sparks put a hand on his shoulder. "You want to talk about it?"

Blake jerked away and stood up, facing him. "If I'd wanted to talk, I would have knocked on your door and said so."

"Look, I get you're pissed, but I'm your friend. You've heard enough of my shit that the least I can do is return the favor."

Blake let out a heavy sigh, running his hands over his head. "She's just obsessed. She wants me to go down for this memorial thing they're doing at Fort Hood, honoring Jenny and other people killed in service and support to the US military. She thinks that I haven't let Jenny go, that I'm still holding on."

"Are you?"

Sparks's searching look seemed to have detected something, but Blake scoffed anyway. "No. I've moved on, and I'm happy. Hannah *makes* me happy, but she can't see that."

"Have you told her you love her?"

Blake's lips compressed, and Sparks nodded.

"Is she wrong? It's been more than a year since you left Texas. Maybe it's time to go back and face your past head-on."

Laughing bitterly, Blake started to walk away from him. "Jesus, you, too? What does it matter, anyway? She left me with a note. Saying she needed more than what I was giving her. Pretty much tells me she is done with us."

Sparks shrugged. "Well, I have it on good authority that if you pulled your head out of your ass and at least tried to see things from her point of view, she'd probably take you back."

Blake eyed him suspiciously. "Whose authority is that?"

"Let's just say, women talk."

"If you know something and you're not telling me—"

Sparks stepped into him, and although he had several inches in height and muscle on Blake, he didn't back down.

"You'll do what?" Sparks asked.

Blake finally stepped back, not really wanting to get into it with one of his best friends. "Nothing."

"Kline, listen to me. You don't need to be here picking fights with your friends and screwing up your love life. Why don't you take some leave and head down to Texas? When you're ready, I bet Hannah will listen."

Sparks left Blake standing in the training field, staring off into space. He pulled out his phone and scrolled through his contacts. When he saw Hannah's name, his thumb hovered over it again, wishing he could call her again.

He kept looking and finally tapped Dr. Stabler's number.

Blake was actually surprised when she answered, expecting to get her voicemail.

"Hello, this is Dr. Stabler."

"Dr. Stabler, it's Blake Kline."

"Blake, is everything all right? Do we need to move up your appointment?"

He sat down in the grass, leaning his head against the fence.

"I just need to ask you something. It's about Jenny."

"Okay, sure, I've got a little time. What's on your mind?"

Blake told her about the memorial, that he felt like he'd finally been making progress toward putting his guilt aside and making a new life, but Hannah didn't believe him, and neither did Sparks.

"Do you think I should go, if only to prove them wrong?" he asked.

She was quiet for a moment, and he could practically see that pensive expression on her face.

"I don't think you should do it to prove them wrong. I think you should go for you. This is a huge moment, celebrating Jenny's life, and yet, you didn't want to even go. You say that you're moving on, but if that were the case, then you'd want to be there."

Blake hated that her words struck a chord inside him he'd been burying deep. "I'm afraid I'm not ready to go back."

"Blake, it's time to sink or swim. The only way you are really going to know whether or not you've truly let go of Jenny's death and are ready to move on is to face what you're scared of."

"Did you read that on a coffee mug?" he joked.

"A T-shirt, actually."

Blake chuckled and then took a deep, shaky breath. "Thanks for picking up the phone, Doc."

"It's what I'm here for. You have a safe flight."

Blake hung up the phone and leaned his head back against the chain-link fence, the sun warming his face.

Finally climbing to his feet, he stopped off at Sparks's office and stepped inside. Sparks looked up from the papers on his desk and sat back in his chair expectantly.

"I've decided to take you up on your offer of a couple of days of leave. I'm going to book the first flight I can get to Texas."

Sparks nodded approvingly. "I think that's the right thing to do."

"Yeah, I'm sure you do." Blake thumped his fist against the doorframe, pausing with his back to his friend. "And thanks for always looking out for me, even when I didn't want you to."

"It's what brothers do."

Blake swung by the study hall and apologized to his guys, promising to make it up to them, and as he walked out to his car, he realized he did that a lot to the people who cared about him. He hurt their feelings and promised to make it up to them. He'd always been that way.

Maybe it really was time for him to change.

He got in his car, and putting aside his pride, he called Hannah. He wasn't surprised when it went to voicemail, and he waited for the beep.

"Hey, Han, it's me. I got your note. I just wanted to let you know I'm going out of town, but if you want to call, I'll have my phone on me." He paused briefly and went for broke. "I'm going to miss you, baby."

He hung up with that and slowly inhaled.

Then drove home to pack.

HANNAH LISTENED TO Blake's message for what felt like the hundredth time while waiting for her OB-GYN to come into the room. She still hadn't told anyone but Nicki and Dani, mostly because she was confused about what to do. And Blake's message had really messed with her head. She'd told him she just needed a break, but his *I'm going to miss you, baby* had made her think this might actually be permanent. That Blake would hate to lose her, but he'd get over it.

But how was she going to get over him?

There was a knock on her door, and in walked Dr. Grant, smiling widely. The heavyset older woman was in her late forties, with silver-streaked black hair. Her nurse stood behind her, pulling an ultrasound machine.

"Well, Hannah, that's an affirmative on being pregnant, but I thought we'd do an ultrasound, and then I'll be able to tell you how far along you are. Sound good?"

"Sure."

"Can you lift your shirt up, exposing your abdomen, and lower your pants?" Hannah pushed down her leggings and lifted her shirt, jumping a little when the nurse sprayed warm goo on her stomach.

"No daddy?" Dr. Grant asked.

"No, he's out of town." Not that it was any of her business.

"Okay, well let's see what we got. Here is your uterus." Dr. Grant pointed to the screen. "And that little peanut in there is your baby. I'd guess you're about seven weeks, but we'll take some measurements."

Hannah stared at the screen, her heart stuttering at the blip. It was real.

"Are you taking prenatals yet?"

"No, not yet."

"You can pick them up in any pharmacy section over the counter, and make sure you take them. I'd avoid foods with too much salt and sugar. If you're nauseous, there are suckers and tea that can help with that. We'll get you some pamphlets. Now, it says here that when you made the appointment, you wanted to discuss your options?"

The nurse handed her a printed ultrasound picture, and Hannah smiled. "No, that's okay. I think I have all the information I need."

"Great, here, let's clean up the goo, and we'll see you back in four weeks. You can make the appointment at the checkout desk." Dr. Grant touched her knee with a sparkling smile. "Congratulations, by the way."

"Thank you."

When they left the room, Hannah almost dialed Blake's number but chickened out. Instead, she listened to his voicemail again, her eyes closed, letting his voice drift over her.

Then, she hung up and slipped the phone back into her purse.

Chapter Thirty-Eight

ON SATURDAY AFTERNOON, Blake stood in his dress blues, staring at the fountain wall with thousands of copper plaques covering it, all with different names and birthdays. The ceremony had been brief, with hundreds of people watching as they turned the water on. Afterward, Blake had gotten up and walked along the pool until he'd found what he was looking for.

Jenny's name sat right at eye level, the water running over it lovingly.

"We are glad you could come, Sergeant."

Blake turned toward Colonel Major's voice. The man was an imposing, barrel-chested figure. He had dark hair sprinkled with salt and pepper, and his mustache was thick enough to make Tom Selleck jealous.

He shook the colonel's hand. "So was I, sir. It was a beautiful tribute."

The colonel nodded. "I'm just sorry we couldn't do it sooner."

"To be honest, Colonel, I don't know if I'd have been able to come back any sooner."

The colonel patted his shoulder as if he understood. "It was a horrible tragedy. I lost my wife to breast cancer four years ago, and there isn't a day that goes by that I don't miss her."

Blake appreciated the colonel's attempt at empathy as he said good-bye. It was true that he missed Jenny, but where before the pain of her loss had been sharp and constant, it had slowly faded.

He'd done what he'd come to do, what Hannah had asked him to do, but it still felt unfinished.

He had one more stop to make.

Blake left the base and drove, stopping at a local market for a bouquet of pink carnations before heading to the cemetery where Jenny was buried. He parked and got out of his car, making his way through the headstones as if he'd just been here yesterday. Finally, he stopped and stared down at her grave.

Dropping to his knees, he laid the carnations across the green bed of grass, fingering the words on the headstone.

Wife. Daughter. Friend. She will always be missed.

The words were true. The world had lost a wonderful human being, and yet, it had kept turning. He'd survived and continued on with his life.

Even found love again.

The death of his parents had introduced him to a new kind of pain, one that suffocated and consumed. It was worse when Jenny had died, because he hadn't expected to experience it again, at least not so soon. He had thought he was safe.

Until Hannah had left him.

Only now, the pain was nearly debilitating.

So, if working through his feelings about Jenny's death was the only way to get Hannah back, he was going to try.

"Hey. I brought your favorites, carnations. I know you always said they were underappreciated." Sighing and trying not to feel foolish, he kept going. "I don't know if you're there, but I know that you're here." He held his hand over his chest. "You'll always be with me. My girlfriend, Hannah—I don't know if you've seen her, but she thinks I haven't let you go. I swear I didn't think that was the case, not until I got here. I drove by that hole-in-the-wall shake and burger place we used to love, and it just hit me. Why it's been so hard to move on. I didn't say goodbye. You left the house and called out that you loved me, but I didn't say it back because I was too busy watching football. Because I figured I'd see you in an hour. Because I thought you already knew. But when you were killed..." Blake wiped at his wet eyes. "When you died, I felt like things were left unfinished. That our story wasn't over."

The only response was a wind whispering through the trees above him, rustling the leaves.

"I almost didn't make it that first year. I don't know if you were watching me, but I alienated just about everyone we knew and was almost arrested. If it wasn't for Captain Marshal, I'd probably be dishonorably discharged and drinking my money away.

"But he got me a transfer, and I moved to California. I got some help. I know I always said that therapy was a joke, but it actually helped a lot. It was group therapy, but that's where I met my friends. You'd like them, especially Best. He's got your perverted sense of humor."

A car with squeaky breaks drove past, breaking through his monologue, and he almost stopped, but it was as if he could hear Jenny telling him to go on.

"I love my job, although I'm not sure my squad will ever talk to me again after the way I treated them the other day. You see, a little over a year ago, I started going into this diner every day after my run, and there was this girl there. She was pretty, a little shy, but she can make me feel so good, Jen. Even before I realized I liked her, she was the brightest spot in my day.

"But it felt like I was betraying you, being with her, so I resisted for a while, until I just couldn't help it. I think you'd like her. And she loves me. God, how she loves me."

Taking that last leap, he continued. "I love her, too, you know? I haven't been able to tell her, but I do. I love that she has the sweetest spirit and that she can turn me inside out with just a look. She's loving and kind and funny, and it's hard because that was you, too, but it's different. I'm different, but with her, I'm better.

"Why am I telling you this? I guess I just hope that this somehow helps me to let go. I'll never forget you or stop loving the person you were, but if I am going to give

Hannah everything I have, I have to take back my heart. My whole heart."

For some reason, a weight he hadn't even known had been there lifted off his shoulders, and as strange as it seemed, he actually felt Jenny. Felt her letting go.

Pressing his hand against the grass, he stood. "Goodbye, Jenny."

Chapter Thirty-Nine

ON MONDAY MORNING, Hannah could hear a thumping noise through the haze of sleep and reached out toward her alarm, hoping to shut off the awful racket. School was out, and it was her day off, so why would she set her alarm?

Sitting up in bed, Hannah realized it was someone knocking.

Milo whimpered from his cage next to her bed, and she let him out.

He tore down the hallway barking up a storm as she followed. She opened the door, expecting to find her mom or dad, but her jaw dropped when she found Blake, holding two coffee cups and a white plastic sack.

"Kenny gives his regards and asked how you were feeling."

"From the diner? I just saw him yesterday." Hannah brushed her hair out of her face, stuttering, "What…what are you doing here?"

"I'm bringing you breakfast and coffee. Are you going to leave me out here looking like a jackass?"

Stepping back, she let him in and Milo out to do his business. When he finished, he marched past her into the kitchen with Blake, who was grabbing forks from the drawer.

"Blake, why are you here?"

"I told you—"

"No, I told you I needed space and you needed to deal with your baggage, and you just showing up here like everything is the same is confusing and wrong. We can't just pretend that we don't have a problem."

He set the containers of food and cups on the table. "Have a seat."

"No, I want—"

"I heard what you want, and I'll give it to you if you'll just sit your cute little ass down."

Hannah pulled out the chair and flopped in it with a glare.

"Now," he said as he sat across from her and took a drink of his coffee, "I have a few things to say. First of all, it was pretty shitty of you to take off in the morning with a Dear John note."

Hannah's cheeks burned at his scolding. "I couldn't take the chance that you'd kiss me until I changed my mind."

Blake's smile was understanding, if a little cocky. "Fair enough. Second of all, I went to Texas for Jenny's memorial."

"That's where you went?" Her breathless whisper drew his hazel eyes to hers.

"Yes, and I realized you were right to a degree. I hadn't let go of Jenny, and I was wrong. I was wrong to start something with you without being completely available."

Hannah realized where this conversation was going. He was going to tell her she was right, that he couldn't give her more and that she was right to break up with him. That they could still be friends, and then he was going to say good-bye.

"However, I have discussed my feelings for you, mostly out loud, and come to a conclusion."

Here it was. "Which is?"

"I love you."

Hannah thought she'd heard him wrong. "You…"

"Love you." His gaze seemed to be caressing her face, and her own eyes stung. "I love you. I have for months, but I couldn't tell you. I wanted to, but I was scared. I was terrified that I'd love you and lose you."

"But now…"

"Now"—he reached across the table and took her hand in his—"I don't want to regret not being all in, not loving you with everything I have. Because I do, Hannah. I love you so much. The day you left, I wasn't even human anymore. I screamed at my squad and lashed out at my friends. I need you. You keep me balanced and make me happy. I can give you anything you need; just tell me I didn't blow it. That you forgive me."

Hannah started to squeeze his hand before something occurred to her. "Dani didn't say anything to you, did she?"

He cocked his head with a smile. "Sparks told me that if I just got my shit together, he had it on good authority that you would take me back."

"I would. I want to. But there's something I should tell you first."

"As long as it isn't that you're in love with someone else, we're good."

His teasing tone made her more anxious. "Come on, Blake, be serious. What I have to tell you, well…it is kind of a big deal."

"What?"

Hannah took a deep breath. "I'm pregnant."

Blake looked shocked. "How?"

"Maybe there was a hole in one of the condoms? All I know is I'm seven weeks, and I'm going to keep it."

"Wait, were you not going to keep it?"

Blake's tone was outraged, and Hannah raised her chin up in defiance. "I wasn't sure what I was going to do yet. I wasn't sure if we were going to work or whether I wanted to raise a baby on my own. And then I saw the ultrasound picture, and I knew."

"Ultrasound?"

Hannah got up and went to the cupboard, pulling down the picture. As she handed it to him, she smiled.

Blake stared at the picture for several seconds, shaking his head. "I can't believe it."

Hannah bit her lip with worry. "So, if you want to take it all back, I understand."

Blake's gaze lifted to hers, and then he reached out, pulling her against him so his head rested at the top of her abdomen.

Hannah held him against her, shocked when she realized his shoulders were shaking with sobs. His lips pressed to her stomach, and he murmured, "I love you."

Hannah's heart melted as he gazed up at her with hazel eyes shining.

"And I love you, too," she said. Her voice came out raspy with unshed tears. "I guess that means you're not taking it back?"

He shook his head and stood up, holding her to him gently.

"Never."

Epilogue

Three Years Later

BLAKE PULLED UP to the house and let Charge out of the back. He held onto his leash and reached in for the trophy they'd won in Montana for the third year in a row. The Hound It Search and Rescue Tournament had been theirs, but Blake figured it was their last, with Charge being six and starting to get a little arthritic.

But it was still fun to win.

The hot July sun beat down on him as he climbed up the walkway and opened the door. He'd been gone for ten days, and it felt good to be home.

All of their friends and family were inside, milling around the house. His in-laws stood in the doorway to the kitchen, talking to Nicki and her latest boyfriend. Sitting on the couch was Hannah, with all of his friends and their wives and girlfriends spread out around the room.

Hannah's hazel eyes widened when she saw him. "Hey, I didn't think you would be here for another hour."

"I was rushing," he said sheepishly.

"Hey, there's Daddy!" Hannah hopped up from the couch, but before she could reach him, Blake's leg was clasped by a black-haired imp with golden eyes.

"Daddy, up!"

Blake took the leash off Charge, who was jumped by an excited Milo. Apparently, Blake hadn't been the only one missed.

He set the trophy down to pick up their daughter, Maggie, tossing her in the air. Her delighted squeal was too adorable not to smile at, and he pulled her in, squeezing her little body in his arms.

"Daddy missed you."

"Noah!" Maggie started struggling until Blake put her down, and the toddler started stalking Dani and Best's son, laughing when he ran from her.

"I guess I've been replaced," Blake said grimly.

"Not to me." Hannah grabbed the front of his shirt and pulled him down for a kiss, which he gladly sank into.

"Shit, we come over here to celebrate, and they're too busy making out to get on with it," Sparks griped.

Violet smacked Sparks on the arm. "Shut up, and let her tell it."

"Her?" Blake asked. "I thought we were celebrating Charge and me?"

"You've won that thing enough, Blake. Let Hannah have a chance in the spotlight," Dani said, rubbing her swollen belly. Best bent over and gave her a kiss, his hand joining hers.

Blake stared down at Hannah questioningly, and Hannah held out a letter to him.

As his gaze scanned the contents, his eyes widened. "You sold your series."

She nodded. "For all four books. Look at the advance."

His eyes scanned the paper, and he whooped, picking her up and spinning her around.

"I am so proud of you! How could you not have told me?"

"Because I wanted to see your reaction."

Blake kissed her again and hugged her tight. Although her parents hadn't been happy about the cart-before-the-horse situation—as her father put it—they hadn't held it against him. They'd gotten married in Tahoe that July, after Blake and Charge had won their first search and rescue competition in Montana, and spent their honeymoon in the suite again.

After that, life had been pretty great. Hannah worked at Fairview Elementary until she couldn't work anymore, and while she was on bed rest, she sent out query letters to agents and publishers. Blake had figured it was a pipe dream but tried to be supportive.

And then she'd gotten an e-mail from a big literary agency in New York wanting to represent her.

Blake had been so proud of her for getting that far, but this…

"I can't believe I'm married to a big-shot author. You're going to be famous."

"Okay, let's not exaggerate."

Bryce stood up, raising her beer bottle with a grin. "To Hannah, we are all so proud of you and wish you nothing but success." Bryce started to take a drink, then added, "And to Blake, for being smart enough to take her off the market."

"Hear! Hear!" Blake said.

HOURS LATER, HANNAH tucked Maggie in for the night and quietly snuck out of the room. When she walked into their bedroom, Blake was bare chested under the blanket and rubbing her side of the bed suggestively.

"You need to get over here and let me show you how much I missed you."

Hannah smiled seductively and pulled her simple black and white skater dress over her head. "Before I do that, I think there's something I should tell you."

"You have more secrets you've been keeping? Didn't we make a vow to stop playing games?"

"You like playing games, sometimes."

His hazel eyes darkened, and she unsnapped her bra, sliding it down her arms.

"Woman, I haven't seen you for ten days, and you are trying my patience."

Fingering the necklace around her neck, she slowly walked toward the bed, rolling her hips with every move. She climbed up the bed until she hovered over him and said, "You're going to have to get me another one of these."

Hannah held up the tiny white-gold peanut, a joke gift when she'd been pregnant with Maggie. After Hannah had told him that the baby was the size of a peanut, he'd come home with the custom legume, and to his surprise, it was actually her favorite piece of jewelry, besides her wedding set.

Blake's jaw dropped, and her smiled widened.

"No. Really?"

"Yep. Seven weeks tomorrow."

Blake pulled her under him and kissed her long and lingeringly, curling her toes with every stroke of his tongue. They'd decided two months ago that Maggie needed a sibling, and Hannah had stopped taking her pill.

From the doctor's calculations, they'd hit pay dirt the first try.

Blake finally pulled up with a laugh, that deep throaty chuckle that made her want to purr.

"If I'm not careful with you, I'm going to end up with a dozen kids, Fertile Myrtle."

"Not my fault you have bionic sperm," she quipped.

Blake kissed her again playfully, and when they broke apart, she whispered, "Are you happy?"

"Every day that I'm with you."

Who could ask for more?

"Then come down here and kiss me again."

"Anything for you."

Acknowledgments

As with every one of my books, there are so many amazing people to thank. My family, for their unwavering support and love. My agent, Sarah, who is always on my side and there when I need to talk. My amazing Avon editor, Nicole, thank you for all of your patience and insight. To my friends, Ellie McDonald and Tina Klinesmith, for helping me sort through the muck. To Catherine Crook and Crystal Biby: Love you, girls. To Victoria Colotta, for the beautiful teasers you make and all the help and support you offer! Avon Art and Publicity and Marketing, thank you for making my fantastic cover and for all the support. My Rockin' Review Crew, which is the best group of ladies in the world! And to all the readers out there who have been falling in love with the Men in Uniform series: You are awesome.

About the Author

An obsessive bookworm, **CODI GARY** likes to write sexy contemporary romances with humor, grand gestures, and blush-worthy moments. When she's not writing, she can be found reading her favorite authors, squealing over her must-watch shows, and playing with her children. She lives in Idaho with her family.

To keep up with new releases, contests, and more, sign up for Codi's Newsletter at http://www.codigarysbooks.com/newsletter.html.

Discover great authors, exclusive offers, and more at hc.com.

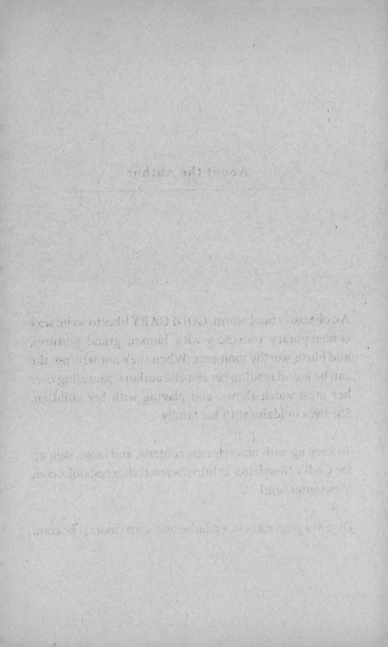

Give in to your Impulses . . .
Continue reading for excerpts from
our newest Avon Impulse books.
Available now wherever e-books are sold.

ALONG CAME LOVE
by Tracey Livesay

**WHEN A MARQUESS
LOVES A WOMAN**
THE SEASON'S ORIGINAL SERIES
by Vivienne Lorret

An Excerpt from

ALONG CAME LOVE

By Tracey Livesay

When free-spirited India Shaw finds herself in trouble, she must rely on the one man she never planned to see again—her baby's father.

Michael Black's cellphone vibrated against his chest and he pulled it from his inner pocket. The caller ID showed an unfamiliar number with "San Francisco, CA" beneath it, but no other identifying information.

His brows converged in the middle of his forehead. It was probably a wrong number. And yet his finger hovered and then pressed the green button.

"Hello?"

"Mike."

He straightened. Her voice stroked his hedonistic hotspots. The tingle caused by every whispered declaration, every lingering caress, hit him all at once.

"Indi."

"Long time, no hear."

Her forced gaiety jarred him loose from her vocal web and allowed his brain to function. Why had she left? Where had she been? What did she want? Why was she calling?

"I know I'm probably the last person you want to talk to and I understand, considering how I ended things and I—"

He remembered this about her, the stream of talking on an endless loop. His favorite remedy? A cock-stirring, toe curling kiss.

"Indi, spit it out."

A thick silence, and then—

"Can you post bail for me? I've been arrested for burglary."

Well *that* happened.

The door to the precinct closed behind Indi. Exhaustion weighed her down, leaving her head throbbing and her sight unfocused. She shivered, her cable knit sweater offering inadequate insulation from the chill.

If she had a bucket list, she could confidently check off this experience: get yourself arrested in an unfamiliar city. It hadn't been anything like *Orange is the New Black*—Thank God!—but she had met some interesting women while she'd been booked and processed. Turns out, her unstable living situations and various relocations equipped her with the unique skill set needed to survive the city's holding cell.

But she didn't do bucket lists. They were created for people who scurried through life afraid to take chances, regretting their caution when faced with their mortality. Indi's life *was* a bucket list. Hence, her current predicament.

"Where's Ryan?"

The brusque voice wrapped itself around her heart and squeezed. She stilled and her breath went on strike.

Those words. That tone. This situation. It wasn't how she'd pictured their reunion.

Though their best friends were married to one another, careful planning on her part would've given her several years to let time and distance erode the memories and allow them to communicate without her recalling the way he'd made her body quake with ecstasy. She'd be cool, look polished, and possess the proper grace to put them both at ease.

That had been the fantasy BN—Before Nugget. Now she'd settle for an encounter where she didn't look and smell like a cat lady's ashtray, and she possessed something other than an unplanned pregnancy and a felony charge.

Despite his harsh tone, the man leaning against the metallic silver Porsche Panamera—new; the last time she'd seen him, he'd been driving a Jaguar—was as gorgeous, as powerful, and as autocratic as the luxury sedan he drove. He'd tamed his blond curls—what a shame—into a sleek mass that shone beneath the street lamps and his body looked trim and powerful in a dark tailored suit and crisp white collared shirt without a tie. He could've been waiting for his date to a society gala and not standing in the street in front of the sheriff's office after midnight, waiting for the state judicial system's newest enrollee.

Indi hefted her backpack onto her shoulder, ignored the dips, swerves, and inversions occurring in her belly, and slowly descended the concrete steps. "He's finishing up the paperwork."

She'd forgotten how big he was. She was a tad taller than average and she knew from experience her eyes would be level with his chin, a chin now covered in downy blond fuzz. Experience also taught her the stubble would be a delicious abrasion against her skin.

"Do you have anything to say to me?"

She blinked. She had much to say to him. But here? Now?

She'd hated calling him. Truthfully, she would've hated calling anyone in this situation. Would rather have stayed behind bars and figured a way out of this mess. But this wasn't about her personal preferences. She needed to make decisions in Nugget's best interests. And *that* meant doing what was necessary to ensure she spent as little time in jail as possible.

She hadn't seen Mike in three months, since she'd awakened to see his face softened in sleep. Terrified of the feelings budding to life within her, she'd stealthily gathered up her belongings and left without looking back. And despite her behavior, when she'd called, he'd shown up. He deserved many things from her, starting with gratitude.

But did he have to be an arrogant ass about it?

She balled a fist in the folds of her skirt. "What else would you like me to say?"

He pushed away from the sex-mobile. "How about 'Thank you for canceling your plans and coming to get me'?"

Crap. She'd pulled him away from something. Or someone.

It was none of her business. She'd given up any say in who he spent time with the night she'd walked away.

"How in the hell did you get arrested for burglary?"

She swiped at the allegation. "Those are trumped up charges."

"So you didn't do it?"

"Of course not. I mean, breaking and entering makes you think of a cat burglar or someone in a ski mask robbing the place. That's not how it happened."

Mike narrowed his eyes and subjected her to his self-righteous stare. "Then why don't you tell me what happened."

An Excerpt from

WHEN A MARQUESS LOVES A WOMAN
The Season's Original Series

By Vivienne Lorret

Five years have passed since the Max Harwick
shared a scandalous kiss with Lady Juliet, only to
have her marry someone else. He's never forgiven
her . . . but he's never stopped loving her either.

Some days Lady Juliet Granworth wanted to fling open the nearest window sash and scream.

And it was all the Marquess of Thayne's fault.

"Good evening, Saunders." A familiar baritone called from the foyer and drifted in through the open parlor door. *Max.*

Drat it all! He was a veritable devil. Only she didn't have to *speak* his name but simply *think* it for him to appear. She should have known better than to allow her thoughts to roam without a leash to tug them back to heel.

"I did not realize Lord Thayne would be attending dinner this evening," Zinnia said, her spine rigid as she perched on the edge of her cushion and darted a quick, concerned glance toward Juliet.

Marjorie looked to the open door, her brows knitted. "I did not realize it either. He said that he was attending—"

"Lord Fernwold's," Max supplied as he strode into the room, his dark blue coat parting to reveal a gray waistcoat and fitted blue trousers. He paused long enough to bow his dark head in greeting—at least to his mother and Zinnia. To Juliet, he offered no more than perfunctory scrutiny before heading to the sideboard, where a collection of crystal decanters waited. "The guests were turned away at the door. His lordship's mother is suffering a fever."

Juliet felt the flesh of her eyelids pucker slightly, her lashes drawing together. It was as close as she could come to glaring at him while still leaving her countenance unmoved. The last thing she wanted was for him, or anyone, to know how much his slight bothered her.

Marjorie tutted. "Again? Agnes seemed quite hale this afternoon in the park. Suspiciously, this has happened thrice before on the evenings of her daughter-in-law's parties. I tell you, Max, I would never do such a thing to your bride."

Max turned and ambled toward them, the stems of three sherry glasses in one large hand and a whiskey in the other. He stopped at the settee first, offering one to his mother and another to Zinnia. "Nor would you need to, for I would never marry a woman who would tolerate the manipulation." Then he moved around the table and extended a glass to Juliet, lowering his voice as he made one final comment. "Nor one whose slippers trod only the easiest path."

She scoffed. If marriage to Lord Granworth had been easy, then she would hate to know the alternative.

"I should not care for sherry this evening," Juliet said. And in retaliation against Max's rudeness, she reached out and curled her fingers around his whiskey.

Their fingers collided before she slipped the glass free. If she hadn't taken him off guard, he might have held fast. As it was, he opened his hand instantly as if scalded by her touch. But she knew that wasn't true because the heat of his skin nearly blistered her. The shock of it left the underside of her fingers prickly and somewhat raw.

To soothe it, she swirled the cool, golden liquor in the glass. Then, before lifting it to her lips, she met his gaze. His irises were a mixture of earthy brown and cloud gray. Years ago, those eyes were friendly and welcoming but now had turned cold, like puddles reflecting a winter sky. And because it pleased her to think of his eyes as mud puddles, that was what she thought of when she took a sip. Unfortunately, she didn't particularly care for whiskey and fought to hide a shudder as the sour liquid coated her tongue.

Max mocked her with a salute of his dainty goblet and tossed back the sherry in one swallow. Then the corner of his mouth flicked up in a smirk.

She knew that mouth intimately—the firm warm pressure of those lips, the exciting scrape of his teeth, the mesmeric skill of his tongue . . .

Unbidden warmth simmered beneath her skin as she recalled the kiss that had ruined her life. And for five years, she'd paid a dire price for one single transgression—a regretful and demeaning marriage, the sudden deaths of her parents, and the loss of everyone she held dear.

By comparison, returning to London to reclaim her life as a respected widow should have been simple. And it would have been if Max hadn't interfered.

Why did he have to hinder her fresh start?

Of course, she knew the answer. She'd wounded his ego years ago, and her return only served as a reminder. He didn't want her living four doors down from his mother—or likely within forty miles of him.